turn
on the
light
so I
can
hear

I hope you enjoy
the story!
Best Wishes,
Teri Kanefield

12-26-2014

turn on the light so I can hear

Teri Kanefield

Armon Books
San Francisco

Portions of this book originally appeared in *The Iowa Review*
and *Cricket Magazine*.

Armon
Books
San Francisco
945 Taraval Street, #130
San Francisco, CA 95116
Cover design by Streetlight Graphics

For Andy

1

The note said: "I think this one will just do the job and stay out of trouble. She's young but eager. Lucinda couldn't possibly have any objections."

I wondered who Lucinda was. Feeling shaky, I refolded the note, replaced it on the desk, and returned to my chair.

I didn't feel eager. I felt desperate. Maybe if I had pulled my hair up instead of letting it fall down my back, I would have looked older. I was of average height but so slender that my roommate caricatured me by drawing me as a tendril.

Mrs. Eakle walked back into the office, and I caught the pungent scent of her perfume. She wore a white blouse that looked as if it had been starched. It didn't surprise me that Mrs. Eakle had written a note like that. She struck me as sharp, competent, and inflexible, the kind of secretary who told the boss what to do.

I opened my notebook and pretended to read, hoping that I looked the picture of innocence instead of like I'd just crossed the room to read something I wasn't supposed to.

If Mrs. Eakle were a color, she'd be metallic silver, an iridescent shade you can't mix yourself but have to buy ready-made. The color I had in mind was made with real fish scales.

The school district office was housed in a New England–style residence with plank floors probably built at least a hundred years ago, now converted to office space. The trim around the doors and windows was painted white, the floors were knotty and scuffed, and the chairs had straight ladder backs. The interior smelled of damp wood and lemon polish.

I turned a page of my notebook and reread the ad I had printed out the day before:

Part-time tutor and interpreter for a deaf student in a public high school. Job classified as classroom aide. Must have proficiency in sign language for the deaf, and proficiency in high school math and English. Contact Mr. Givens. Begins September. $18 hourly.

Sign language was the catch. The only thing I knew about sign language came from watching Children of a Lesser God. Well, I had five months to learn. Hadn't I done things that were much harder?

Mr. Givens opened his office door. He was thin with rounded shoulders and a jacket that seemed a few sizes too large.

Mrs. Eakle handed him my résumé and her note.

"Bretna, please come in," he said.

His office smelled of old coffee. His desk was dark wood without a single piece of paper or speck of dust. It was the kind of desk you'd expect to find in corporate executive offices, not a school district office.

I sat across from him and watched him read my résumé and Mrs. Eakle's note.

Without looking up, he said, "You have no teaching or tutoring experience?"

"No."

He still didn't look up. "You're an artist."

It wasn't a question, but I responded: "Yes."

Now he looked up, one of his eyebrows cocked higher than the other. I'd seen that look before, a look that said, You're willing to admit a thing like that? Mr. Givens would be a murky tan: burnt umber mixed with a touch of Mars black and lots of titanium white—nondescript and lacking emotion.

Then he asked the question I dreaded: "When did you learn sign language?"

"I have some deaf friends. They taught me. I haven't signed for a while, so I'm rusty. I'll take a refresher course this summer."

Fabricating a few friends seemed safest. If I invented a job or volunteer work, he could easily check. The evening before, studying a sign language book in the library, I'd taught myself to sign, "My signing is rusty," finger-spelling "rusty." If he tested me by signing something and expecting me to respond, I'd perform the sentence.

"Why do you want this job?" he asked.

I needed the money, that was for sure. But something else, too, drew me to the job.

"I had a brush with deafness myself," I said. "I lost most of my hearing when I was five. An operation helped, but I still have trouble in one ear." This time I was telling the truth.

"We need someone who can tutor Alejandro in his academic subjects," he said, "math, science, English."

"I'm sure I can do it."

"Yeah. He's in low-level classes." He said this flatly, as if unaware that he'd just said something insulting. Then he said, "I can only offer a one-year contract."

"That's fine." With luck, I'd only need the job for a

year.

"Do you have any questions?" he asked.

I wanted to know who Lucinda was. Instead, I asked, "Can you tell me something about Alejandro?"

"He's thirteen. He'll be the only deaf student in the school."

I waited for him to say more—like why Alejandro wasn't attending the prestigious school for the deaf in Boston. He drummed his fingers idly on the desk and remained silent, so I asked, "Is he worried about being the only deaf kid in the school?"

"He's in a program for the deaf now, housed in a regular high school. He really wants to be mainstreamed."

"Is he a good lip-reader?"

"Oh yes," he said, perking up for the first time. "Very good." He stood up and said, "We'll call you in a few days, after I've checked your references." His tone was off-hand, as if to say, "You'll do."

When I stood up, my knees trembled. Thank God that was over. I can lie when necessary, but I don't like doing it.

I had to change buses in Harvard Square to get home, so I stopped at a thrift store to root around for vintage clothing. The week before, I'd found my interview outfit, a 1950s dress made of muted olive-green worsted wool with covered tab buttons and a flared box-pleated skirt. Today I found a chocolate-brown velvet hat with a wide oval brim. I tried it on, and liked it: A woman wearing that particular hat in 1945 would have meant business. The hat, still in mint condition, cost $3.99, so I bought it.

Back at our apartment, Janae was at the kitchen table, drinking blackberry tea so strong I could smell it from the entryway.

"How did it go?" she asked.

"Fine," I said. I hadn't told her much about the job, and I didn't plan to tell her that I was hopelessly unqualified.

Janae and I first lived together in the dormitories at the Massachusetts College of Art, and since graduating, in our Kendall Square apartment. Janae's real name was Jane. She wasn't the only person to change her name in her first year of art school: Tammy Lou became Tamara, and Martina, who'd always been called Tina, said Marti suited her better. I considered my own name one of the few things my mother had done right.

"Bretna," Janae said. "You're eccentric." She was looking at my hat.

"You don't like the hat?" I asked. Then, recovering: "How many cats do you have at your parents' house?"

"Eighteen. Why?"

"I don't think a person with eighteen cats should be calling other people eccentric."

She laughed and put the kettle on for more tea. "Someone else answered our ad. She's coming tomorrow at six."

"Good. I hope she's better than the last two."

The first person who came to interview for our spare room said she liked ferns and had a few dozen plants that needed to be protected from dry air, so she'd have humidifiers going at all times. The first thing she looked at in the apartment was the heater to evaluate whether the air would be moist enough for her ferns. I imagined a few dozen ferns—and the three of us—dripping with perspiration. The second person insisted on a strictly vegetarian household. Neither Janae nor I liked being told what to do.

"This one's name is Rosie Pym," Janae said. "She

sounded nice enough on the phone. Exuberant but nice."

"Is she an artist?"

"Nope. She works for a place called Outdoor Adventures."

"Outdoor Adventures? Maybe that means she'll be gone a lot." I considered making a joke about how she might have to explain to a couple of hermits like us what an outdoor adventure was, but Janae had opened a book and started reading, so I pulled the latest issues of The Art Quarterly and Art World from my handbag and started reading. For the first time in three years, I wasn't listed as a recipient of the Foundation for Sculpture fellowship. Was it a coincidence that at the same time, my sculptures stopped selling, or was I already a washed-up has-been? Whatever the cause, for the first time in three years, I needed a real job.

Late the following afternoon, my phone rang. The caller was Mrs. Eakle.

"Congratulations, Bretna," she said crisply. "You've been selected for the job."

Something about her use of the word "selected" made me think I'd been the only applicant. "Great!" I said. "Thanks!"

"I take it you accept the job," she said.

"Yes, of course."

"Very good. We'll send you a packet of forms to fill out. We look forward to seeing you in September."

Metallic silver, while coolly competent and confident, was rarely sincere.

Rosie Pym was startlingly pretty: glowing skin, sparkling eyes, a wide smile, a small upturned nose with a sweet sprinkling of freckles. She breezed into the loft, radiating joy and energy and enthusiasm. "This place is great!" she said. "I love the exposed brick and beams, and real wood floors. And what could be better than a bakery downstairs?"

Janae showed her around the loft.

"Look at all this space!" Rosie said.

"We use ours for studio space," Janae said.

"I'll use mine for storage. I have hiking gear, rock climbing gear, camping equipment, skis, the works."

I sat on the couch, and Janae perched on a straight-backed chair.

"So what do you do at Outdoor Adventures?" I asked.

"I'm a program director. Mostly I train the program instructors, but I also get to lead hiking and climbing groups. And I teach courses in ecology. It's a great job. Imagine getting paid to go rock climbing and camping—things I want to do anyway!"

Rosie's unrestrained enthusiasm for camping and rock climbing made me feel vaguely uneasy. Something in her intensity and pitch seemed off.

"I can go right up the side of a cliff," she said. "With the right equipment of course."

"Really?" I said politely.

Rosie played with a lock of her hair, combing it with her fingers, tossing it back with a flick of her hand. "Not too many people like whitewater rafting or survival camping," she said, "but a lot of people like hiking and bike riding. How about you two? Do you like to hike or bike ride?"

Janae and I looked at each other. Neither of us had a car and we both had bikes, but our walking and bike riding were entirely for the practical purpose of getting from one place in the city to another.

"I like hiking downstairs to get a croissant on weekends," Janae said. "I don't mind climbing back up the stairs to eat in peace."

Rosie laughed. "You'll have to try it. You may like it."

I couldn't think of any reason not to let Rosie move in. We needed someone else to help with the rent and utilities, and Rosie seemed nice enough. I gave a little shrug to show Janae that she was fine with me. Janae returned the look.

Later, after Rosie left, I said, "What kind of animal?"

Janae's last boyfriend was a basset hound: droopy-eyed and affectionate, but stout, lazy, and stubborn.

"Maybe she's a boxer: a little skittish, but mostly friendly."

"Or a monkey," I said, "playful and enthusiastic."

"She's definitely over-the-top. I hope she doesn't swing from the rafters."

Rosie did seem over-the-top, but it occurred to me that anyone listening to our conversation about boxers and monkeys would think Janae and I were the odd ones.

Rosie moved in the following evening. She said, "Do you mind if I rearrange some of the furniture? This room could feel so much more intimate if we pull the furniture away from the walls and group it together."

"Go ahead," I said, and watched as she pushed the furniture around until the arrangement suited her. As before, her exuberance made me vaguely uneasy, but I shrugged it off. After all, what's wrong with unrestrained enthusiasm?

She moved some plants away from the window so we could see the sky and said, "Don't artists need to see nature for inspiration?"

She didn't seem to expect an answer, so I remained

silent. Next she unpacked an espresso machine. "The bakery downstairs closes at five," she said. "So we'll need this."

She made us lattes—decaf because it was evening—all the while chattering away. It turned out that Rosie was thirty-four and had worked for a journal at Harvard before landing her current job.

"Both of my husbands were crazy," she said.

"Were they always crazy?" Janae asked.

I glanced up and saw that Rosie had missed the significance of the question.

"They were," Rosie said, "but I didn't really notice it until after we were married. Both deteriorated after being married for a few years. One even tried to kill me."

Janae shot me a look. I had known Janae long enough now to guess exactly what she was thinking. She was thinking that if one of Rosie's husbands had tried to kill her, there was probably a reason, and we may end up wanting to kill her, too. But I thought Rosie would at least cheer up our loft, which did seem gloomy at times. Besides, maybe her husbands *had* been crazy.

2

The classroom at the Deaf Association wasn't a room at all. It was a space enclosed by the kind of movable panels used to create cubicles. Inside, four white, laminated tables formed a square. I sat on the side facing the portable chalkboard. Several people, who already seemed to know one another, whispered together. Chairs scraped. More people came into the room and sat at the table.

A man in his late twenties entered, wrote "English" on the board, and drew an X through the word. Then he wrote "Voice" and drew an X through it as well. He pretended to take both words from the board and throw them out the window. Students looked around and smiled.

Next he wrote "Curtis" and pointed to himself.

Curtis was large and bearish with a round face and curly hair. There was a slight squint to his eyes, as if he closely examined everything and missed very little.

He drew a stick-figure girl and made a sign, touching his thumb lightly to his jaw and stroking downward. His lips formed the word "girl," and he indicated that everyone should imitate him. Feeling awkward, I stroked my jaw with my thumb and looked around. Others were doing the same. Curtis next drew a boy and taught us a sign similar to a boy gripping the visor of an imaginary baseball cap. After everyone imitated him, he drew a heart around the boy and girl, crossed his wrists, and held them against his chest in a sign that conjured affection. "Love," he mouthed as the students imitated the sign.

He grinned a conspirator's grin and drew a large diamond ring on the girl's finger, and made the sign for "marriage," a clasping of both hands into a tight bond. His hands then followed the contours of a swollen belly, and he made a sign as if cradling a baby in his arms.

He signed with the grace and purpose of a dancer or athlete. I sat up straighter in my chair and realized I was entirely enjoying the lesson.

"Baby," his lips formed. Like everyone else, I imitated him, rocking an imaginary baby. On the chalkboard, Curtis drew a small boy standing with his parents. After another pregnancy and cradling motion, he drew a girl. In this nursery rhyme progression, the signs for sister, brother, mother, father, grandparents, and family followed easily.

When the chalkboard pictured an extended family of fourteen members, Curtis wrote, "15- minute break" on the board. I was startled by whispers and scraping chairs. Having become accustomed to a silent classroom, I found this to be a strange reminder that the world was filled with noise.

In the reception area, a dark-haired girl wearing hearing aids and a T-shirt that declared "Deaf Pride" stood by the stack of books. A sign announced the required books for each course and the prices. The girl made change from a metal box.

I bought my American Sign Language textbook and a collection of essays called *American Sign Language: The Language of the Deaf Community* and stood off to the side, thumbing through the essays.

A telephone rang. A guy at the reception desk answered the phone and said hello in a surprisingly clear voice. I thought everyone who worked at the Deaf Association was deaf. I wandered over to the reception desk and waited until he hung up.

"What's happening?" he asked me.

"I was just wondering how long it takes to learn sign language."

"After a year of classes, you should have the basics. Then you have to practice."

A year of classes? My heart thumped. "How much will I learn over the summer?"

"You can get started, have some basic conversations, stuff like that. Why?"

I steadied myself and said, "I just wondered."

I was five years old, playing in the kitchen with my neighbor Kimmy, waiting for my mother to get off the telephone so we could ask permission to go outside. I went to the family room door every few minutes, peeked in, and saw that she was still on the phone.

"What are you doing?" Kimmy said.

"Looking."

"At what?"

"To see if my mom's still talking."

Next time I got up, Kimmy said, "She's still talking. And she's closing cabinet doors."

"How do you know?"

"I can hear her."

I went to the door, and sure enough she was still on the phone, and just then was looking in a cabinet. "You knew," I said. It seemed like a magic trick that Kimmy could sit in one room and know what was going on in the next.

My mother was always moving. She had the quick, nervous gestures of a hummingbird. Her hands twitched. Her legs jiggled. Even when she watched television, she was moving, folding laundry, or straightening a sewing basket. She had tranquilizers prescribed by the family doctor. In another century, people would have said she had a nervous condition. To me, my mother was a bewildering mystery.

One evening my mother sat me down at the table and said, "Bretna, stand up." I stood up. She put her hand in front of her mouth and said something. I knew she was talking because I heard her mumbled voice, but without seeing her lips, I couldn't understand a word. Then she uncovered her mouth and told me to sit down. I sat down.

My parents looked at each other.

"Mrs. Conn's right," my mother said. Mrs. Conn was my kindergarten teacher.

"Sure is," agreed my father.

"Maybe that's why this child never pays any attention to anything," my mother said.

She took me to see Dr. Kutler, who poked inside my ear with an otoscope. He said, "First we're going to have to drain the ear." I watched his mouth and knew exactly what he said, but when he went on to explain what had caused the buildup of fluid, I couldn't understand him. He picked up a long, needle-shaped metal instrument and held my shoulder to steady me.

No way was I going to let him put that needle into my ear. I pulled back and said, "No!"

"Hold still!" my mother said.

"No!"

"It's okay," the doctor said. "We'll take care of it all in

the hospital."

The next week, my mother drove me to the hospital. Two nurses took me into a white sharp-smelling room, dressed me in a loose white nightgown that tied in the back, and put me in a bed with railings on the sides.

"I'm too big for a crib," I told them, but they laid me down anyway. I expected the nurse to give me a spoonful of something bitter to make me sleep, but instead a doctor came in wearing a watery-green smock. He fiddled with a machine that looked like a TV set, then put a black rubber mask over my nose and mouth. "Take a deep breath," he said, "like you're going to blow up a balloon."

I held my breath as I'd been taught to do in the swimming pool. Again he said to breathe. I shook my head. One of the nurses gave my ribs a tickle, and I was forced to breathe the sweet, heavy fumes. When I woke up, I had a gauze bandage on my head, and when I tried to sit up, I felt dizzy. The doctor came and took the bandage off, and everything sounded magnified and close: footsteps on the tile floors, voices, the distant closing of doors.

The noise driving home was like something out of a nightmare. Every time a truck drove past, creating an earth-splitting roar, I squeezed my hands over my ears and cried. Each time I screamed, my mother grinned awkwardly and kept driving.

Many days passed before I could accustom myself to the blaring and uncomfortable noises. I didn't like the honking of horns, the rattling of dishes, or the grinding hum of the dishwasher. I didn't believe the doctor when he said I still had hearing loss. Could it be that for others the noises were even more grating?

3

I arrived for the second sign language class to find the guy at the reception desk, whose name plaque said "Jake," engaged in a spirited sign conversation with Curtis. I stood about five feet away and watched. It occurred to me that spending more time with Curtis would be one way to learn sign language in a hurry. I had to do something, that was for sure. Eighteen dollars an hour for a six-hour-a-day job would pay the bills and leave time for my art work.

Curtis turned to me and made the sign for "hello," which resembled a salute with the fingertips touching the forehead. I saluted back and signed, "How are you?"

It was a small comfort to understand his standard response: "Fine, and you?"

"Fine," I signed. I was trying to figure out how to continue the conversation, but he backed away and made the sign for "See you later."

After he left, I turned to look at the assortment of photographs thumbtacked to the movable wall behind the reception desk, candid shots of what appeared to be large social events. Curtis was in several of the photos. In one, a group of fifteen or so people were huddled together, their arms around one another, smiling at the camera. In another, Curtis appeared with a tall, willowy girl with sandy-colored hair.

"Is that Curtis's girlfriend?" I asked the guy at the

desk.

"Nah. That's Lauren. Lauren is hearing."

That was an odd thing to say. I turned to look at him. "So what if Lauren is hearing?"

"You asked if she was his girlfriend. Curtis doesn't date hearing girls."

"Never?"

"Never."

I smiled. *Oh yeah?* I thought. *Maybe I'll have to change that.*

I went the long way to the classroom, through the maze of offices and cubicles, and found the cubicle with "Curtis" on the nameplate. I peeked in. On one wall was a poster of deaf artists, none of whom I recognized. On another wall was a graphic of a fist and the slogan "Deaf Pride." Just outside the door, by Curtis's nameplate, was a business card that looked as if it had been printed with a high-quality laser printer: "Teacher, Private Lessons: American Sign Language."

I smiled again. Private lessons were a good idea.

Curtis started that day's class with a question: "Why are you all learning sign language?" He went around the table as each student gave an answer. He read lips and nodded appreciatively when a student was able to supplement with signs. Most students were learning sign language because they had deaf relatives. One had a deaf colleague.

When Curtis stood in front of me, I downplayed my job by telling him I would be a classroom aide in a public high school. I figured that wasn't exactly a lie, because the ad had used the phrase "classroom aide." I also explained that part of my job would be tutoring a deaf boy. I left out the interpreting part.

"Will the deaf boy also have an interpreter?" He spoke as he signed, his voice coming from deep in his throat, low and hoarse, like a gravelly whisper.

I shrugged as if I honestly didn't know. "I will tutor him in all his academic classes," I said, using my voice and supplementing with the sign for "tutor" and "day."

Curtis pointed to himself, then made the sign for "see"—I see.

I wasn't sure from the unblinking way he looked at me whether or not he believed me.

After class, I sat on a bench in the glass-enclosed bus stop with my sketch pad on my lap, sketching the street scene: a row of shops and restaurants, including a florist and coffee shop with striped awnings. With cobblestone sidewalks and old-fashioned streetlights, it was a picture of New England charm.

A group of students from my class came out of the building in a cluster and crossed the street to wait for the T. Ordinarily I took the subway also, but a bus went directly from this corner to Kendall Square.

I looked up to see Curtis and another guy walking toward the bus stop, signing and laughing about something. When Curtis saw me, he stood up straighter and stopped smiling. I went back to my drawing. In my peripheral vision, I saw the motion of their hands. Sometimes one of them made a grunting sound.

A bus came, and Curtis's friend boarded it, leaving Curtis by himself. We were the only two people at the bus stop. I stole a look at him, and he saluted stiffly.

I signed, "Hello," then looked back down at my sketch pad. I felt him watching me. I looked up to see that, in fact, he was looking at my hat.

He signed, "I like your hat." The signs were easy to follow: he pointed to himself, then he made the sign for "like," lightly touching his chest and snapping his fingers together. Then he pointed to my hat.

"Thanks," I signed. I made the signs for "you have good" and finger-spelled "taste" because I didn't know the sign.

He showed me the sign for "taste," touching his lips with two fingers and his thumb. Awkwardly I imitated him.

If Curtis were a color, he'd be a reflective blue mixed with green, the color of a tropical ocean—cool but teeming with life and enormous depth. All my confidence evaporated. I hadn't had a real boyfriend for years, so I was definitely out of practice.

"Where are you going?" he asked.

I made the sign for "home."

"You know a lot of signs," he said.

"I've been practicing." Then, to change the subject, I asked, "Where are you going?"

He pointed the other direction and made a sign by first pointing to his temple and then making the sign for "tree." It took me a moment to understand: Braintree, a town south of Boston. When I got it, I laughed, and repeated the sign for practice.

"I'll show you another one. This one always makes hearing people laugh." He made a sign by closing his fist into the manual letter S then pointed to his ear.

This one also took me a moment. "Sears?"

"Right!"

I smiled and spelled "clever," on my fingers.

He pointed to my sketch pad. "Can I see?" Again, he signed as he spoke.

I shrugged and showed him the drawing I was

working on. He looked at the drawing for a long time, then looked at me, astonished. "It's beautiful! You're really good."

I felt a little thrill. "It's okay," I said aloud. Then, remembering that he couldn't hear, I shrugged modestly and made the signs for "just okay."

He looked back at the drawing, and I looked, too. The drawing was pleasing, whimsical and light, like a whisper.

I took advantage of the moment to say, "I have to learn sign language by the end of the summer."

"Why?"

"That's when my job starts." Despite his rule against English, he was obviously a good lip-reader.

"But your student will have an interpreter, right?"

"I guess so," I said, making an exaggerated shrug. "I think I'll be a better tutor if I can sign with him. I saw the card that says you give private lessons."

He said, "I gave lessons last summer. One hour for twenty dollars."

I thought about eighteen dollars hourly in the fall and figured it was a good business investment. "How about two hours for twenty-five dollars?"

He smiled again. "Okay. It's a good cause. Most tutors for deaf kids don't care this much."

I felt uncomfortable under his stare. What could I say? Obviously, I did care, although maybe not for reasons I wanted to admit.

"Should we start next week?" he asked. "After class?"

I made the sign for "fine," touching my thumb to my chest with my palm open and my fingers spread like a fan.

At the start of our first lesson, Curtis had to explain his instructions twice before I understood. He would finger-spell a word, then I would respond with the correct sign. I watched, but his fingers flew so rapidly I could only catch a few letters. I shook my head helplessly.

"Watch again," he said.

I spelled back the only three letters I had caught: "*D-P-Y*."

"No, no, no," he said. "When you read a word, you don't say each letter then think of the word. Watch again."

This time I caught an *S* between the *D* and the *P*.

"Display?" I guessed, making the sign.

"Good. Try another."

I watched his hand, caught the first letter, *C*, and *M-P* in the middle. The others flew by too fast. I guessed, making the sign for "computer."

"Good," he said.

Next time his fingers flew, I caught a *T* a few *R*'s and a *B*.

"Terrible," I said.

"Great! One more."

This time I was distracted by the supple movement of his hands. I'd never realized how sexy a man's hands could be, particularly moving as gracefully and competently as Curtis's hands now moved.

He stopped and looked at me. I felt a warm flush, which I was sure he'd notice—and I felt embarrassed, as if he knew I'd been having sensuous thoughts about his hands.

"I'm lost," I said, trying to recover. "It's hard, like lip-reading. Mostly you're just guessing."

"It's exactly like lip-reading. How do you know what it's like to lip-read?"

I told him how I'd gradually lost my hearing when I was about five, all the while teaching myself to lip-read, until a surgical procedure restored most of my hearing. "I still have hearing loss," I told him.

He looked at me curiously. "Were you raised hearing?" he asked. The sign for "raised" was the same as the sign for "grow up."

I made the sign for "yes," nodding my fist up and down.

"I see. Well, back to work."

His fingers flew again. This time I caught an F at the beginning of a short word, and N-D at the end.

"Friend?" I asked, making the sign.

"Amazing improvement," he said. "I'm a good teacher."

It seemed to me that I was a quick learner, but I signed, "Yes, you are." A little flattery wouldn't hurt.

One day, in the middle of one of our private lessons, he stopped and asked, "Will your student be the only deaf student in the school?"

I made the sign for "yes."

"Why are they doing that to him?"

"He wants to be mainstreamed. The guy who hired me said he's motivated to do well." Between our weekly class sessions, our weekly private lessons, and the dozens of hours I practiced each week, I'd gotten pretty good at signing, but Curtis still had to mostly read my lips.

"Poor kid," he said.

"But you lip-read and speak."

"My parents put me into an oral school. For twenty hours every week I was drilled like this: To make the F, put your lower lip against your upper teeth and make a sound. For V, do the same but add voice. I still can't make D sound different from T."

"Why an oral school?" I asked.

"I didn't lose my hearing until I was two, so I already had some speech. Our family doctor told my parents if they weren't careful, I'd become 'very deaf.' Naturally, my parents didn't think 'very deaf' would be a good idea."

Because I couldn't evaluate his tone of voice, I wasn't quite sure how he felt about this. "Isn't it nice, though, that you can speak so well?"

"I don't speak so well."

"Yes, you do!"

"I used to think so. Then once I tried to say, 'Happy Hanukkah, boys,' and everyone laughed like they'd die."

"Why did they?"

"Nobody wanted to tell me. Finally, someone told me that my words came out sounding like, 'Have a hand job, boys."

I wanted to say something sympathetic to assure him that they shouldn't have laughed. He said, "I guess it's kind of funny."

"It is a bit obscene."

With that, we both giggled—my giggles silent, muffled by my hands covering my mouth, his louder, like a series of grunts.

"That stuff happens all the time!" he said. "I was visiting my sister, and she asked me, 'Where's the baby?' and I said, 'In the trash.'"

Again, we both burst into a peal of laughter. After we stopped laughing, I lingered a few more moments, hoping he'd ask me to stay, but the usual awkwardness descended again, so I gathered my things, gave what I felt was a lame smile, and waved good-bye.

4

I was eight years old when my mother told me I could go to a sleepaway summer camp. "Bretna isn't afraid to go off by herself," she said, making me want to live up to this image of bravery, even though I was secretly a little frightened. She asked if I wanted to stay at camp for one week or two. Some campers would stay for two weeks; others would return after one. Two weeks sounded like a frightfully long time. She said, "It's your decision. But remember: you might be having so much fun after one week that you won't want to come home yet."

I went to camp for two weeks. I wrote letters home and received responses. I thought it odd that my mother wrote back in a large rounded hand. Usually her writing was small and tight. I also thought it odd that she accommodated my rather unusual request. Some girls at camp received packages from home, mostly containing clothes or sweets. I wanted a package, too. I didn't much care what was in the package, but I envied the girls who, at mail call, were handed boxes that they got to unwrap. So I wrote home:

> *Dear Mommy,*
> *Will you please send me my blue felt pen and my green sweatshirt and some Chips Ahoy cookies? Please send everything together in one box. Love, Bretna*

Five days later, I received a package with everything I had asked for, which wasn't like my mother. Odder still was that she hadn't sent my favorite blue pen, as I expected. Instead she sent a new pen, still in its plastic casing.

After I returned home, my mother told me that she, my father, and my younger brother and sister had gone to the Bahamas while I was at camp. She knew just how to tell this to get the reaction she wanted: she emphasized that my brother and sister, Teddy and Hannah, had gone along because she couldn't find a camp for them, but they had stayed in the cabin with baby-sitters most of the time while my parents had their vacation.

"Because I knew you'd be understanding," my mother said, "we brought you back lots of presents. Teddy and Hannah didn't get any presents. You understand why we had to do this, don't you?"

I said yes, because I wanted to be a good girl. As a result, I was rewarded with an evening in my mother's good graces. She smiled at me, she sat on the floor and played with me, and she laughed appreciatively when I made a silly joke.

I felt warm and happy—but it didn't last. When I looked at the presents, I felt somewhat disturbed, even though the presents included an interesting straw doll, a necklace of colored shells, and a violet T-shirt. Violet was my favorite color.

Hannah started to say something about their trip to the Bahamas, but Teddy said, "Shh. Remember we're not supposed to talk about our vacation around Bretna." This irritated me deeply. I was also disturbed to find out that our neighbor, Ellen, had opened my mail and answered my letters and signed "Mommy." I learned this the day

Ellen asked, "Did I send you the right sweatshirt?"

I felt that everyone was in conspiracy against me. I felt cheated and betrayed. I went to look for my mother, who was busy in the kitchen. "You shouldn't have gone without me."

"We finished that discussion, Bretna."

"But maybe I would have wanted to go to the beach, too."

"Bretna. It's done. I have work to do."

"But why didn't you tell me?"

"If you want to be mean and selfish about it," she said, "just give back the presents."

I wished I could stop myself and be good, but I couldn't. I felt too angry. "Fine." I went into my room and got the presents and flung them. She left the presents on the floor.

"Look what you are doing to me," she said. "Look!" She showed me how hard her hands were trembling. She took a medicine bottle from high on the pantry shelf and shook two white pills into her palm. Before washing them down with water from the sink, she said, "Because of you, I have to take tranquilizers." She pinched the bridge of her nose and closed her eyes. "Go ahead and treat me this way. Just keep this up. One day I'll be dead, and you'll be sorry." Again she held out her hands to show me how badly they were shaking.

I wandered back to the living room and picked up the presents from the living room floor—an admission of defeat. Back in my bedroom, I sat down listlessly, an ache in my chest. I longed for something, but I didn't know what—something beautiful perhaps, and harmonious and lovely.

I propped the straw doll up on my dresser and sat for a long time, looking at the doll's linen patchwork dress, the gold hoop earrings, and straw hat woven with a zigzag pattern of greens and grays. The doll fascinated me, even though it utterly lacked beauty and harmony. Her eyes were outlined boldly in black, set too closely together and opened wide, as if someone were squeezing her too tightly. It seemed that she, too, felt some nameless and deep loss.

I was at work in my studio when a key rattled in the door to the apartment. There was no door to my studio, so from my workbench, I had a clear view of Rosie entering the apartment and putting her handbag and keys on the table. She crossed the common area and came into my studio and looked at the sculpture I was working on.

The sculpture was formed from pieces of shattered glass glued into shapes and brushed with glaze to heighten the shimmer and round the edges. The figure seemed to be resting on a bed of grass, but in fact what appeared to be grass was a series of rods that looked like spikes. The doll and spikes were glazed in muted mauves and beiges, imploding into a chaos of purples and yellows, overlaid with a shimmering and melancholy violet.

"Oh, my!" Rosie practically squealed with delight. "That is so creepy!"

Creepy? I felt hurt that she could so reduce what I felt was a complicated interplay of emotions down to a word like creepy.

"Is your real name Rosie?" I asked. Her name now struck me as too perfect for her.

"Roseanne," she said. "For Roseanne Cash. My mother is a country music fan, especially the oldies— Willie Nelson, Loretta Lynn, Patsy Cline. Thank God my name's not Patsy!" She walked away singing: "*I'm crazy for feeling so lonely!*"

It was mid-August, warm and humid. Curtis and I were sitting in his office for our last sign language lesson. He planned to be out of town for two weeks, and after that, my job would start. With only a few weeks to prepare for the semester, panic should have helped me concentrate on the lesson, but my arms were fatigued.

"I'm tired," I told him.

He looked at his watch. With twenty minutes left, it was too soon to quit for the day. "Let's take a little break," he said.

I stood up to get a better view of the pictures on his wall. Facing the door was a bulletin board with a medley of snapshots thumbtacked in place. Also tacked to his bulletin board was an old student identification card from the Massachusetts Institute of Technology.

I looked at him. "You went to MIT?"

"I studied architecture."

He must have read in my eyes an accusation of hypocrisy, because he said, "My situation is different. I wasn't born deaf. I could hear for my first two years. Someone deaf from birth never gets English this well."

"So you were mainstreamed, too?"

"When I was young, until I could insist on a deaf school."

There was a pause as I did a mental adjustment, imagining Curtis moving with ease in such a place as MIT. I sat back in my chair and studied him. Wouldn't he have to admit that maybe all deaf students might benefit from learning to make their way in a hearing environment?

He was also watching me. "There's something I've been wondering." His signs were gentle, his movements slow. "I've been wondering all this time. Why did you want this job?"

"I need the money."

"Tutoring pays that well?"

"It's better than slinging hamburgers."

His gaze was steady and questioning.

"I'm an artist, remember? We're always looking for work that *pays*."

"I remember." Then: "We have agencies that take care of deaf students. I can send in a representative to see that your student is getting what he needs."

"I'm not sure they'd want to talk to you," I said, working to keep my expression neutral so I wouldn't show my alarm. "His parents, and probably the school officials, are confirmed oralists."

"Our representatives know how to talk to those people. They probably haven't hired the right kind of interpreter."

That was for sure. What I said was, "I'll know more after school starts."

"All right. Let's talk then. You're a struggling artist, right? So maybe I should buy you dinner."

"Maybe," I signed, glad that I didn't have to use my voice, which would probably betray my fears. Ordinarily, I would have welcomed dinner as a chance to practice signing—but not if his motive was to hunt down and root out impostors not qualified to work with deaf students.

5

The Carmichael High School building had classic New England charm: brick with white-painted trim, a lawn dotted with elderly maples, a wide walkway leading to the entrance. The interior, though, felt like any other high school with scuffed floors and walls, the dusty smell of chalk, and a steady hum of laughter and voices echoing in the corridors.

I followed the signs to the special education office, where a gray-haired woman sat at the reception desk. "Elaine Weathers?" I asked.

"Over there," she said, pointing.

Elaine Weathers was leafing through a stack of paper. I approached her. "Hi, I'm Bretna Barringer."

"Yes, yes, sit down. I'll be with you in a moment."

She put a file back into a drawer and took another out. I had the feeling she was trying to look busier than she was. She wore a cranberry-red blouse with a silk tie in a bow at her throat, the kind of prissy bow that made me want to yank one end and pull it apart.

Elaine finished with her files, and handed me a computer printout and three books. "This is a copy of Alex's ed plan. Here are the teacher's additions for his books. He has three academic classes in the morning, then an hour for tutoring." She looked at her watch and said, "In ten minutes there'll be a welcome assembly in

29

the auditorium. You can interpret it for him."

An *assembly*? "Fine," I said, as if interpreting assemblies was something I did routinely.

"At noon, Alejandro goes to lunch. After lunch, he has PE, then Resource Center. Can you meet me briefly before lunch?"

"All right," I said. Then: "Where is the auditorium?"

"Straight down that way," she said, pointing. "I told Alejandro to sit in the front row so he can see better."

"How will I recognize him?"

Elaine shot me a look. "He has dark skin, and he wears hearing aids."

In the auditorium, three custodians were setting up chairs. A few kids were already seated. Others were streaming in. One custodian fiddled with knobs on the microphone control box, sending a low-pitched beep through the auditorium.

I took a chair and turned it to face the front row, selecting a place to the left of the microphone so that my good ear would face the speaker.

When the kids came in, the laughter and shouts and pounding of feet made me feel entirely self-conscious. I rested my hands in my lap. I'd been practicing so much the past few weeks that my arms were beyond tired.

I spotted the boy wearing the tell-tale hearing aids. "Hello," I signed. "You must be," then finger-spelled "Alejandro."

He spelled "Alex" on his fingers, then turned away and didn't look at me again. His jeans were so new they still had creases. His cotton shirt, a deep indigo with an insignia near the breast, was tucked neatly into his jeans, giving the impression that he'd fussed a long time getting dressed.

30

He sat about fifteen rows back, toward the center of the auditorium. I waved to get his attention and pointed to the chair in front of me. "Please sit here so you can see me."

"No," he answered. "I can see from here." What he signed was "I see here."

I signed back, "I don't want to stand up." If I stood up, I'd be on view for everyone. This could very well end up in disaster.

Alex looked away. When he looked at me again, I signed, "Sit here."

"No," he signed.

Just great. We were off to a wonderful start. He stole a sideways look at me, and I signed, "This is silly." The kids in the front row were watching me.

The corners of his mouth lifted into what was almost a smile. He was playing games with me. By then all the seats in front of me were taken.

A bell rang, and a thin man wearing round glasses and a celery-green shirt climbed the steps to the stage. He took the microphone and said, "Welcome. I'm the principal, Mr. Richards, and I want to tell you how happy I am to see you and. . ."

I signed, trying to keep up, but Alex was looking around at the other kids. Once in a while he looked at Mr. Richards, but I knew that from his angle, he wouldn't be able to lip-read at all. Not that it mattered. A few curious kids watched me, but Alex never once looked at me.

I was the interpreter, so it seemed to me that if Alex had no idea what was going on, the fault would be mine. On the other hand, if he didn't watch me, who could blame me if he missed things?

Now Mr. Richards was talking about a pep rally. I had no idea what the sign was for "pep rally," so I spelled it out on my fingers. Alex chose that moment to look at me. "What's that?" he signed.

I was surprised to have him stop me with a question. Maybe it wasn't quite right, but I wanted him to leave the assembly with some idea of what had been said. But how could I describe a pep rally?

"It's like a party." That was the best I could do. He perked up when I made the sign for "party."

I added, "For school spirit before a football game."

It didn't seem right for us to have our own private conversation right there in the assembly in front of everyone, but who was I to determine what was right and what wasn't?

"Spirit?" he said, frowning and repeating the sign. The sign for "spirit" was the same as the sign for "ghost." He could really be lost.

I tried to think of a way to explain school spirit, but he'd already lost interest and was looking around at the other kids. I kept on signing, and he kept on not paying attention. The consolation was that I was being paid eighteen dollars hourly for this.

The coach was saying, "Fall sports will be football, soccer. . ."

Alex perked up again and signed, "I like sports. Especially football and hockey."

Again I had the feeling that we shouldn't be having our own private conversation, but I needed to succeed in this job, and for that, I needed Alex's cooperation.

"That's nice," I responded.

At nine fifteen there came the startling metallic jingling of a bell announcing the end of the assembly. I'd survived—sort of. At the flurry of motion, Alex looked at me. "First period," I signed. I looked at the printout

Elaine had given me and signed, "Science, room thirty-seven."

He jumped up and followed the other students out of the auditorium.

Alex and about a half-dozen kids were in room thirty-seven when I arrived. The kids sat at black-topped lab benches. At the head of each bench was a sink and three metal gas taps. Alex was sitting by himself at a bench near the back of the classroom. I pointed to a chair in the front and said, "This is a better seat for you. You can see the teacher, the blackboard, and me."

He looked down, visibly annoyed. He didn't look up again, even when the teacher came in. I introduced myself to the teacher and told him where I wanted Alex to sit and why. The teacher told Alex to move into the seat I had selected. Alex shot me an angry look.

"Why this seat?" he demanded in sign language.

"I don't hear well in this ear,"—I pointed to my left ear—"so I want to make sure my good ear faces the teacher."

He looked at me as if trying to assess whether I was telling the truth. Well, I was, and I couldn't interpret for him if I couldn't hear.

A girl walked into the classroom wearing pink glasses and a fuzzy green sweater. Seeing her, Alex sat up straighter in his chair and watched while pretending not to. I had the feeling he already knew her. The girl's face was all curves with rounded cheeks and a dimple in her chin. The pink reflection from her glasses made her cheeks rosy and soft.

The teacher called out names and handed out index cards. I signed the instructions, but Alex didn't look at me. Next to him a boy wearing a green plaid flannel shirt unbuttoned over a faded blue Led Zeppelin T-shirt slouched in his chair. Alex imitated his posture. The problem was that Alex couldn't slouch and look at the floor and pay attention to what the teacher was saying at the same time. *Sorry, Alex*, I wanted to say. *You're deaf. You have to watch. You can't be rude like the others.*

Alex looked around, saw the kids going up to get their cards, and signed to me, "What's going on?"

"You'd know if you paid attention," I signed back.

"I am paying attention." He snapped his hands angrily.

He went back to watching the teacher's lips. When the teacher said, "Alejandro Palacio," he stood up and went to get his index card. The teacher was explaining what they should write on their cards. Alex wasn't watching me, so I kept my hands in my lap.

After a while, he looked at me and signed, "Is the teacher talking?"

"Yes," I signed.

"Why don't you interpret?"

"You're not watching. Why should I get sore arms for nothing?"

He grinned and signed, "You're supposed to interpret."

"You're supposed to pay attention." Then I signed, "You're stubborn, like a mule." The sign for "mule," one hand imitating a floppy ear, made him smile.

He spent the remainder of the class period looking around at the other kids. I continued interpreting. When the teacher said, "Carbon dioxide," I was at a loss. Not that it mattered; Alex wasn't watching.

Alex looked at me and, keeping his signs small, asked, "What's that girl's name? The girl with pink glasses?"

I shrugged to show him that I didn't know, and continued signing. When the class ended, he asked again,

"What's her name?"

"I don't know," I told him again.

He gave me a disgusted look and said, "Why not? Are you deaf?"

"A little."

"You sign like a hearing person," he told me. "Your face like this." He made his face stony.

It occurred to me that Alex, too, signed like a hearing person. "By the way," I said, "what's the sign for 'carbon dioxide'?"

He blinked, thought for a moment, and finger-spelled, "*C-O-2.*"

Of course. I should have thought of it.

I entered the math classroom shortly after Alex. This time he sat near the front without being told. His face was flushed, and he was sitting awkwardly.

"What's the matter?" I asked.

He signed something, but he mumbled his signs so I couldn't read them. "Pick up your hands," I told him. "I can't see."

He looked around to see if any of the kids were watching.

"You shouldn't be ashamed of sign language," I told him.

"Ha!" he said. "You're ashamed! You didn't want to stand up in the auditorium and have people see you!"

"That wasn't why I didn't want to stand up." I paused until I could think of a lie. "I just haven't done this for a long time."

'Ha," he repeated, clearly not believing me. Then: "That girl with pink glasses talked to me outside. She said something about a moving laser cot."

"A what?"

He picked up a pencil and wrote, "Lazer cot." He signed, "Something like that."

I shrugged to show that I, too, was puzzled.

"How is your first morning going?" Elaine asked. Her tone was light and intimate, even coaxing – so different from her previous briskness. I sat in a yellow vinyl chair across from her. On her desk were piles of folders and papers in perfect order, and two wooden plaques. One said, "Just one more thing . . ." The other said, "When this crisis is over, I'm going to have a nervous breakdown. I earned it, I deserve it, and nobody is going to cheat me out of it."

"It's going fine," I said.

Elaine raised her eyebrows. "Fine? Really?" She was watching me closely, the way the deaf stare. "Alex isn't giving you any trouble?"

"A little. But I like him. He's very. . ." I paused to think of the right word. "Spirited."

Elaine nodded, her lips pressed together. She probably knew I wasn't being completely honest, but what could I do? Telling the truth, the whole truth, and nothing but the truth was out of the question.

"I've known Alex a long time," she said. "As a teacher consultant, I monitored his performance at Brandon. But I know him personally as well. But of course, it's inappropriate to bring personal relationships into the school."

She sounded almost as if she was boasting. "Hmm," I said.

"If you have any problems," Elaine said, "I want you to come to me right away."

"His signing doesn't seem to be very good," I said. "I can't really tell because he doesn't sign much."

"His signing is terrible. He didn't learn until two years ago. His family doesn't sign at all."

Once I got over my surprise, I realized how entirely I had lucked out.

"All you have to worry about is tutoring Alex," she said. "His parents can be, well, rather difficult, but they can't do anything to you. Just remember: You work for the school, not them. If they start making unreasonable demands, let me take care of it."

"All right."

"In particular, any militant ASL anti-oralist attitudes will irritate his family. But you don't strike me as one of those."

"I'm not," I said.

"That will make things easier. Still, for everyone's protection, all important communication should go through me."

By the time Alex and I were settled in English class, his last academic class of the day, I was worn to a frazzle. Alex asked me, "What should I do?"

I wasn't sure whether the problem was his poor signing, my limits as an interpreter, or the fact that he rarely paid attention.

"You're supposed to write an essay," I signed, "about your favorite movie." Because he watched my lips instead of my hands, I mouthed the words while signing them. His lip-reading skills were obviously better than his signing. I didn't know the sign for "essay," so I spelled the word on my fingers.

He grunted and signed something, but his signing was so sloppy I couldn't tell what he'd said.

"Repeat," I signed.

This time he spoke louder: "What that?" The boys

sitting nearby looked at him.

I asked, "What's your favorite movie?"

"No. That other word. *E—*"

"*E-S-S-A-Y*," I spelled slowly.

He made an unintelligible grunting sound supplemented by the angry signs: "Not real word."

"Of course 'essay' is a real word."

"I don't like that word." He turned away and raised his hand for the teacher. When she came over, Alex said, "What am I supposed do?"

The teacher looked at me, alarmed. His voice was coarse and throaty—much harder to understand than Curtis's voice. I understood what he was saying because I knew the context, and because he made the signs for "what" and "supposed" as he talked.

"He doesn't believe he's supposed to write an essay about his favorite movie," I told the teacher. Then something occurred to me: "Maybe he doesn't know what an essay is."

The teacher wrote on his paper, "Write a few paragraphs about your favorite movie." Alex looked at the paper, his expression positively glum, and doodled on the margins. The teacher turned to help another student.

"What's the matter?" I asked.

"I don't like that word 'essay,'" he said.

"Why not?"

"Because it sounds stupid."

I had no idea how to respond to that. He was profoundly deaf. How would he know what something sounded like? Besides, why would he care?

He took a fresh piece of paper from his notebook and wrote, "Lethel Wepan." I watched him write about how Lethal Weapon was his "favit movy" because it had a lot of "axshon." I thought back to how many times that day

I had interpreted by spelling out what was said on my fingers. If this was any indication of his reading and spelling ability, he hadn't understood a single word I'd spelled. This job was going to be harder than I'd thought, for reasons other than I'd expected.

With all the kids busy working on their compositions, the only sounds were the shuffling of chairs, an occasional cough, and the clicking of the teacher's heels as she walked around the classroom.

Suddenly, Alex let out a terrific belch. Every head in the classroom bobbed up. When he realized everyone was staring at him, he turned pink.

Keeping his hands in his lap and his signs small, he signed, "Me? I made noise?"

I nodded my fist, making the sign for "yes."

The kids were laughing and Ms. Montgomery looked around for the guilty kid. Alex looked at me, completely panicked.

Discreetly, so no one else would notice, I signed, "Say, 'Excuse me'."

Alex turned to face the class. The word "excuse," came out sounding like "cooze," but once he voiced the words "cooze me," Mrs. Montgomery relaxed.

Alex looked down at his paper. I could see he was deeply humiliated. He signed, "I burped before. Nobody heard it."

"Some burps are louder than others," I explained.

He looked to the side and saw that two of the boys were still laughing. He kept his signs small. "They're laughing at me."

"It's okay," I signed back. "Laugh with them."

He hesitated, as if trying to decide whether to believe me. Then he looked at the boys and gave a silent chuckle. One of the boys said, "That was funny" clearly enough so

Alex would have no trouble reading his lips. Then he gave Alex a good-natured punch on the arm.

When at last even the boys returned to their compositions, Alex grinned at me and signed, "They think I'm funny."

"It was funny once," I signed. "But it won't be funny a second time, I promise."

He looked down at his paper, but a moment later he looked back up and signed, "What did it sound like?"

How do you describe a loud belch? "It sounded big."

That pleased him. He smiled, picked up his pencil and hunched over his desk. From this angle, I could see the young child in the curve of his cheek and his awkwardness. In that moment, when he wasn't fighting against me, he seemed brave instead of difficult, independent instead of stubborn.

After class, in the corridor, I came face-to-face with the girl with the pink glasses. Seeing me, she squealed and said, "You're the sign language interpreter!"

I smiled and said, "Hello," while making the sign.

"Will you teach me to say something in sign language?"

"Okay. How about, 'What is your name?'" I showed her the signs, and she repeated them, her arms awkward.

Alex came up beside us. I could tell he was deliberately slouching. I could also see he was tense and nervous. The girl turned to Alex and signed, "What is your name?"

She made the signs well enough so that he understood. He spelled, "*A-L-E-X*" on his fingers and said, "Alex." Then he signed, "What is your name?"

"Mona," she said.

"Like this," I said, and showed her how to spell her

name on her fingers.

She tried it and smiled. "Cool," she said. Then "Bye!" and disappeared into the crowd.

Alex stood perfectly still, as if dazed. Then he said, "I didn't think I'd be able to talk to a girl like her."

"Next time," I told him, "we have to figure out what the heck she meant by a moving laser cot."

6

I had already seen the Renoir exhibit at the Fine Arts Museum three times, but after so many hours in the high school, I needed to relax and look at something beautiful.

"Can I join you?" Rosie asked.

"Sure," I said, although I would have rather gone alone.

Standing in a room with Renoir landscapes all around quiets and humbles me. Few artists will say, "Renoir is my favorite," because he's so famous and popular. It would be like saying, "I think Shakespeare and Dante and Chaucer were the best writers, ever." Like, duh. But when I look at one Renoir after another, I feel sheer astonishment at the brilliant play of light and darkness, and the control and variety of brush strokes.

"These are so beautiful!" Rosie said. "I mean, I've seen reprints and photographs of some of these paintings, but actually seeing them is really an experience. This makes me want to get a member pass to this museum, too."

We were standing in front of "*Landscape at Wargemont*" when my cell phone vibrated. I answered it and said "Hello," still gazing at the picture, which like a dream, with sparkling hills of translucent greens, blues, and purples. This particular painting, the images done in swirls, was audaciously close to surrealism.

Nobody was on the line. I felt another vibration. It was a text message, so I had to look away from the painting. The message was from Curtis: *"Hello and how was the 1st day of school?"*

"Fine," I texted back, *"and tiring. I didn't know 13 yr old boys can be so difficult!"*

"Ha ha."

Feeling jittery, I looked back up at the painting, waiting for the rest of the text to come through. When I looked back at my phone, Curtis had written: *"I promised you dinner. Can you meet me tomorrow at 7?"*

Dinner would probably also include questions about the job. In fact, for all I knew he was asking me to dinner just so he could ask about Alex. But I may as well go. Janae had been telling me lately to stop living like a recluse—as if she had room to talk.

"OK," I wrote.

"Great. Meet me at the Deaf Association?"

I wrote, *"Sure."*

By then the crowd had pushed me back so I was no longer standing under the *"Landscape at Wargemont"* and I had to wait my turn to rejoin Rosie. She looked at me eagerly, obviously expecting me to tell her who had texted, but instead I pointed and said, "It looks like Renoir did this one from a hallucination."

"Oh, yes! Reminds me of college and my drug days! So who was that?"

"Just a friend," I said lightly. To keep her from asking any more questions, I pretended to look closely at the hills of the next landscape, which reminded me of the creamy gold color of a Pomeranian.

There were no classes held in the Deaf Association

the following evening. The lights over the classroom cubicles were dimmed. In a corner by the reception desk, a group of five guys sat at a table playing a board game. Curtis was hovering over the table, watching them. He looked up when I entered and waved casually to me. He signed his good-byes to the group, and came to the door.

A straggly man who had been standing near the bulletin boards made a grunting noise and stopped Curtis with a question. I could not understand the question, but I understood Curtis's response: "No. C'mon. We have to talk about some important things." Curtis gave him a good-natured punch on the arm, evidently to soften the refusal.

The man then signed, "I'm hungry!" His hair was uncombed and his shirt was torn at the elbow.

Curtis reached into his pocket, took out his wallet, and gave the man a ten-dollar-bill. Curtis signed rapidly, pointing toward the street. I caught the signs for "Good-bye," and "See you later."

To me, Curtis signed, "Let's go." We walked out to the street and down the block to a Chinese restaurant with red awnings and café curtains. Inside was burgundy carpeting and deeply paneled walls. The smell from the kitchen was mouth-watering.

"The best Chinese food in Brighton," Curtis told me, signing as he spoke. His signs were sharp and clear, making me realize how much Alex slurred his signs.

"Smells great," I responded.

We sat at a table for two in the center of the room. I said, "That man wanted to come with us?"

"His name is Reuben. He used to beg on the streets with one of those cards that say, 'I'm deaf.' We brought him into the association and helped him apply for disability checks."

I made the sign for "interesting." The sign for "interesting," I'd learned, was a catch-all conversation filler.

People at nearby tables were watching us while pretending not to. The way the other diners watched us, furtively then quickly looking away, was more unnerving than the open, curious way the kids in the high school stared.

The waiter approached our table and stood with his pencil and pad ready. Then, to my surprise, he leaned close to me as if he would whisper something, but instead he shouted in my ear, "What do you want?"

The force of his shout thoroughly startled me. Everyone in the restaurant, it seemed, turned to look at us. Curtis put his hand over his mouth to hide his smile. I almost laughed aloud.

I turned back to the waiter and said, "Chicken with cashews, please." To my own ears, my voice sounded softly modulated and clear. The waiter, appearing confused, wrote my order.

"Tell him I want the shrimp dish, number fourteen." Curtis's eyes were shining. I repeated his order for the waiter. After the waiter turned away, Curtis said, "He turned purple when you used your voice."

"He shouted right in my ear," I said.

"At least you're not wearing a hearing aid. When people do that to me, I feel like. . ." He made a gesture of shock so exaggerated it resembled electrocution, reminding me of Wile E. Coyote.

We both laughed again. To keep him from turning the conversation back to Alex, I asked about his new class. He was now completely relaxed, no longer speaking as he signed. He signed about his new students, and about how he enjoyed his Wednesday nights teaching at the Deaf Association, but that teaching was tiring, too, and after having done the same lessons so many times, it was getting boring. Then he told a funny story about what had happened during the first class meeting. I caught familiar signs and phrases, but once he launched into his story I couldn't make sense of what he was saying. I didn't want to ask him to slow down, so I nodded, pretending to understand.

He leaned forward and signed, "Your signing has improved."

"I've been practicing."

"It's still straight English, no ASL grammar at all. And stiff."

I pretended to be insulted. "Well. Thank you very much."

He softened. "You're doing fine."

"For a hearing person." I stressed "hearing" by shrugging my shoulders in a sassy gesture.

"Well you *are* a hearing person," he said. Then: "So do the kids want anything to do with Alex?"

"I think they will." I told him about the burp incident, and he laughed. I liked the way the corners of his eyes crinkled. "Something like that happened to me, too," he said. "But it was even more embarrassing, and not a suitable story for a restaurant. Let's just say I made an embarrassing sound." He laughed again, remembering. Then, leaning forward with an expression of genuine concern, said, "Does anyone try to talk to Alex?"

"One girl, Mona, wants to learn sign language. She tried to talk to Alex, but he couldn't understand what she said—I guess something about a moving laser cot."

"Lesser God," he said. "Looks like 'laser cot' on the lips. She was probably talking about the movie, *Children of a Lesser God*."

"Now why didn't I think of that?"

He smiled, then spoiled the moment by asking, "So what's your day like? What kind of schedule do you have in the school?"

"Alex has three academic classes, plus a special reading class, and three times each week he goes to speech. I spend a few hours in the learning center tutoring him."

I left out the fact that I also interpreted his classes for him. He was gazing at me steadily, with the look that seemed to take in everything. What I thought was, *He knows. He has to know. He isn't stupid.*

"What do you do when he's in class?"

I was about to say, "I tutor other kids with special needs" —a direct lie, but what choice did I have? Fortunately, our waiter chose that moment to come through the swinging door to the kitchen carrying our tray so I was spared the necessity of lying, and given the excuse to look away and watch as the waiter put our plates in front of us.

"Will that be all?" the waiter asked loudly.

"Yes," I said, making the sign as I spoke. "Thank you."

I looked back at Curtis, and he was watching me with something like amusement. I put my napkin in my lap and picked up my fork. Thank goodness it was too difficult to converse in sign language while eating. We managed some small talk, but mostly we ate without signing. He had a hearty appetite, and was clearly enjoying his meal, not minding at all if his enthusiasm showed on his face. At one point he paused, gave his fork a little shake in my direction, and, using only his voice, said thickly, "I told you it's good."

I smiled and made the signs for "yes" and "excellent."

After we ate, Curtis paid the bill. "It's on me," he said firmly. We were walking toward the bus stop when he startled me by signing, "I want to study for the state architecture exam. I need tutoring in English. I need a hearing tutor."

"A tutor?"

"I can do the designing, math, and engineering parts fine," he signed. "It's the reading comprehension and vocabulary that's difficult. I can sit and memorize vocabulary lists, but I thought it would be more fun to drill."

"OK. Thirty dollars an hour."

"Ha ha," he said. "Two hours for twenty-five dollars."

"OK. It's a good cause."

"I'll need enough lessons to pass," he said, "and to give you back the money you gave me for sign lessons."

Now we were sitting on the bench in the glass-enclosed bus stop. From down the road came the grinding of an engine. I looked, but it wasn't a bus; it was a silver pick-up truck.

"Okay," he signed. "Once and for all, I want to get something straight about Alex. Exactly who is his interpreter?"

I drew in my breath. We looked at each other. I said, "His interpreter is me."

I expected him to be angry. Instead, he gave me an odd smile. "You are really something else." I waited for him to get angry, but he didn't. He said, "Gutsy beyond gutsy. Nerves of steel."

"My nerves are not steel. Mostly, I was in a panic. Why do you think I practiced so much?"

"So that was why you wanted private lessons. I thought maybe you liked me."

How was I supposed to answer that? "I could have asked someone else."

"You lied to me all summer. You lied to me in there," he said, pointing back toward the restaurant with his thumb.

"I didn't lie to you in there. The food came in time so I didn't have to."

"Bretna," he said and shook his head.

"It all turned out all right," I said. "Alex doesn't even know ASL grammar or idioms, and his signing is worse than mine. Besides, he's in low-level classes that go slowly. I can easily keep up."

He stared at me with his most penetrating gaze.

"I got lucky," I said.

"You got lucky because he's being raised orally, so he can't really sign. That poor kid. An ASL interpreter might have helped him get to the point where he could fit in with the deaf culture instead of being stuck between, not fitting in anywhere."

"Maybe he can fit in everywhere," I said.

Instead of responding to that, he pointed to me and signed, "You are exactly what we don't want. We advise schools not to hire interpreters with less than two years experience."

"I know. I'm sorry. I needed a job. I needed a job paying eighteen dollars hourly."

"You're *sorry*? If people at the association knew." He shook his head. "Just don't tell anyone, okay?"

"What do you think I'm going to do? Stand up somewhere and announce that I'm in the habit of telling lies that might hurt a deaf kid?"

"I don't know, Bretna. But I wouldn't put anything past you."

I lifted my chin and looked straight at him. A crinkle

came into his eyes.

"Where do you get your nerve?" he asked, his expression so soft I felt myself smiling. Just then the bus pulled up in front of us, the engines whining. I boarded the bus, found a seat, and looked at him out the window. He made a sign as if punching keys in his palm, then pointed to me, which I took to mean, "I'll text you."

7

I sat across from Alex in the Learning Center, wishing the windows had shades so I could close them. The sunlight fell onto our table in the shape of a trapezoid.

We'd spent the first hour of his tutoring time going back over what had happened in class. He insisted on lip-reading the teacher, which meant he got nothing out of class so I had to tell him what he missed.

Alex was distracted by the glowing trapezoid on his desk, but I was distracted by his black eye. Evidently he'd gotten the black eye in the locker room after school the day before. From the moment he'd walked into school in the morning, everyone who saw him, including me, asked, "What happened to you?" Each time, he said, "I ran into a locker." I knew from the way he said it that he hadn't run into a locker. I assumed it had happened when kids were horsing around. It could have been an accident, or someone could have been picking on him.

He put his head down on the table. When he looked up again, I traced the outline of the trapezoid with my finger and said, "Isn't it an interesting shape?"

"You're strange," he said.

"I like shapes," I said.

"Nobody likes shapes. That's weird." He tilted his head, and added, "Your vest is weird, too."

The vest was one of my thrift-store finds, a black

velvet vest delicately embroidered with brightly colored birds and flowers. I wore it with a shimmering white silk blouse and black twill pants that had a slight sheen. If by "weird," Alex meant "different," he was right. I'd never seen a vest like it.

"We need to get working," I said, signing as I spoke. "You have a test on Tuesday."

He burst into a loud guffaw. "Tuesday!" he signed emphatically. He turned his hand so that the sign became "toilet."

I realized my mistake. I'd turned my hand the wrong way while signing "Tuesday," making the sign for "toilet" instead.

He guffawed again, and signed, "A test on the toilet!" and slapped his knee. I put my finger to my lips and said, "Shhh." He stopped laughing and looked around to see if he'd been too loud and drawn attention to himself. Seeing that nobody was paying attention, he put his head back down on his desk. I was getting tired of prodding him. I sat back and waited for him to begin work.

He looked up and said, "I am not good at football."

"I know. You told me. Maybe you'd be better at soccer."

"I like football. But it's hard to practice. My dad can't throw or catch."

He had already told me that his father was a nuclear physicist at Draper Labs in Cambridge. I said, "Maybe your dad is just not a natural athlete."

"That's for sure." He put his head back down.

I looked out the window. Already the maples were turning. I wished I had an easel and oil paints so that I could paint instead of sitting here trying to get Alex to work.

He picked up his head and said, "I want an A on the

math quiz tomorrow."

"Then we'd better start working."

He guffawed again. "A test on the toilet! That was a good one!"

"Shhh," I warned.

"I want an A," he said, sitting straighter and picking up a pencil.

"If you want an A you better stop laughing and start working."

Just then Mona poked her head into the Learning Center. Seeing us, she waved. Alex sat up in his seat. She mouthed, "Look what I can do!" and began performing the manual alphabet. "A-B-C-D—" she got stuck with "E," then began again with "J."

A boy passing by in the corridor stopped and mocked her, forming his hands into random shapes. She put her hands on her hips and said something. I caught enough of what she was saying to interpret for Alex. "She's telling him to shut up, that sign language is cool. Now the boy said, 'Who are you? His mother?'"

"Mother?" Alex was alarmed.

"He means she's *acting* like your mother, protecting you."

Alex blushed. I realized my mistake: The sign for "protect," the wrists crossed in front of the chest, was similar to the sign for "love."

A hall monitor came and put a stop to the conversation in the hallway, gesturing for both Mona and the boy to get going. When they were gone, I said, "Alex. I forgot to tell you. 'Laser cot' was probably 'Lesser God.'"

"Yes! That's it!" Then his expression darkened and he said, "My mom doesn't like that movie. She doesn't like how the girl is so mad at hearing people and doesn't want to learn to speak."

I heard the clicking of heels across the tile floor and looked up. Elaine Weathers was walking toward us. I felt a momentary guilt—Alex and I had been sitting here at least twenty minutes without getting a single thing done.

She smiled tightly, lips closed. Her shirt was bright yellow and she wore another of those ties in a bow at her neck.

"Hello, Alex," she said. Then, surprised, "What happened to you?"

"I ran into a locker," he said. I'd grown accustomed to his speech. When it was just the two of us, I could understand everything he said because he supplemented his speech with signs. When he relied just on his voice, as he did now, I realized how thick and hard to understand his speech was.

"That eye doesn't look good," Elaine said.

Unlike the other teachers, she knew just how to speak to a deaf person. She held her head perfectly still, spoke quietly, and enunciated her words without exaggerating them.

"I'm fine," Alex said.

"I understand you're trying out for football," she said.

"Yes," said Alex.

"Very good," she said. Then she turned to me. "I have to talk to you for a few minutes."

"Now?"

"Now. Tell Alex you'll be back soon."

I told him to do the problems himself, and I'd check them when I got back. Once Elaine and I were in the hallway, I said, "There was an announcement about Parent's Night. What's that?"

"Nothing you have to worry about."

"I'd think Alex's parents would want to meet me."

Wasn't I spending the better part of every day with their son?

"You really don't have to go," she said as if doing me a great favor. She stopped and gave me a look. "Remember: you don't have to worry about Alex's parents. You work for the school."

"Why do you keep warning me about them?"

She stopped and pursed her lips, as if trying to decide whether to tell me. "Let's just put it this way," she said. "Alex's mother did not get along with the interpreters at Brandon last year."

She turned and walked into her office. This was how Elaine was. She talked in riddles. She dropped hints. She had a stern, businesslike manner that discouraged questions or protests.

She sat at her desk and I faced her. "I just talked to Walter Givens," she said. "He wants me to tell you what is going on with your contract."

"What contract?" I asked.

"Your union contract. All the teachers and aides have one. The union decided you will be classified in Unit D because you are a classroom aide. So your salary will be the same as the other employees in Unit D, eight seventy-five an hour."

"Eight seventy-five! No. I was promised eighteen dollars!"

"I'm sure Walter told you he couldn't promise that much because the teachers hadn't yet agreed on their new contracts."

"He told me nothing of the kind! The ad said 'eighteen dollars hourly.'"

She looked at me suspiciously. "He didn't tell you that the final offer and contract depended on what happened in the union meetings?"

"He did not!"

"Didn't the ad say that your job was classified as a classroom aide?"

"Yes, it did. But the ad also said eighteen dollars an hour."

"Well. It doesn't matter. There's nothing that can be done now. The union is all about being fair to everyone. They've been trying for years to get increases for the people in Unit D, and when they found out that Walter wanted to pay you eighteen dollars hourly. . ."

"How many school holidays are there?" I asked.

She blinked, startled, and handed me a school calendar. I flipped through. Each month had at least two holidays, except March. Then of course, there were two weeks off in the winter and a week in spring.

She said, "In Unit D you get paid for four holidays, and three sick days."

"That's crazy. How do people in Unit D support themselves?"

"Most classroom aides are retired, or married and working an extra job—"

"I'm not retired, and I'm not married. Eight seventy-five is not enough."

"Walter has been trying to convince the union to make a special exception for you, but they are not willing to do that. It wouldn't be fair to the other non-credentialed employees. So there's nothing that can be done—"

My mind was spinning. I'd depleted my savings account paying for sign language classes and lessons in anticipation of eighteen dollars hourly.

"This can't happen," I said, fighting panic. "If he had told me last spring, I wouldn't have applied for the job. Now he thinks I'm stuck."

"He knows you're not stuck. He knows as a sign language interpreter, you can go into the city and earn at least twenty-five dollars hourly."

How was I supposed to answer that? Tell her I had no choice because I wasn't a *real* sign language interpreter?

My hands were shaking. I stood up. "I need to think. I'd better get back now."

Elaine said, "I know you and Alex are getting along, but trust me. He and his family can be difficult. I'm just saying that with your skills, there are better jobs out there."

"Fine," I said.

"Please sit back down," she said.

I sat down.

"Remember the first day," she said, "when you told me your day was going fine? Well. Alex was at Brandon for two years. Never once did an interpreter ever describe a day with Alex as 'fine.'"

"Maybe I can do what they can't do."

"That's not the point. The point is that you weren't leveling with me. Your day wasn't going fine. It couldn't have been going fine. First days with Alex never go fine. I'm not going to be able to help you if you don't level with me."

"At first he was difficult, but I can handle it. I wanted you to think I could handle it."

She sat back, considering this. I brought the conversation back to the point: "I was promised eighteen dollars an hour."

"You're every bit as stubborn as Alex. If you can't get by on eight seventy-five an hour, it won't take you long to find something else. There's just nothing we can do about the union."

"I'd better get back now," I said.

The corridor was eerily quiet between classes. I went back to the Learning Center and sat across from Alex. He hadn't even opened his notebook.

"What's the matter?" he demanded.

"Nothing," I signed.

It was clear from the way he glared at me that he knew I was lying. How would I get him to trust me and tell me the truth, if I lied to him? I'd held enough back from Elaine. So I signed, "Well, actually, something is the matter."

"About me?"

"No. Of course not. About the job."

"You get in trouble?"

"No."

He squinted as if he didn't believe me.

Next morning, at the start of first period, I sat in my usual seat across from Alex. He pointed out a boy sitting in the back row. "That kid is weird."

"Why?"

"He sits in the back and draws pictures. In the lunch room he sits by himself and draws pictures."

"His name is Rodney," I said. "He draws pictures of cars, and his drawings are good."

The day before, I'd stopped in front of Rodney's desk to look. The drawing he was working on was a race car with the hood up. The motor was drawn with such precision I had the feeling he was a boy who could not only draw motors, but take motors apart and put them back together.

"He's weird," Alex said again. Then he perked up and said, "I have this for you." He handed me a sealed envelope.

I opened it and read:

> *Dear Ms. Barringer:*
>
> *We just returned from Parent's Night and would like to express our appreciation for the kindness, care, and invaluable help you are giving Alex. We sincerely thank you for making Alex's mainstreaming possible. We are impressed to see how your presence enriched (in the teacher's words) the classroom experience for all children, as well as for the teachers and staff. You are not only providing an invaluable service to Alex, but you are also influencing positively attitudes toward deafness and mainstreaming in our public schools. We want to assure you that you have our total, active support as well as our gratitude.*
>
> *Sincerely,*
> *Esteban and Lucinda Palacio*
> *cc: Walter Givens and Elaine Weathers*

It took me a moment to remember why the name 'Lucinda' was familiar. Then I remembered the note Mrs. Eakle had written to Mr. Givens the day I interviewed.

Alex was watching me. I smiled and said, "Thanks."

"My mom wants to meet you. She said I should give you her phone number. She wants you to call her."

"Thanks," I said. "Maybe I will."

After class, I saw Rodney and Alex nod to each other. Earlier I'd seen Alex and Rodney entering the PE building at the same time. I had a hunch Rodney knew something about how Alex got the black eye, so next time I had the chance, I stopped in front of Rodney's desk for the outward purpose of looking at his drawing. After complimenting his drawing—an antique car with fins—I said, quietly enough so that others wouldn't hear, "Hey, how did Alex get that black eye?"

"We were throwing around one of the padlocks. We shouted to him to duck!"

"Sweetie. He's deaf."

"I know he's deaf! That's why he talks funny! But he hears the bell ring. He *told* me he can hear the bell ring. We yelled 'duck' loud."

"He might have felt somehow the bell was ringing, but that doesn't mean he understood 'duck.'"

Rodney gave an irritated grunt and went back to his drawing.

It occurred to me that even if Alex figured out that the boys were saying 'duck,' he may have thought they meant the noun. I imagined Alex wondering why the boys were talking about ducks just before a padlock came crashing into his eye.

8

"I have a friend coming over tonight," I said.

Janae understood immediately. "What kind of animal?" she asked.

Rosie, who had been standing at the stove, cooking, turned around, her expression incredulous. Rosie cooked frequently. Since she'd moved in, the loft always smelled faintly of spices and meats. She kept a bottle of red wine on the counter, and invited us to have a glass whenever we wanted. Her philosophy of life seemed to be: If one is good, two is better. If climbing a small mountain is a challenge, how much more thrilling to climb a large one.

"I'm not sure," I said. "Solid, friendly, and good-natured."

"Sounds like a French bull dog," said Janae. "People think they're unfriendly because of the name 'bull dog' and because of their pug faces, but they're very outgoing and good-natured."

"Just a minute," said Rosie. "Did I miss something? Bretna has a French bull dog coming to visit?"

"She has a date," Janae said. "She's describing him."

In the spirit of full disclosure, I said, "He's also deaf. He was the teacher of my sign language class."

"Oh, a teacher!" said Rosie. "My first husband was one of my professors. We met when I was in college, but we didn't get married until two years after I graduated."

Neither Janae nor I responded. I honestly didn't know what to say when Rosie made comments like that one.

Curtis and I sat on the floor in the common area, on a tweed rug in front of the couch, his study guides open. The tweed rug was one of Rosie's many additions to the apartment. When she went around adding furnishings, she made clear she did not like minimalist decorating. "Who said less is more?" she demanded. "If you ask me, less is less." Now, both Rosie and Janae were out for the evening. Janae, the soul of tact, had suggested to Rosie that they go out somewhere, so Curtis and I were alone in the apartment.

I signed, "What's the opposite of confluence," finger-spelling "confluence."

"Separation," he signed.

"Right."

He looked glum and said, "I'd never be able to pronounce this word."

"Nobody ever actually says words like 'confluence.' You just have to know what it means for silly tests." My signing had improved so much that he didn't need to use his voice or try to read my lips.

"This is exhausting," he said, setting aside the books. "So how is Alex?"

"He seems to be in love."

"With a hearing girl?"

"Yes, the one who wants to learn sign language."

"Does he have a chance?"

I thought of how pretty and appealing Mona was, and how mature, taking on the boy who made fun of sign language. She was so poised. Alex was so youngish. "I don't know. Maybe not."

The shelves in the living room were mostly filled with art books. Curtis looked at the books, and asked about the sketches on the wall. I told him they were Janae's. On the top shelf was a stack of sketchpads. "How about these?" he asked.

"They're mine."

"Can I see?"

"Sure."

He pulled one out and looked at the first sketch for a long time. "Where is this?"

"The Mohave Desert in Southern California, just before you get to Arizona." I recalled that the town nearby had a strange name, Needles.

"When were you in the Mohave Desert?"

"I passed through a few times. Once, going to California with my mother, brother, and sister when I was ten. I sketched this from the window of a Greyhound bus, going the other direction, when I was eighteen."

He turned to the next page, an Arizona sunset, done in pastels. There's no point in drawing an Arizona sunset with pencil because an Arizona sunset is all about color— the dramatic purple and fire-orange of the sky set against a backdrop of hills and cactus.

"Where did you go on that bus when you were eighteen?"

"To St. Louis, where my family came from." He was staring at me, as if expecting me to say something more, so I said, "It took fifty-two hours."

He turned a page. "That's Texas," I told him.

"I've never been to Texas," he said. Then: "Why did you go to St. Louis?"

"To get away from my family. To try to understand my family. To try to understand what went wrong."

"What are your parents like?"

I weighed whether he really wanted to know, or whether he was just asking a polite question. He was watching me, expecting an answer, so I went into my room, opened my closet and stood on a step stool and pulled down a stack of canvases from a shelf.

I returned and handed him a canvas and signed, "This is what my mother is like."

The canvas was an explosion of orange with a touch of red. Two images, one larger and done in deeper shades of scarlet and carmine, the other smaller, in shades mixed with yellow. The larger figure covered and overpowered the other. The painting was angry, dangerous, and full of rage.

Curtis looked at me, alarmed.

I suspected he didn't believe me. People never seemed to believe me when I tried to tell them what my mother was like, so I rarely talked about her. In fact, I hadn't talked to her since shortly after I moved out of Myrna's house, when my mother called to tell me my father had moved out and they were getting a divorce. "Good riddance," she said. "I should have kicked him out a long time ago."

I turned away from the painting and pointed to Curtis's portfolio. "What's in there?"

"Work stuff."

"Can I see?'

He signed 'sure' so I unsnapped the portfolio and took out a sheath of architectural drawings. One, sketched by hand, showed a façade with trees and shrubbery.

"This is good," I told him, even though the drawings were stiff and fussy and slightly distorted.

"It's all right. I got through architecture school. I would have never gotten into the Massachusetts College of Art. I'd certainly never have any work displayed at the Museum of Fine Arts."

"You just haven't had the right teacher."

He turned to a blank page and said, "All right," he said. "Give me a drawing lesson."

"Relax," I signed. "Look closely at something and draw exactly what you see."

From his bag, he took an ordinary number two pencil. He watched his pencil as he drew the outline of my face, glancing at me occasionally as he sketched in my features, the curve of my chin, my pale eyebrows.

He turned to a fresh page. He reached over and touched my chin, turning my face slightly to the side. He drew me again, this time with my eyes slightly narrowed, the curve of my lip and small pertness of my nose and chin exaggerated. It wasn't quite right because it wasn't quite me. He continued sketching and something emerged in the expression that I didn't recognize as mine: a light mischievousness. A few more strokes near my pupils added a steely determination.

I took the sketchpad and looked at the drawing. "See! It's good."

"It's all right. Your turn." He handed me the sketch pad and pencil.

I looked steadily at him and sketched in his face, the curls of his hair, his neck and shoulder. He had good bone structure, so I emphasized the square of his jaw and the slant of his eyes. I drew sinewy lines suggesting the muscles of his neck and arms—then, feeling a flood of warmth through me, I stopped, suddenly self-conscious. It occurred to me that either I was a prude, or I had gone way too long without romance if drawing the lines of his neck and shoulders had such an effect on me.

He reached for the drawing and looked at it for a long

time. "It's really good, like it's alive. I always wished I could draw like that."

"You can—"

"No, I can't. I took enough art classes to know what I can do and what I can't."

Just then, my phone rang in the kitchen. The ringing was a shock after sitting so long in absolute silence. I gave such a start that my foot hit the trunk. He stared at me. The phone rang a second time.

"My telephone," I signed. When the phone rang a third time, I signed, "It's probably a telemarketer."

Curtis stood up. He closed the study guide, gathered his pencils, and put everything back into the portfolio. "I guess I'd better go now."

Suddenly closed and tense, he picked up his coat and waved good-bye. The phone rang once more, then the apartment was silent.

Next day, Curtis sent a text message: *"I'm sorry, Bretna. That was stupid. And rude."*

I searched for a response. "That's okay," seemed wrong, as if encouraging him to vanish without notice. So I tried for a joke: *"I agree. I told the telephone that ringing like that was stupid and rude, and the telephone promised never to do it again."*

"Ha ha," he responded. *"My phone doesn't listen to me either."*

I was trying to figure what to say next when he sent another text inviting me to dinner at his favorite Italian restaurant.

As it turned out, his favorite Italian restaurant was only a few blocks from his apartment. I wasn't, as they say, born yesterday. I knew his design was for us to end up in his apartment.

His apartment surprised me—bare walls, lamps without shades, white scruffy walls, brown shaggy carpet. The only attempt at decoration was a photograph of Frank Lloyd Wright's *Falling Waters* tacked to one wall. I didn't expect his apartment to look like a prison cell, or interrogation room.

I said, "What's with the lamp shades?"

"Lamp shades?"

"You don't have any."

He laughed. "I'm lazy."

The apartment seemed to have been built in the twenties, with real carved wood trim on all the windows and doors. From where I sat on the couch, I could see that the floor tiling in his kitchen was kiwi green.

"Can I look at your kitchen?"

"Go ahead."

The kitchen, unbelievably enough, had a dusty-pink refrigerator with a single door that looked like it dated from the 1940s. The tile on the countertop was orange and peach. The kitchen was no more than five feet across. I poked my head back into the living room and signed, "This kitchen is brilliant."

"I don't so much mind the green floors and orange tile," he said. "But the pink refrigerator I can do without."

"I love it. It's zany and playful."

He said, "Since you're being nosy, I'm reading this."

From the outside flap of my purse, he pulled a folded copy of Alex's ed plan. It was ten pages, single spaced, full of information about Alex.

While he read, I went back into the kitchen and opened the refrigerator. Inside were several cans of Diet Coke, a loaf of wheat and honey bread, cheese, peanut butter, condiments, and milk. The refrigerator had a small icebox, the kind that probably had to be defrosted every few weeks. In the ice box were three plastic ice trays and a carton of Ben and Jerry's Cherry Garcia. I closed the refrigerator and went back to sit on the couch.

He refolded the ed plan and signed, "That kid has learning disabilities in addition to his deafness. He is functioning way below grade level. His English skills are like that of a third grader. How can anyone believe he can function in regular ninth grade?"

"Mostly he's not in regular ninth grade classes. He only has three academic classes, and they're low level. Plus he gets two full hours of tutoring. Anyone can do that."

"You know," he signed, "seeing this, I am really glad you're the one in that job. The usual person who takes a job like that in a public school would just walk in, sign rapidly, tutor him and leave without really paying attention to his needs."

I said, "Just recently—"

He shook his head. "Like this." He made the sign for "recently," placing his right index finger curved against his cheek.

I imitated him, but he shook his head again. Taking my hand, he corrected my sign by curving my fingers inward with the fingers facing back. I held still, letting him shape my hand, not drawing back even when I should have.

He turned my palm upward. With his index finger, he drew a horizontal line across my palm followed by a curved line, making the sign for "what?" in my hand.

I couldn't answer without pulling my hands back. Instead, I turned my hand up, and asked, "What, what?" in his palm. He smiled directly at me. With great difficulty, I didn't look away. I had thought his eyes were hazel but now I saw they were a pure watery green without a touch of hazel.

I looked away first, glancing at my hand resting in his, then his knees. When I looked back at his face, he was still watching me. We stared at each other for what seemed like forever. I knew he would kiss me, but the moment of waiting went on and on until it felt absurd that we were just looking at each other. He shifted again, moving closer so that our knees were touching.

I made the sign for, "Well?"

He blinked, startled. "Well, what?"

"Well, are you going to kiss me, or do I have to kiss you?"

He laughed and looked at me the way he had at the bus stop when I told him that Alex's interpreter was me. He touched my chin, then kissed me.

I surprised him again by pulling back and saying, "There's a rumor about you."

"Me?" he was genuinely startled. "What?"

"Rumor is that you don't date hearing girls."

"I might have said something like that. But obviously that rumor is outdated—unless you have a different word for what we're doing."

He pulled me close and kissed me again. When he signed, "It's too late for you to go back," it took me a moment to realize what he meant.

"I guess I'll have to sleep on the couch," I signed.

"No," he signed. He took my hand and led me into the bedroom. Feeling awkward, I reached for the light switch, but stopped. With the light off, we couldn't talk.

"Leave it on," he signed.

Hours later, when we fell asleep, the light was still burning.

9

I painted my father in washed-out grays and watery blues—cool and distant, radiating nothing, passive, silent and immobile—but always with an edge, generally a harder, steelier gray. He was lifeless and empty, with occasional flashes of meanness.

Mostly he spent his evenings watching the news and reading the newspaper. He watched the news over and over, first at six, then at six thirty, then again at ten. When a commercial came on, he changed to a different news program. He never talked about the news, though. He never talked about much of anything. If anyone said something to him, he'd say, "That's right!" or "Absolutely!"

Sometimes he invented goofy songs and sang them over and over, like the time he wouldn't stop singing, "Grizzlies and ghoulies and goblins and ghosts and things that go BUMP in the night." He had scarlet fever as a child, and the fever had so ruined his eyesight that he wore glasses as thick as the bottoms of glass bottles, which distorted his face and made his eyes too big.

When I was five and learning to swim, I asked him to stand a few feet from the edge of the pool so I could swim to him. But as I swam toward him, he backed up until I was at the center of the pool, my arms too tired to keep me afloat. I swallowed water and cried. He caught me and laughed. Next time he promised not to back up so far, but he did it again, and once again I was crying and swallowing water.

He was gray, but a cold steely gray, not one of those warmer grays with green undertones.

One summer, at a carnival, he took me up in the Ferris wheel and rocked the gondola until we almost tipped over. No matter how hard I cried, he just chuckled and kept rocking the gondola. I never once heard him say he loved anyone, except for those times my mother poked him and poked him until finally he said, "I love you too, Lenora."

I was about seven and liked to invent games. The game that day was "The Great Penny Hunt." I shook pennies from my father's purple plastic piggy bank and hid them for my five-year-old brother Teddy and two of his neighborhood friends.

After losing interest in the game and returning to my room, I heard my mother yelling. I went to the door to listen, and gathered that my mother had found Teddy and his friends' pockets filled with pennies. The boys evidently thought they could take the pennies home. She called all the children into her bedroom and demanded to know who had taken the pennies from the bank.

It was clear whoever had taken the pennies was in deep trouble. Each child said, "Not me." When it was my turn, I said, "Not me." I figured I wasn't the one who had tried to take the pennies from the house. My mother persisted until I admitted the game was my idea. It seemed to me all the children were at fault. I tried to explain this, but my mother, impatient with my explanations, said, "I can see you are a liar. But I'm not going to spank you. Your punishment is that from now on you will be known as the Family Liar. We will always know who the liar is. Once a liar, always a liar."

"Once a liar, always a liar," became her refrain. If a dispute arose between me and anyone else, the fault was automatically mine because I was the family liar.

When I put my mother's orange-red next to my father's watery gray, the result utterly lacked harmony. From mixing paints, I understood that my parents had come together uneasily for reasons of convenience.

I was ten and my father was at work when my mother took me into her confidence and told me secrets about what he had done to her. "He hit me," she said and showed me bruises on her legs.

"What are you going to do?" I asked.

"I don't know. I have to think about it."

I had to readjust my thinking about my father to imagine him as a wife beater.

One night after I'd gone to bed, something happened in my parent's bathroom and my mother screamed. My father walked calmly out of their bedroom, past my room, and into the kitchen. I crept from my bed. My mother was in the bathroom crying, leaning over the sink, wearing her bathrobe, her hair wet on her shoulders.

"Mommy?"

"Go to bed," she said, breathing in gasps as if she were choking.

Next day she told me that he had slapped her in the shower. "And you saw it," she said. She described how he had lost control and hit her. When she repeated, "And you came in and saw it all," I imagined my father hitting my mother on the cheek with the back of his hand. Before long, I believed I had seen it happen.

So I became my mother's witness. To win an

argument with my father the next night, my mother said, "Bretna, tell your father what you saw."

"I saw you slap Mommy in the shower."

He picked up his newspaper. My mother smiled. Now that she was pleased with me, I understood how Teddy and Hannah felt being the good children. It was comforting and safe to be my mother's ally.

On a Wednesday in April, my teacher told me I had to go to the office. This worried me. Going to the office usually meant trouble. "Your mother is here to take you to a doctor's appointment," the teacher said.

My mother was waiting in the principal's office.

"I didn't know I have to go to the doctor," I said.

"Come on," she said. Teddy and Hannah were waiting in the car. My mother had packed the station wagon with suitcases, boxes, pillows, and the picnic cooler. After we pulled out of the school driveway, she said, "We're not really going to the doctor."

Something exciting and tense was happening. "Where are we going?" I asked.

"To California," she said.

She had left a note for my father telling him that we'd left, but not telling him where we were going. Her brother Oliver, who lived outside Los Angeles, was expecting us.

And so we were off on our adventure. "Hey," I said, thinking of a joke. "We are going to the doctor. Uncle Oliver is a doctor!"

"Is Daddy coming too?" Hannah asked.

"No," my mother said. Hannah knew not to ask any more questions. I thought Hannah would miss him. She was still young enough to enjoy the games he played and the songs he invented. I wouldn't miss him. I'd long since grown bored with his goofy songs, and besides, wasn't he a wife-beater?

We stopped at a Mobil gas station out in the middle of nowhere. I struck up a conversation with the gas station attendant. "We're going to California," I told him.

"That's nice," he said.

Back in the car, my mother said, "Bretna, don't tell strangers where we're going. Remember it's a secret. We don't know who might try to find us."

My mother certainly had a taste for drama—as if my placid and complacent father would actually put detectives on our trail.

Because I was the oldest and knew how to read a map, I sat in the passenger seat. My mother and I were a team. I read the Triple A Tour Book and helped choose the motel for the night. To compliment me on how helpful I was being, she said, "Bretna, when you're good, you're very, very good. Just like the girl in the nursery rhyme."

Sitting in the front seat, keeping track of where we were on the map, watching the fields of Oklahoma stretching to the horizon, I felt my mother and I would always be in perfect harmony. She was pleased with me, so it seemed that the troubles were solved and gone forever. The little girl who could be very bad had been left far behind.

Traveling through the desert put my mother into a melancholy mood.

"Take a good look, Bretna," she said. "You never know when you'll get a chance to see this again."

I watched the arid and desolate-looking hills, trying to feel the emotion my mother seemed to think I should feel, but instead, I felt a thrill of expectation, and relief that we were, perhaps, going to a more peaceful and harmonious place.

Passing through the hills reminded me of a different nursery rhyme: *Come with me and fondly stray, over the hills and far away.*

We arrived at Uncle Oliver's house in mid-afternoon. Nobody was home except the housekeeper and their many animals: three dogs in the back yard, cats, and a bird in a cage. Teddy and I ran through the house, a rambling three-story, six-bedroom house with a swimming pool and separate recreation house. Outside was a marble fountain and inside were two fireplaces. I understood that Uncle Oliver had such a fancy house because he was a doctor.

We lived with Uncle Oliver and Aunt Pat for two months. Teddy and I attended school with our cousins, Janet and Laura. We waited for the school bus in a damp fog so heavy we couldn't see more than twenty yards in any direction. The school had outdoor corridors instead of indoor. Everywhere were palm trees and a succulent ground covering called ice plant.

School ended for the summer and we moved into our own apartment seven miles from Uncle Oliver's house. It was a simple, single-story wood-framed apartment complex consisting of a row of rectangular units each housing five apartments, lined up like barracks. The metal numbers nailed to the doors reminded me of a motel. My mother fixed up the apartment with furniture she bought at garage sales. Our apartment had two bedrooms. Teddy and Hannah shared one room, my mother and I shared the other. My mother found an old comfortable chair, covered it with a red checkered cotton throw, and positioned it so I could sit there and turn the chair to face the window. "This will be a good drawing chair for Bretna," she said. I was happy living in that apartment and often sat in that chair with my sketch pad.

We never talked about my father, except once when I asked her why she'd stayed married to him so long. "He's a good provider," she said.

On my birthday, a package arrived at Uncle Oliver's house. Inside, wrapped in birthday paper, were six board games and a card from my father. Teddy and I played with one game after another. My mother watched for awhile, then started crying. She went into the back bedroom and closed the door. Teddy and I sat still and looked at each other. Neither knew what to do, so we continued playing with the games, all the while listening for sounds of what she would do next.

Teddy, who mysteriously picked up cues that I missed, pointed out the randomness of her moods. He said, "Sometimes she wakes up cheerful and says, 'come on, guys, let's clean up.' Other times she wakes up angry and yells at us for making such a big mess." I paid attention and noticed that Teddy, completely in tune with her moods, adjusted accordingly. If she was cheerful, he made jokes and acted silly. If she was in a bad mood, he became quiet and accommodating. He did indeed have a special gift for being good.

After my father sent the birthday presents, my mother wrote him a letter. One morning, she told us he was coming for a visit. Teddy and Hannah were excited about this, but I was not. He arrived late one evening after Teddy, Hannah, and I had gone to bed. I heard my parents talking in the living room, but couldn't make out what they were saying. I must have drifted to sleep because I was startled when my mother came in and turned on the light.

"Bretna, we want you to come into the living room for a few minutes."

She woke up Teddy and Hannah as well and called them into the living room. She and my father sat on the couch. Teddy, Hannah, and I stood in front of them.

"We want you children to be part of this decision," my mother said. "Your father wants to come back and live with us. We'd like to live together here in California." She looked at each of us in turn and asked, "Do you children want Daddy back?"

Teddy and Hannah, excited and happy, said, "Yes! We want Daddy back! We want to live in California!"

It was my turn, but I couldn't give the same response. How could I forget those stories about how he'd beaten her? I knew they didn't love each other and I didn't see why they wanted to be together. And for reasons I didn't understand, we got along better when he wasn't around. Moreover—and this struck me as the main point—why let him back if he was a wife-beater?

So I told the truth. "No. I don't want Daddy back."

"Bretna!" My mother stood up. Teddy had the alert, uncomfortable look of someone expecting trouble.

"But I don't," I said. "Mommy, he beat you, remember—"

She glared at me, but I just couldn't go along like Teddy and Hannah if it wasn't right. My father was angry too. He said, "I know why you're saying that, Bretna. When I wasn't around, your mother spoiled you rotten."

Spoiled me rotten?

I knew what he meant, though: When he was gone, he was the enemy, and I got to be my mother's ally, a position I was reluctant to give up.

10

The Palacio's house was large, square, and neoclassical with a graceful, pilastered doorway flanked by shrubs that appeared to be the kind that flowered in springtime. I tapped lightly using the brass knocker, but nobody answered. Lucinda had said three thirty, and I was on time. Not sure I had tapped loudly enough, I tried again. Still no response.

The living room curtains were open. Inside was a glass-fronted hutch and a darkly polished dining room table. In the next room, down a step, was a white sofa and two white wing-backed chairs. The sculpted wooden figures on the end tables with arms reaching upward in a graceful dance gave the stark luxury of the room a touch of the exotic. Alex seemed like such a regular kid in his hooded jacket and dusty white sneakers, I hadn't expected his home to be so, well, rich.

Alex walked into the living room eating an apple. I waved to get his attention.

He grinned, embarrassed, and walked over to open the door.

"Is your mother home?" I asked signing as I spoke.

"Not yet," he mumbled through a mouthful of apple. His free hand dangled by his side. "She's late."

"I'll just wait."

He mumbled, "Fine," and went back into the kitchen.

I listened to his noises as he opened and closed cabinets. The house smelled faintly of spices, as if a stew were simmering somewhere.

In the dining room was a collection of photographs in antique silver frames, scrolled and flowery. Several were old black-and-whites, slightly faded and softly out of focus with a touch of sepia. The people in the newer, colored photos shared Alex's wide, toothy smile. Alex and a boy who must have been his older brother dominated the pictures. One photo, smaller than the others, pictured a beautiful teenaged girl who had Alex's oval face, her eyes slanting upward like almonds. She wore a string of baby pearls and black dress with tiny lace collar and cap sleeves.

A key rattled the front door and a tall woman entered, her loose double-breasted taupe suit a shimmering elegant silk. "I'm Lucinda Palacio," she said with the hint of an accent. She extended her hand. She was the girl in the picture, about thirty years older. "I'm terribly sorry I'm late. I hope you haven't been waiting long."

"Not at all," I said.

"Good." She put her briefcase down and pulled off her scarf and set it on the mirrored mail table. "Please make yourself comfortable. I'll get us some tea."

I sat on the sofa. Lucinda went into the kitchen and came back carrying a tray with a silver tea pot, a creamer, and a bowl of sugar cubes with silver tongs. She sat down beside me and handed me a white porcelain cup and saucer. "Milk or sugar?"

"Both, please."

In the white porcelain cup, the tea was golden like honey, minty with a hint of lemon.

"After everything I've heard about you," said Lucinda, sitting down and resting her elbow on the back of the sofa. "I feel like I know you already. Alejandro told me he got an A on his algebra quiz."

I'd pushed him to study, then the teacher, seeing how hard he had worked, gave him a few extra points as a bonus to bring the grade up to an A. "Yes, he did."

Lucinda said, "You don't know how many times I've listened to teachers and administrators tell me that he's learning disabled. But nobody can convince me of that."

I didn't answer. I had no experience determining who was and who wasn't learning disabled, but it did seem to me that it took Alex a long time to grasp new ideas.

"He's hearing impaired," she said. "That's all. Nobody can tell me that he can't succeed in a public high school."

It was obvious from her tone that people had told her just that. "Who said that?" I asked, wondering if one of those people was Elaine.

"The administrator and a few teachers at Brandon. They said Alejandro was not a good candidate for mainstreaming because of what they called his 'other' limitations."

"His ed plan says—"

"The conclusion in his ed plan are from language-based tests that cannot accurately measure the aptitude of a hearing-impaired child."

Well. There was no arguing with *that*.

"I didn't expect his first few weeks to go so smoothly," she said. "Nobody did. We have you to thank for it. If you only knew what we've been through. All Alejandro ever wanted was to fit in with the hearing kids."

She took a sip of tea and said, "Last year the kids had to give oral reports. The hearing-impaired kids signed theirs, letting their interpreters talk for them. Alejandro wanted to say his aloud. After all, it was an oral report. But the interpreter told him that he shouldn't speak in front of the hearing kids because they'd laugh at him."

"That's terrible," I said.

"If the hearing children laugh," Lucinda said, "the solution is to educate the hearing children, not silence the non-hearing children. Last year Alejandro got suspended when he lost his temper. Ever since, he had the reputation of a troublemaker."

I didn't answer. It wasn't hard to see Alex as a troublemaker.

Lucinda said, "He was frustrated, that's all."

She expected me to say something, so I said, "I'm sure he was."

"We had a meeting with Elaine before school started. Alejandro told Elaine that he wants to prepare for college. Elaine handed him a list of entrance requirements for Gallaudet. Alejandro said, 'I don't want a deaf college. I want to go to Harvard like Marcus.'"

I took another sip of tea, keeping my expression neutral.

"Elaine actually looked hurt," Lucinda went on. "Just because something is good enough for her son—"

"Her son?"

"Her son, Jeremy."

I shook my head to show that I didn't understand. Lucinda said, "Her son is also hearing-impaired. She didn't tell you that?"

"No," I said. I'd assumed that Elaine knew how to talk to a deaf person because of her special education training.

"Jeremy is studying at the Rochester Institute. They have an excellent program for the deaf. Jeremy is happy there. I can tell you that Alejandro wouldn't be." Lucinda smiled. She was strikingly lovely—and as relaxed as if we were old friends. She was perfectly groomed, but unlike Elaine, who went for bright colors, Lucinda had a more natural look: neutral clothing, hair the color of burnt sienna, a tinge of peach on her cheeks, clear nail polish.

"Alejandro was nine months old when his babbling suddenly stopped," she said. "I thought hearing English and Spanish confused him, so I switched to just English, but that didn't help. Then one day a gust of wind came through the house and slammed the kitchen door. He was asleep on a blanket, and didn't flinch. I touched him and he calmly opened his eyes and smiled at me. That was when I knew."

I said, "You must have been shocked."

"It took days—no, it took *weeks*—for me to accept it and tell Esteban. I went to the doctor to make sure. We got books from the library, and followed all the advice, picking one new word each day and using it over and over, varying the sentences. That's when I became interested in special education. You can't even imagine how hard it is to raise a child who can't hear. One time he disappeared from the backyard and after three hours of frantic searching, I found him riding his tricycle three blocks away. I got him a bracelet with our phone number and an explanation that he was deaf."

The way she talked about Alex pulled at something inside of me. I might have felt jealous of this perfect example of motherly love, in other circumstances.

"When he was about three, he didn't understand about sound. He thought everyone lip-read, but that everyone lip-read better than him, so he was always frustrated. He thought hearing was a magical way of knowing things. I asked him once how he knew the cookies were on the top shelf, and he said he heard them there."

I said, "He didn't know that burps can be loud."

She laughed. "He told me about that. He also told me that you told him exactly what to do so that the kids wouldn't laugh at him."

She set her cup down and said, "He's been in four different schools, and each time, something went wrong. But now we have you to help us. I told Walter Givens how difficult your job would be. Most teachers don't want someone else sitting in their classroom observing them. I told Walter that Alex's success depended on hiring the right person for your job."

I understood I was being flattered and cajoled, and that the flattery was working. I'd wanted to succeed because I needed the money. But now I felt warmed by the knowledge that I was truly succeeding, and doing some good.

She said, "The interpreter's job is extremely difficult, much harder than Walter or Elaine really understand. The interpreter has to facilitate communication among everyone."

I said, "Elaine thinks she's the facilitator of all communication."

"Of course she does, because she's Elaine Weathers. But she isn't the one sitting in the classroom when the teacher doesn't understand how to communicate with Alejandro, or when the teacher just doesn't understand his impairment. Elaine isn't the one right there when one of the kids wants to talk to Alejandro, but doesn't know how." She paused for a drink of tea. "Elaine probably told you not to speak with me directly, that all communication should go through her."

"How did you know?"

"An easy guess. It's the kind of thing Elaine would

do. My older son uses the term 'control freak.'"

I smiled.

"Now, tell me." She turned to face me, resting her elbow comfortably on the back of the couch. "What is happening with the union?"

"How did you know something was happening with the union?"

"I sit on the school board."

I blinked, surprised. "The latest," I said, "is that I have been classified in Unit D, and there seems to be no way for me to be moved out of that unit. My choice is to take the lower salary or leave."

Lucinda did "tsk-tsk" with her tongue, and said, "Leave it to Walter. If it's possible to muddle something simple, he'll find a way. Things go much more smoothly when he's away fishing and leaves the work for Elaine and Beverly."

"Who is Beverly?" I asked.

"Beverly Eakle. His secretary."

"I saw him this afternoon at the school," I said. "When he saw me, he hurried away like a frightened mouse."

She laughed. "I can imagine. Sometimes I wonder what his wife must be like." She grew serious again and said, "What did Elaine say?"

"She said with my skills, I can easily find another job."

"You'll do nothing of the kind. You're perfect for this job. Absolutely perfect. It's probably galling Elaine that she was wrong about Alejandro and that he's going to do just fine at Claremont High."

So Elaine, too, had advised Lucinda against mainstreaming Alex.

"Now," said Lucinda. "Let's get down to business.

What hourly wage did Walter promise you?"

"His ad said eighteen dollars hourly."

"Do you still have that ad?"

"As a matter of fact, I do."

"Good. Make a copy and give it to Alejandro tomorrow so he can give it to me. In the meantime, have you received a paycheck?"

"I got the first one on Friday."

"For the Unit D salary?"

"Yes."

She stood up and went out of the room. She came back with a leather-bound checkbook and a calculator. She pushed buttons on the calculator and said, "Hm. Two weeks, that means we owe you, let's see, three hundred and seventy dollars."

"Wait a minute," I said. "You can't do this."

"It's only fair that you get what you were promised. Ridiculous for Walter to think he can get away with telling someone a week into a job that she will get a salary lower than what she was promised."

She uncapped her fountain pen and wrote the check.

"But," I said, feeling I needed to tell her what I'd learned earlier that day: "Interpreters at Brandon Middle School are also considered classroom aides and they earn only twelve dollars an hour."

"Calling an interpreter a classroom aide is a neat way to get out of paying a professional salary. Besides, interpreters at Brandon Middle School are grossly underpaid. Maybe if they were paid better they'd put more effort into their jobs, the way you do, instead of just spouting all that deaf pride nonsense about how hearing and non-hearing children should be segregated."

Lucinda folded the check and handed it to me. Taking her check would embarrass Walter Givens and annoy

Elaine. But what else could I do? I needed to do something. Eight seventy-five would not be enough to cover my bills. Besides, I couldn't exactly tell Elaine that in fact, I had no other options.

"But I can't take your money."

"When I get this mess straightened out—and you can be sure that I will get this mess straightened out—I will see if I can get reimbursed. If not, so be it. I won't let Alejandro go without an interpreter because Walter can't figure out how to do his job. And I certainly won't let them pay eight seventy-five per hour for an interpreter. Look what they get at Brandon for twelve dollars. Your job is difficult, as difficult as a teacher's, and you deserve more compensation than a classroom aide or file clerk."

"Elaine isn't going to like this," I said.

"Don't worry about Elaine. I know how to talk to her."

Just a few days earlier Elaine told me not to worry about Lucinda. I felt as if I were stepping directly onto a mine field.

Lucinda took a business card from her wallet, wrote something on the back, and handed it to me. "Here's my card. Feel free to call me any time of the day."

I looked at the card. Lucinda Palacio was a professor of special education at Leslie College. I blinked, surprised. "A professor of special education?"

Lucinda smiled. "You didn't know that?"

I shook my head.

"I also earned a law degree in Barcelona, many years ago, before we came to the States, before the boys were born. Elaine and Walter both earned their master's degrees at Leslie while I was on the faculty. I sat on Elaine's committee. I was not on Walter's committee. If I had been, he would not have graduated."

Lucinda gave me an impish smile much like Alex's and said, "Come to think of it, maybe we shouldn't have let Elaine graduate."

11

The following week I received a letter on Claremont district office letterhead, signed by Walter Givens, stating that the school would pay me a salary of eighteen dollars hourly.

I asked around, trying to figure out how Lucinda had done it. From the science teacher, who was also head of the union, I learned that Lucinda raised hell and embarrassed everyone. Elaine was tight-lipped when I saw her, but I could tell she wasn't pleased. I imagined Walter Givens wasn't either.

On Saturday morning, sitting in Curtis's living room, I told him the whole story and concluded with, "This means Lucinda is my only ally. Which worries me."

"I don't know what else you could have done," he said, "other than quit."

"Here I am, aligned with a confirmed oralist and mainstreamer. She even says 'hearing-impaired' instead of 'deaf.' How do you like that?"

"Being aligned with Elaine wasn't much better. She's a confirmed oralist, too. Besides, if you quit, they'll just get someone else, and whoever they get might not do as much for Alex as you do."

"I think Elaine has me pegged as a troublemaker. She told someone I'm a loose canon."

Curtis laughed. "Well, you are! She probably thought

you were a timid and sweet artist type because at first you seem like that. Then she found out that you're capable of walking into a job you're not qualified for and raising hell with the unions."

"She never knew I wasn't qualified. Besides, I'm qualified now."

"H-A." He finger-spelled the word the way Alex did. "Walking into that school after a few months of sign language classes took some nerve."

"Or stupidity." The sign for "stupidity," rapping the knuckles lightly against the forehead, always made Alex smile, and now Curtis smiled as well.

I liked being in Curtis's apartment, even though it had bare walls and lamps without shades. Two of his bedroom walls were completely lined with books. Most were art and architecture books, but he had lots of literature and science as well.

"Have you read them all?"

"Yes, but I prefer the ones with pictures." He grinned.

"Me, too," I said.

That's when I saw a model he was building on a table. I wandered over to look. It seemed to be a resting place in the woods—a rounded bench in a half-covered structure just large enough for two people, or maybe three. The small structure was set off from the main trail. A set of steps cantilevered over a stream in a lovely interpretation of a bridge.

Next to the model were computer generated drawings of the model. The architect, who I assumed was Curtis, had gone back over the drawing with a regular pencil to create a sense of light playing through the trees, a peaceful place where a traveler could come to rest.

"It's beautiful," I told him.

When I returned home, Rosie was in her room, crying. Her door was open and she was lying face down on her bed, sobbing loudly. I knocked on her door and said, "Rosie?"

She sat up, her face wet with tears. "Oh, God," she said, "I'm sorry to be blubbering like this. He's not worth it. He's *so* not worth it."

"Who?"

She gave me a look and said, "Luke! The guy I've been seeing! He's scum—I mean, seedy, seedy, seedy."

I hated to ask a stupid question, but I had to know: "Then why are you seeing him?"

She let out her breath in a deep sigh. "It's a problem. I know. I'm working on it with my psychiatrist."

Her *psychiatrist*?

"Breakups are horrible," I said, feeling like I needed to say something.

"Isn't that the truth." She put her head back down. "It's even worse when you want to break up, but can't." Her sobbing resumed. Seeing Rosie crying like this was something of a shock. Usually she seemed so upbeat and sure of herself.

"It's really Rocco's fault," she said.

"Who is Rocco?" Hadn't she just said the guy's name was Luke?

"My psychiatrist. One year ago, he said he'd cure me of this addiction. It's been one year, and I'm still addicted!"

I felt confused. "What are you addicted to?"

"Not what. *Who.* I am addicted to Luke. I just can't let go, or get over him." She put her head back down and said, "Maybe you'd just better let me cry for a while." She started sobbing again, her entire body convulsing.

Janae came in through the front door and put a bag of groceries on the table. She looked at me and waved, but didn't come over. I went to the kitchen and said, "She's upset."

"I can hear that. She's been upset for days."

"Did you know she was seeing someone named Luke?"

"Of course I knew. She talks about him all the time. Honestly, Bretna. Get your head out of the sand."

All right, it was true—sometimes I didn't pay much attention to what was going on around me. So I caught up on what I'd missed. After Rosie emerged from her room I spent a full hour listening as she told me all about Luke, who was married, but separated from his wife, and evidently liked to be involved with several women at once.

"He drives a truck, mostly between here and New York," she explained. "I've ridden with him sometimes. He left a week ago, and he promised, he *swore*, he wouldn't sleep with anyone while he was gone. I told him, 'if you sleep with Debbie, you may as well just hand her your cell phone because she'll call to tell me before the sweat dries.' He didn't sleep with Debbie. I guess he knew she'd tell me. He slept with someone else. I realized it when he got back tonight."

"How did you know?"

"From his smell."

I thought maybe I hadn't heard her correctly. "You could tell from his *smell* that he slept with someone other than Debbie?"

"Yes!"

"Come on, Rosie—?"

"I can just tell, okay? My sense of smell is very sensitive. I could smell that he was with someone else. It wasn't like I could smell *her*."

It didn't seem to me that anyone's sense of smell could be that acute. "Maybe you were wrong."

"I wasn't wrong. I confronted him. I said, 'You were with someone else, weren't you?' He looked like a deer in the headlights. I could see he was trying to figure out how I knew. I said, 'Admit it,' and he said, 'It was only once, in New Haven. I don't care anything about her.'"

She gave me a minute to absorb this, and said, "I told you he's seedy." She went to the kitchen and poured herself a glass of wine. "Does anyone want any?"

Janae and I both said no thanks. Rosie said, "I may as well go to bed." We all said goodnight, and she took her glass of wine into her room and closed the door.

Janae whispered to me, "Maybe you have the right idea, being oblivious. She lives on an emotional roller coaster."

Next day, I was in my studio working when Rosie breezed in, her hair cut into a shorter bob, and said, "You'll never believe this! The woman who cuts my hair is wonderful, about fifty years old, and knows everyone in town. So she was cutting my hair, and I mentioned Luke, and it turns out she's friends with his wife!"

"Oh, really," I said stupidly, unable to reconcile her joy and gaiety with the story she was telling, and her sobbing the night before.

"Yes!" she practically shrieked. "You can imagine how scared I was! She knew right away who I was—I mean, how many people are named Rosie, and of course, Luke's wife knows all about us. I was terrified! Here she was, cutting my hair! Luke's wife's friend!"

Rosie ran to the mirror and looked. She ran her fingers through her hair and shook her head. "Whew! It looks fine. I was sure she was going to cut it weird, or put in multicolored streaks, or *something*." She laughed.

Growing serious, she said, "I made an extra appointment with Rocco. He's going to see me twice this week."

"Good," I said. "I hope he can help."

I had a mailbox in the special education office at the high school, but I rarely received any mail. So I was surprised one morning to find a card in my mailbox. It was from one of the librarians, Carole Lowry, asking if I would please stop by to meet with her about something. During my next free period, I went to the library.

I was greeted by a woman who I did not remember having seen before. "I'm Carole Lowry," she said. "You know my daughter, Mona."

"Of course I know Mona." I hadn't known Mona's mother was a librarian.

"Please come in and sit down," she said, gesturing toward her office. After we were seated in the school's standard saddle-backed chairs, she said, "We have some money to fund an after-school enrichment program. We thought it would be a good idea for you to lead a sign language club. So many of the kids are fascinated by sign language, and after all, we do have a deaf student in the school."

"It's a great idea," I said.

"Good! So you'll lead it?"

"Sure."

"What day are you available?"

"I'm pretty flexible," I said.

"How about Wednesdays? We can pay you fifteen dollars hourly, and we'd like the enrichment program to meet weekly for an hour."

"All right," I said.

I had a few minutes before English class to tell Alex the idea. He balked. "Why should hearing kids have to sign?"

"They don't *have* to. They *want* to. It's like learning another language."

"No, it isn't. It's like using crutches." He signed 'using crutches' by pantomiming hobbling along on crutches.

"The librarian is organizing it," I said. "The librarian is Mona's mother. I have a feeling Mona helped think of the idea."

At the mention of Mona, he sat up straighter in his chair. The more I saw of Mona, the easier it was to understand the effect she had on Alex. She was more than just pretty: She was alert, sensitive, and graceful, but also playful—definitely a poodle.

Turned out I was right about the idea being Mona's. Next day, Mona and her friends distributed flyers and hung signs. The first meeting of the sign language club was the following Wednesday after school.

"It will be so much fun," Mona told me. "I hope lots of kids come."

The club met in a room in the back of the library. The room had large windows facing the library, and a chalk board. When Carole showed me which room we would be using, she said, "This room was Mona's idea. She thought if anyone came into the library after hours, they might see inside, feel intrigued, and want to join."

At the first club meeting, Mona and seven other girls showed up. The girls sat in desks, watching me. Alex positioned himself carefully to one side of the room, leaning back against the wall. Someone who didn't know him might think he was relaxed and at ease, but I knew from his studied nonchalance he was feeling intensely self-conscious.

I sat on a desk facing them. "What shall we do?" I asked.

"Give us a sign language lesson," said one of the girls, in a tone that said, *Duh. What else?*

I knew how to give a first lesson in sign language. I picked up a piece of chalk, and on the board, wrote, "Voice," and drew an "X" over the word. I then pretended to take the word and throw it out the window.

Alex and the girls smiled. The girls watched me. Alex pretended to watch me, but he watched the girls.

I drew a stick-figure girl, and made the sign for "girl," forming the word "girl" on my lips. The girls just stared, so I indicated that they should imitate me, which they did. Next I drew a boy, and made the sign for "boy." After they all imitated me, I drew a heart around the boy and girl, and made the sign for "love."

Alex blushed. The girls smiled.

I marched through the lesson. After I'd taught fifteen signs, I stopped and wrote on the board: "Now it's time for practice!" and reminded them not to use their voices by pointing to the crossed-out word, "voice" on the board.

The girls clustered in groups, practicing their signs, occasionally giggling. Once in a while, one of them would glance at Alex, who tried to be helpful by showing the right way to make the sign, but he usually mumbled his signs so badly that he wasn't much help.

Through the window I could see that the library was entirely empty except for Carole, who was working behind the desk. I gestured for Mona to come talk to me. "Do you think any boys would be willing to come?" I whispered.

"High school boys are so immature. They'll just make fun. If this was college, that would be different."

"Too bad," I said. What Alex really needed were some friends.

Then she startled me by saying, "I know *my* boyfriend would like to come, but he goes to U Mass."

"Your boyfriend goes to U Mass?" I asked, stunned.

"He graduated high school after three years. He's seventeen."

"I see," I said.

When Mona went back to join her friends, Alex demanded, in signs, "What did you say to her?"

"I suggested that she try to get some boys to come."

He nodded. A more secure freshman might have enjoyed being the only boy in an after school club. But Alex needed to fit in, and fitting in meant being like the other boys. He couldn't be like other boys if no other boys participated.

12

The Sunday before Thanksgiving, Curtis and I were in his apartment when he asked, "So what are you doing for Thanksgiving?"

I made the sign for "nothing."

He looked curious. "You don't go home?"

"I never go home."

He turned away to pour himself some more orange juice. Now wouldn't you think a person should at least respond when someone says, "I never go home?" Not that an introvert like me should go around criticizing people who don't immediately gush over with questions and sympathy, but still.

I waited until Curtis looked back and signed, "What will you do?"

"My family expects me to join them. They have a house on the Cape."

"That's where they live?"

"They live in New Hampshire, but they have a house down there."

"That's nice," I signed.

I went back to my drawing. We passed the morning quietly. I sat in the window and sketched each object on his back patio, and he studied his chessboard.

At noon, as if no time had passed he looked up and

signed, "Would you like to come to the Cape with me for Thanksgiving?"

The house was in Chattam, on the elbow of the Cape—a clapboard house painted mossy green with white shutters and white trim. All the windows were lit up. We pulled into the driveway, and lights over the garage came on. The front door opened and a slender woman with graying hair appeared on the doorway. Seeing Curtis, she waved and ran outside.

"My mother," he explained.

Curtis stepped outside, and she ran to hug him. Then she came around to my side of the car. "Hello, Bretna!" she said, and threw her arms around me and hugged me tightly.

"It's nice to meet you," I said, entirely startled by the embrace.

"I've heard such wonderful things about you, Bretna. Please, come in." She loosened her grip on me, and went to hug Curtis again.

Inside was bedlam. I moved through the introductions: This was Daniel, Curtis's oldest brother, these were Daniel's children, that was Clare, Daniel's wife. Curtis's other siblings were Adam and Caleb. There was an Aunt Melissa, and an Uncle Syd and their children. There was hubbub and hugs and shouts of delight the likes of which I'd never seen before.

Everyone was busy. Even the children had jobs: One was carrying the vegetables to the table, one was putting serving spoons in the dishes, another was taking care of the infant. I stood helplessly by, watching. Most family members signed as they spoke, except for the children, who obviously tried, but kept forgetting. When the children remembered to sign, their signing was as awkward and mumbled as Alex's.

Dinner was noisy and chaotic, with everyone reaching for the food and talking across the table. So many conversations were going on that I had trouble following any of them. I was most comfortable when I felt nobody was looking at me, when I could just watch everything going on. The scene seemed staged, but the excitement in Curtis's mother's voice, the giggling and shouting and sheer volume of noise of the younger children made me think the warmth was genuine. I felt like I'd been dropped into a Norman Rockwell painting. I felt grateful to be there, and awed.

The dinner dishes had been cleared away and everyone was gathered in the living room. Curtis, sitting on the couch beside me, was subdued. I thought it was because he was missing so much of what was going on. Then he laughed at something, and I realized he was following a conversation between his uncle and his father.

On the dining room hutch was a menorah. "Is your family Jewish?" I asked.

He nodded his fist up and down, making the sign for "yes."

"So am I!" I said, even though I didn't particularly feel Jewish. The only token of Judaism in my parents' house had been lighting a menorah at Hanukah instead of putting up a tree.

"I know," he signed.

"You knew? How?"

"I just knew."

Well, that was a surprise.

On the other side of the room, Curtis's father was telling a joke. I missed the punch line—in crowds like this one, I felt my own hearing loss. Even if you didn't know exactly what he was saying, you couldn't overlook a person like Curtis's father: He was large and squat with a booming voice. Curtis's mother was his opposite: sweet, small, and affectionate.

His mother moved her chair so she was closer to me and said, "Curtis tells me you graduated from the Massachusetts College of Art. Very impressive." She pulled a little closer and said, in the voice of a conspirator, "He has a great admiration for artists. He wanted to be one himself. I tell him that an architect is a special kind of artist." She smiled, and I thought there was something absolutely magical about her.

Later, when Curtis's parents walked us to the door, his mother wiped her eyes and said, "Don't mind me, Bretna. I always cry when it's time for my boys to leave." She blew her nose.

"She cries," her husband said, "and I sing my song." He sang, signing as he went along: "We're glad you're going, you rascal, you." He sang and signed this sentence over and over.

"The song only has one line?" I asked, signing as I spoke.

"It had more lines," signed Curtis, "but my dad forgot them."

His mother said, "It also had a tune, but as you can tell, he forgot that, too." She blew her nose again.

So Curtis's father sang his line over and over, while Curtis' mother cried. It was quite a routine, and I had never seen anything like it. I wondered what Mrs. Willet would say if she knew my mother hadn't even said good-bye the day I left home at eighteen—and that I'd never been back.

Mrs. Willet said, "Thank you so much for coming, Bretna," as if I had done her the greatest honor. She squeezed me in a tight hug.

In my peripheral vision, I saw Curtis sign, "Sorry."

I wanted to ask Curtis why he was apologizing, but there was no chance with the songs and good-bye hugs and tears.

Outside the air was frigid, easily a few degrees below zero. Once we were in the car with the engine on, I asked, "Are they sincere?"

"Oh, yes."

He shifted into gear. We never spent longer than a few seconds at a stoplight, so there was not much chance to talk during the ride back. I watched out the window at the passing pines covered with snow. The car's heater hummed quietly and the air inside was close and warm, but the sight of those icicles, so sharp and cold and delicate, was enough to make me shiver.

It was late afternoon when Curtis stopped the car in front of his apartment. We went inside and sat at the table in the kitchen. He signed, "Okay. Talk."

"Me? What about?"

"Your family. All I know is that your mother is fiery red, and your father is empty and gray."

"You don't want to know about them."

"Yes, I do."

He waited. I found I couldn't speak. I had no idea how to explain my mother or my father.

At last he said, "I want to see some of your sculptures."

"Do you know the Livingstone Gallery in Brookline?"

"No. Any chance it's open now?"

"Probably not. But two of my sculptures are in the window."

"What is the address?"

I gave him the address. He started up the car and

swung around back toward the city. He parked in front of the gallery and walked to the window. I led him to my sculptures. My sculptures were displayed on podiums covered with black velvet. He looked at each of the sculptures for a long time, so long, in fact, that I went to sit on a bench. After he finished looking, he sat next to me on the bench.

"What did you think?" I asked.

A beat of time passed. Then another. "I've never seen anything like them. They're delicate." Then, after a pause, "They're bright. They're also disturbing. Can I see what you're working on now?"

"All right," I said. We got back into the car and drove to Kendall Square, and walked up the stairs to my apartment. I took him into my studio and showed him what I was working on. The sculpture, like the others, was made from shattered glass, which I glued together and glazed over and over until the glaze was so thick that the sharp edges were smoothed.

He sat on a bench and kept looking at it. He shook his head and said, "It's fascinating." He shook his head as if that were the wrong word, and said, "It's perfect."

I made the sign for "thank you" as softly as I could, like a whisper.

I waited while he went on looking at the sculpture. Then he said, "I always wanted to create work with such emotion, but I never could." He grinned and added, "I figured it's because I'm just a simple guy, with no depth."

"No," I said. "It's because you haven't suffered enough."

I enjoyed his startled expression. He looked as if trying to gage whether I was joking. He said, "This sculpture is a dog, a Pomeranian."

I made the sign for "yes." The title of that sculpture

was "Benji."

"Was that a dog you knew?" he asked.

'Yes. But he wasn't really like that. I wanted him to be my savior, but he wasn't."

"You thought a dog would save you?"

"Sounds crazy, right?"

It's possible to speak softly in sign language. When his hands moved again, they were gentle. "It sounds sad."

Tears came to me. After all this time, remembering Benji could still make me cry.

I looked up at the window. A gust of wind pressed some leaves against the glass. The broken leaves reminded me of a high school art project in which I'd torn colored construction paper into shapes and arranged them on a sheet of white paper. When I finished, I had a vaguely round form, like a pair of arms embracing an abundance of shapes. The arms were curved and flowing and the entire picture appeared to be an organic whole.

13

My parents bought a small house in Daly City, not far from San Francisco—a white clapboard house built in the 1950s. The house was two miles from the ocean.

My mother was thrilled to be living in California, so near a city like San Francisco. What she didn't like was the constant fog. I loved the fog. I loved the gray mist, and how the sky over the ocean was moody, and changed from minute to minute. At sunset, I could see the spectacular colors from my bedroom window.

After buying the house, and renting space for his repair shop, my father complained that he couldn't afford to hire someone to help him, so occasionally my mother helped him out. That was when she learned that when it suited him, he told customers the repairs on their television would be too expensive to be worthwhile. When the customer decided to buy a new set instead of fixing the broken one, he offered to buy the broken set for the parts. He fixed the set and added it to the display of used televisions for sale in his window. He sold his rebuilt televisions for a large profit. My mother berated him for cheating his customers. He just laughed.

I tested his ethics for myself. One day when I was about twelve I sat next to him on the couch while he was reading his newspapers, and said, "Dad, if slavery were legal, would you want to own a slave?"

"Why, sure I would. Wouldn't it be nice to have a slave clean the house for us and water the plants?" He spoke in his usual, jovial voice that made me hope he was teasing. I had the uneasy feeling, though, that he wasn't.

Mostly at home I felt bewildered. Something was wrong. Something was off. But I didn't know what. It was like putting together a puzzle with missing pieces.

For example, there was the time I came out of my room and my mother said to me, "Look at you, grinning. You love to see us fight, don't you?"

My heart suddenly pounded. I had no idea what she was talking about. Just then my father kicked a speaker and stomped on it, breaking it to pieces. He tossed armloads of clothes into his work van, gunned the motor, and screeched up the driveway. After he was gone, my mother showed Teddy, Hannah, and me the speaker and kept saying, "He is a man of violence."

Next day, she called his repair shop to reassure herself that he was still working.

For the weeks he was gone, I was again an insider—my mother's confidant and pal. He came back soon after, changed. He'd always been withdrawn, but now he was completely insulated, taking no interest in anything that went on around him. He reacted only when the situation was so severe that he couldn't avoid it. My mother took jabs at him, pointing out his flaws and shortcomings, reminding everyone that he was a man of violence, but he never responded. I understood that he was following the advice he had given me: Ignore the things that annoy you and eventually they will go away.

My father rarely talked to my mother. He let her know when the house needed cleaning by writing, "Hi Lenora," in the dust.

That was the year I developed a passion for animals. I wanted a dog, but my mother was adamant in her refusal. Her refusal puzzled me. "The problem with getting a dog," she said, "is if something happens to it, you're devastated."

Soon my wish for a dog had become an obsession. I imagined a companion completely in tune with my emotions, a creature who understood me perfectly and accepted me completely. The pet dog in my fantasies was a character from a Disney movie that would know when I was sad and try to cheer me up. With my dog I would feel content, and loved.

I talked constantly about my friends' dogs. Veronica had a giant poodle named Bundles. Karen Halligan had a dachshund named Schnitzel—a name she chose because she thought it sounded German. Lisa Heimann had a cocker spaniel named Beethoven.

Then, to my surprise, my mother stopped saying no. She never said yes, but she stopped giving a flat refusal. Even my father, in response to my ceaseless begging, said, "If you drive us all crazy for the next six months until your birthday, you probably won't get a dog," which sounded to me like I might get a dog for my birthday.

A dog was indeed my thirteenth year birthday present. My uncle in Los Angles picked out the dog, a full-grown five pound Pomeranian. I'd wanted to name him Hercules, but my mother insisted that I name him Fella. She said some famous president had a dog named Fella. I resisted, but my mother said, "I'll call him Fella and you can call him whatever you want." One of the dog books I'd read said it was important to give your dog one name and stick to it, so I had to give in. I was so happy to have a dog of my own, I didn't care that he had a stupid name.

Then, exactly five months after I got Fella, he nipped at Hannah, its teeth grazing her hand. The result was a pinkish scratch. The skin wasn't broken, but the injury qualified, in my mother's view, as a dog bite. She said if I didn't find a family willing to take him, she'd take him to the dog pound, where he would most likely be put to sleep.

I spent four frantic days searching for a family willing to take him. Finally a classmate told me that her mom liked Pomeranians so she'd ask. Her mom came to look at the dog and said he'd make a fine addition to their family. It occurred to me that if Fella was too dangerous for us, he was too dangerous for his new family, but I never brought this up because the alternative, the pound, scared me so deeply. His new family changed his name to Benji.

I cried for hours, days, and weeks until my mother bewildered me by saying, "I know just how you feel." I glared at her. How could she possibly know?

Then she told me how she knew: When she was my age she had a dog named Fella, and after she'd had her dog five months, he was run over by a car. In a matter of mere minutes after my mother told me this, my emotions ran the full gamut: First I felt sympathy and horror that my mother, too, had suffered this way. Then the usual bewilderment returned. How was it that my life so mirrored hers?

The house my parents bought in Daly City was built on two levels. One full wall in the living room was plate glass, overlooking the patchwork of backyards. There were two living areas, a high-ceilinged living room upstairs and a smaller darkly paneled family room downstairs. The design meant there were no corridors.

The four bedrooms were set in opposite corners of

the house, two bedrooms upstairs, one off the living room and one near the front door, and two bedrooms downstairs, one to the left of the staircase, one through the family room. After I'd had my first design class, it occurred to me that the layout of the house was perfect for splitting a family into factions.

In ninth grade I took my first art class.

On the first day, the teacher draped a white sheet over a chair. She told us to put our pencils down on the paper and draw the sheet without looking at the paper.

I looked at the teacher to see if she was joking. She wasn't. I'd signed up for this class because I'd always been able to draw well, and arts and crafts had always been my favorite school activity. I wanted something fun. This sounded flat absurd.

The teacher said, "Look carefully at the sheet, at the folds and contours. As your eye follows the lines, let your pencil move."

Drawing the sheet—painstakingly following each line and contour—put me into something like a trance. As I worked, I heard the teacher telling someone that this was an exercise in learning to see. The teacher coached the kids who were resisting to relax and concentrate on each and every fold of the sheet.

I finished and looked to see what I had drawn. The lines were soft and lovely and flowing. I had actually depicted the draping sheet. I looked around at the other students' pads. Each was different, but most, in their own ways, were lovely.

At home, I closed my bedroom door and turned on my radio to the popular radio station, KCBQ, which my father made fun of by calling "K-C-be-quiet!" That was when I taught myself to mix paints and discovered a whole new world of emotion and depth.

The next assignment I thought was silly, too, until I tried it. The assignment was to select a card bearing the reproduction of a masterpiece painting and reproduce the image exactly, the quality of the master's lines, the shadings, the hues. I selected Renoir's "Girl with the Watering Can." Painstakingly copying the picture taught me to appreciate the delicate beauty of the girl's expression, the harmony of the colors, the perfect curve of her cheek and lips. The colors were vivid—the bright red bow of the girl's lips, the cool greens of the garden, the deep blue dress. The picture shimmered with subtle light.

Losing myself in the painting was like losing myself in a perfect world of quiet beauty and peace—a world I did not actually inhabit until many years later when I arrived at the College of Art in central Massachusetts.

14

Two boys showed up at the next sign language club meeting, Rodney, the boy who sat in the back and drew detailed pictures of cars, and Costa, who was not in any of Alex's classes.

I came prepared for the lesson. I brought handouts illustrating how to form all the hand shapes of the manual alphabet.

The girls sat at the desks toward the front, Costa and Rodney sat at desks in the back, and Alex stood in the same place, to the side of the room, leaning against the wall. When it was time to begin, I distributed the handouts.

Costa took one look at the sheet, crumpled it, and said, "This isn't what we want to learn. We want to learn how to make cuss words in sign language."

One of the girls in the front row made an exasperated expression, turned to face Costa, and said, "Oh, *please*." She pronounced the word with two syllables as in, "Pul-ease."

I interpreted for Alex, who laughed.

"How old are you, Costa?" Mona demanded. "Five? Maybe you want to learn to sign 'poo-poo' and 'diaper' so you can laugh like a kindergartener."

"I'd rather learn 'bra' and 'girdle,' and what goes inside," said Costa.

Alex laughed again, this time a little too loudly.

Rodney, who seldom spoke, poked Costa in the side and said, "Dude. If you read the words instead of just looked at the pictures you'd know they're not called girdles."

I figured they were talking about lingerie catalogues. A few days earlier, a teacher in the lounge explained that no high school teacher dared teach the distinction between "lie" and "lay." Listening, I understood why.

Mona looked at me and said, "I told you. They're just babies."

If the point of this club, at least for me, was to help Alex fit in with the hearing kids, I saw no reason not to use unconventional measures. "Costa," I said. "If you want to learn to swear in sign language, and say any dirty word you'd like, just pay attention and by the end of this hour, you'll be the leading expert in sign language potty-talk. You can start by uncrumpling that paper."

I spent the next forty five minutes teaching the manual alphabet. Rodney and Costa participated, while keeping their hands in their laps so nobody could see that they were, in fact, signing.

At the end of the hour, I said, "Now you can sign anything you can spell. If you want to learn actual signs, I'm going to leave. If Alex wants to teach you a few signs, just don't tell me about it. If any girls want to leave, you're welcome to come with me."

I left the room and waited in the corridor until I heard every one of them, including the girls, rocking with laughter. I knew which signs Alex was teaching them. There were a few delightfully graphic signs for "bullshit." I just hoped nobody translated for the principal or teachers.

Next morning in science class, I learned I'd guessed

correctly. Rodney stopped by Alex's desk and, with a grin, made the sign for "man," followed by, "you are full of bullshit."

Alex imitated Rodney's posture and signed back, "No way, man. You are full of bullshit." Rodney shuffled back to his desk. For the remainder of the class period, Alex looked pleased.

The biology teacher gave Alex his midterm two days early so he'd have plenty of time to work on it. This would be his hardest test—actually, his only test. His English and math classes were basic skills, so there were no actual exams. The kids in basic skills were graded on their class work and improvement through the semester, so Alex would get A's in both classes. And of course, Learning Center and speech would be A's.

Alex worked on the biology midterm all through our tutoring periods for two days, which meant by eleven o'clock on Tuesday, he'd been working on the test for five hours. He wasn't finished yet.

We were in the Learning Center, sitting across from each other at our usual table by the window. He pushed the test away and signed, "I'm tired. Tell me the answer."

"I can't. That wouldn't be fair."

He slapped the table, hard. Kids nearby looked at him.

I signed, "Kids are watching."

He glanced over, saw that it was true, and sank lower into his chair. "I can't remember," he signed. "Tell me the answer!"

"I can't. Stop acting like a prima donna."

He blinked. "What's that?"

How do you describe a prima donna, other than someone who acted temperamental and privileged? I signed, "I think a prima donna is an opera singer," I finger-spelled 'opera singer' and pantomimed an opera singer.

He laughed and for just a moment, the tension was broken, so I signed, "Leave that one, and you can ask Mr. Carlisle about it."

"Let's go see him now," he said.

We found Mr. Carlisle in his office, grading papers. Alex said, "I need help with the last two."

Mr. Carlisle looked at me helplessly, obviously not understanding Alex's speech. I repeated what Alex said. Mr. Carlisle took the test from Alex and looked over his work.

Mr. Carlisle said to Alex, "How much heat would be needed to activate an organism?"

Mr. Carlisle had a long mustache that made lip-reading difficult for Alex, so I interpreted.

Alex said, "I don't know."

"A little or a lot?" asked Mr. Carlisle.

Alex thought about it and said, "A lot." Mr. Carlisle cocked his eyebrow. Then Alex got it. He said, "A little. A lot of heat kills organs." Mr. Carlisle nodded, but didn't tell him that 'organ' should have been 'organism.' Mr. Carlisle walked him through the last unanswered question. then went back through the test and prompted Alex to change one of his wrong answers.

Mr. Carlisle smiled and wrote, "A–," at the top of the test.

Alex was jubilant. To me he said, "Can I go back to Learning Center now?"

I said yes. When he ran from the room—he was always forgetting the rule about walking in the school building—I said to Mr. Carlisle, "A minus?"

"The kid works hard. Really, hard. And it's not like

giving away the crown jewels."

Back in the Learning Center Alex was showing the teacher his A minus. "Congratulations," she said. "That's wonderful!"

We sat back at our table, and Alex signed, "Today the PE teacher assigns activities for next quarter. Some kids get basketball. Some kids get swimming."

"Which do you want?"

"Swimming! What else! Everyone's deaf in the water!"

"How does the coach decide who gets what?"

He shrugged to show he didn't know. "I want you to come interpret for me today." Until now he'd insisted that he didn't need an interpreter for PE, that he'd never had an interpreter for PE

"All right," I said.

I stood near the coach's office, watching as the boys came out of the locker room. Most of the boys went to sit on wooden benches to watch the swimmers. Alex followed and sat nearby. He was watching the boys' faces while pretending not to. From the way the boys mumbled, I knew lip-reading would be impossible.

Two girls were swimming laps, one doing the crawl and the other swimming on her back. Alex looked over at me. I knew he wanted me to tell him what the boys were saying.

From where I stood, I couldn't hear a word. I inched toward the boys, trying not to call attention to myself. I was about five feet away when one of them looked at me. I studied my notebook. Because of the echo and the strange acoustics of an indoor swimming pool, even with my good ear facing the boys, I could catch only a few phrases.

I wondered what Curtis, who believed Alex should have a normal high school experience, would think of me trying to help him out by eavesdropping on honest-to-goodness locker room conversation.

The boys were commenting on the girl in the red tank suit, a large-breasted girl swimming on her back. One of the boys, who evidently possessed a poetic sensibility, said, "—tits like mountains rising from the sea."

I signed enough of this to give Alex the general idea, barely moving my hands so nobody else would notice what I was doing. I listened, and signed, "The boy next to him wants to—" that was honestly all I heard.

Alex turned to the boys and said, "I think so, too."

Alex's voice was harsh and jarring, even to me, and I was used to the way he sounded. I was touched by his bravery in trying to join their conversation. The boys, though, were predictably cruel. They laughed and one said, "How come that dude can't talk?"

Alex turned to me to find out what they'd said. Lying, I shrugged and signed, "Sorry." Then, "They're whispering. I can't hear."

The coach walked out and clapped his hands. "Everyone on the bleachers!"

Alex didn't look at me. He followed along with the others and sat near the top row. Alex looked miserable. I thought maybe Curtis was right. Maybe Alex shouldn't be here.

The coach looked at me curiously. I said, "I'm Alex's interpreter." Then, "He wants swimming. That's easier for a deaf kid because nobody hears well in the water."

"Smart," he said.

He turned to the boys and reading off a list, assigned activities. When he got to Alex's name, he said,

"Swimming."

I made the sign for "swimming." Alex smiled and signed, "Thank you."

The next day, Alex sat down across the table from me in Learning Center smelling like potato chips. His eyes were bright, his face flushed as if he'd been running.

He handed me a computer printout. "It's my schedule for next semester," he said.

I looked at the schedule. He would be taking five classes instead of three, and all five would be intermediate instead of two basic skills and one intermediate. I looked at him to see if he was serious.

"All intermediate," he said.

"Do you feel ready for that?"

"I'm ready! I got all A's this semester."

Responding to that statement by pointing out the truth would be unkind. The phrase "Yes, but," should never follow a kid boasting about grades. I looked back at the schedule. He expected me to be pleased and happy, so I tried to look pleased and happy, but I've never been particularly good at disguising my emotions. What on earth was Elaine thinking, to give him this schedule?

I said, "This will be hard."

"I can do it."

"The intermediate English class reads "Great Expectations."

"I can do it."

I stood up and went to the bookshelf at the back of the room and found a worn copy of "Great Expectations." Even to me, the dense five-hundred-page paperback seemed daunting. I handed it to him and watched as he flipped through the pages.

"I can read this," he said.

I took the book from him and opened to a page in the middle. "Read a paragraph," I said.

I watched him pretending to read. When he finished, he grinned the way he did when he was upset.

After class, I knocked on Elaine's door. She said, "Come in. I've been meaning to talk to you about a problem."

"What problem?" I asked, sitting in the chair across from her desk. She straightened some papers on her filing cabinet and sat down, folded her fingers like a steeple and tapped her fingers against her chin. "Alex is becoming completely dependent on you." She gave me what could almost be described as a mournful look. "If you leave the room, he looks for you. He won't do anything without you there."

That didn't seem to me to be a problem. That seemed the natural result of the fact that without me there, he wouldn't have a clue what was going on. "He has almost no residual hearing," I said. "He can't even distinguish a bell from an airplane—"

"Bretna." Her voice was calm and measured. "I don't need you to explain to me the extent of Alex's hearing loss."

"That's why he's dependent on me."

"No, it isn't. He is too dependent on you because you have been giving him too much help. You've essentially carried him this semester, and now you've set him and his family up for success next semester. You have set him up for a fall, Bretna."

"I did *not* give him too much help. He wanted me to—" I thought about his demand for answers on the test, and said, "but I didn't!"

"You carried him," she said evenly. "Now he is

completely dependent on you. There will be consequences for him because a child his age should not be dependent on an interpreter."

"His teachers gave him extra help! He is in basic skills, so they inflated his grades because he was trying so hard!"

"Don't blame the teachers."

I was aghast. "Now, you're pushing him into intermediate, and he should not be in intermediate classes."

"That is not for you to decide."

"Why can't we just leave him where he is, in basic skills, so he can do well and feel good about himself?"

"He doesn't have to get A's all the time. Besides, his mother thinks he's going to an Ivy League school. You can't get into an Ivy League school with basic skills on a high school transcript."

"Elaine, he's working at capacity."

"It's not your decision."

"Whose decision is it?"

"His parents decide, advised by a team of eight professionals. Bretna, I have explained that you work for the school and not the Palacios. You let me worry about Alex and Lucinda. You just do your job. And I'd advise you to start helping Alex become more independent."

15

Rosie pulled up beside me and rolled down the window. "Bretna!" she called out. Her car was newish, small, and bright red. She told me once that when she bought her car, she didn't care which kind it was, as long as it was red.

"Please come with me!" she called.

I was heading back to the apartment from the Kendall Square subway station. I'd tutored Alex after school for an extra hour, and treated myself to a visit to a thrift store near Harvard Square. I was hungry, tired, and ready to be home.

"Where to?" I asked.

"I'm looking for Luke. I'm all shaky. I don't want to be by myself if I find him."

It was almost six p.m. and growing dark. "Oh, Rosie."

"I just want to see where he is. We'll just look for his car. C'mon, please?" She made a gesture like a dog begging.

I sighed and shook my head, not to say 'no,' but to say, 'Rosie, you are too much.'

"You'll come?" she asked eagerly.

"All right." I walked around to the passenger side and got in.

"First we'll try Nick's," she said.

"Nick's?"

"A bar in Inman Square."

I sat back and sighed.

"Rocco says I have middle class guilt," she said as she wheeled the car into traffic. "That's why I keep going for these seedy blue collar types. My father is a CEO and my mother is a socialite who raises Abyssinian cats. So I'm attracted to 'bad boys' to relieve my guilt."

"Why do you feel guilty?"

"That's the part I have to understand. Guys like Luke, and my second husband, berate me for not being a perfect housewife. Luke expects me to cook breakfast, and then gets mad if I burn the bacon."

"What century does he live in? I didn't know there were still guys like that."

"There are. And I end up with all of them."

"If a guy got mad at me for burning bacon, I'd be tempted to hit him with the frying pan."

"That's because you're strong, Bretna. Not everybody is. Look, there's Nick's! I don't see his car or Debbie's." She drove around the block and said, "We're looking for a green Tercel or a black Jaguar."

"Who drives a black Jaguar?"

"Luke. That car is his pride and joy. He puts all of his money into that car, and all of his time. Well, the time he isn't screwing around. I don't see their cars anywhere. Can you go in and look? Please?"

"Rosie," I said.

"C'mon. Even if he's there, he's never met you so he won't know who you are."

"But how will I know who he is? I doubt he wears a badge that says 'I'm a seedy, sleazy, married truck driver who likes to screw around."

She laughed. "Just see if there's anyone in there who might be them. He's forty-two, with black hair, thinning on top. Perfect body. Think Adonis. She has pale blonde hair, but I think it's dyed."

Seeing that I hesitated, she made her puppy-dog eyes again and said, "Please, please, please!"

"All right." I could see why Janae spent so many evenings talking to Rosie at the kitchen table. Something about Rosie pulled you in.

Nick's was lit by flashing neon signs. To the side was a room with a pool table. Three guys were sitting at the bar. None matched Luke's description. Two girls were at a booth. Some guys were playing pool.

When I was back in the passenger seat, I said, "Nope. He wasn't there."

"All right. Let's try the Blue Moon." She swung back into traffic and said, "There was a message on my cell phone from Luke's phone, but Debbie left the message. Obviously she swiped his cell phone long enough to call me. She told me she's been sleeping with him since April—*April!*—and went on about the terrible things he told her about me. He says I'm spoiled and temperamental and don't know what it means to work."

"You work," I said.

"He doesn't think I *really* work. He thinks my gig leading hikes is just fun and games. He thinks he's superior because the owner of Outdoor Adventures goes to the same country club as my parents, so he thinks that's why I got the job. He says no one ever helped *him* get a job, and he's been working since he was fourteen. He's a reverse snob. He thinks anyone who doesn't work at a tedious job for minimum wage isn't really working."

I looked out the window and said, "Are we really doing this? Driving around looking for some guy in bars?"

"I know. I look at my life sometimes and think,

'Rosie, you're really slumming.'" She said this as if she was pleased.

She stopped suddenly and pulled up to the curb. "There's his car," she said. "He must be in there. Please go in and see who he's with."

"Oh, Rosie—"

"C'mon, please! I'd do it for you!"

I got out of the car and walked into the Blue Moon. Inside, the fluorescent lighting had a deep cobalt blue cast. In a booth in the corner was a man who met Luke's description—broad shouldered and muscular with black hair, thinning on top. Next to him was a beautiful dark-skinned girl with hair as glossy as a mare's.

Luke looked up curiously. For one uncomfortable moment, we looked at each other. Feeling a cold terror, I whirled around and walked outside.

I got back into the car and said, "Rosie, we need to get out of here."

"Was he there?"

"Yes. Please start driving. He had a good look at me. This is too creepy."

She pulled into traffic. Someone behind us honked. "Who's he with? Debbie?"

I considered lying. Seeing my hesitation, she inadvertently stepped on the brake and the car lurched. From behind us came the sound of another horn. To keep her driving, I said, "No. She was dark. That girl could never be blonde."

Rosie looked at me and swerved dangerously. "Is she pretty?"

"No," I lied.

She relaxed a bit, then laughed. "Let's do something to his car."

"No! Rosie, forget it! Let's go home!"

She pulled back into traffic and turned toward Kendall Square. "I have an idea!" she said. "I'll list his car for sale! I'll list it cheap, and put in the ad that interested buyers should call him before seven on Sunday!"

I giggled, mostly in relief that we were heading home. "He'll know it was you."

"So what? He'll know he deserved it. Bastard."

16

I was a high school sophomore and Michael Wright was a junior. He had a youthful face, with pale skin and bright blue eyes. The way he looked around, as if he disapproved of everything he saw, made him seem even older. Later my mother described his eyes as shifty. Michael walked with a sort of swagger even though he wasn't particularly large. Sometimes after school I saw him sitting in the empty field across from the bus stop with his buddies, a ragged motley group, smoking cigarettes and drinking beer. I would have expected him to like the tougher girls, the ones who smoked and wore heavy eye makeup, but by the start of tenth grade, it was clear that I was the one he liked.

The only way to paint Michael was in black and white. No shades of gray. Lots of stark contrasts, lots of clarity. There was nothing weak or halfway about Michael.

He took to waiting for me after school. He was surprisingly polite. When he smiled, his dimples showed and I thought he was cute. When he asked if he could call me, I told him he could, even though I didn't want him for my boyfriend. He called frequently, and I thought of him as a good friend. At school, though, I ignored him. He didn't seem to mind.

When Evan Corey, who was much cuter, asked me to go out with him, I had no trouble choosing him over

Michael. I was proud to have Evan as my boyfriend. Evan, in contrast to Michael's blacks and whites, was glittery and gold, a rich harmonious color with lush undertones of luminous browns and yellows.

The only problem was that Evan kept changing his mind about me. He'd ask me to go out with him, and for a few weeks he'd call each evening and often come to visit. He wrote "Evan loves Bretna" on walls and scratched our initials into trees. Then, without warning, he'd tell me he wanted to break up. The first few times he did this, I cried. But after enough breakups and reunions, I just waited for him to come back, which he always did.

Michael Wright continued to watch me at school and call in the evenings. I still ignored him at school, but on the phone I told him about the woes I experienced with Evan. It turned out Michael knew Evan's family. "Evan and I were in little league together," he explained. "I've known Evan since first grade."

"What do you think of him?" I asked.

"I think he's a goody-goody. I also think he's a spineless wimp without an opinion of his own. I also think he's jerking you around and he won't stop until you get sick of him and tell him to kiss off."

"His friends don't like me," I said. "They don't think I'm pretty."

"His friends are idiots," Michael said.

Michael did have a certain appeal. He was honest, intelligent, and tough, and I had the feeling that if he were my boyfriend, he'd be utterly devoted, unlike the whimsical and unpredictable Evan Corey.

Next time Evan broke up with me, Michael called to ask if I wanted to spend Saturday with him. He suggested going to the beach. "Okay," I said.

That afternoon, I listened, captivated, as Michael told me about his family, stories that were gruesome enough to make me think he'd be able to understand what I went through at home. Michael's father, before he moved out, used to get drunk and beat his mother. Michael often interceded, taking the whipping himself to spare her. Once his father had thrown Michael against the garage wall so hard he'd knocked him unconscious.

Michael had two younger sisters, Candice and Christa. When his father went on a rampage, threatening to beat Candice because he'd seen a boy trying to kiss her, Michael sneaked both his sisters out to the shed. He locked them in and hid the key under a rock. His father had been furious at not being able to get to Candice. Michael took a beating, but wouldn't tell his father where the key was. His sisters remained locked safely in the shed until his father sobered up. He never hit anyone when he was sober.

In return, I told him all about my mother and the problems I had at home. I didn't expect him to believe me. I expected him to wonder what was wrong with me for being in trouble all the time with my mother. But after listening to my stories, Michael gave his opinion of my mother. He said, "What a stupid bitch."

I found that reassuring. "Yes," I said, "she *is* a stupid bitch."

"If you ever need a place to stay," Michael said. "I can hide you in our shed."

We stayed at the beach until dark. He told me that he'd been in love with me since the first time he saw me. He kissed me, but unlike Evan, he didn't try to slide his hand into my shirt. He just kissed me sweetly and told me again that he loved me.

I had an ally now. Every day after school I went to Michael's house. His mother had a job, so we had the house to ourselves. He got along well with his sisters, and I liked being there with them. Most of the time Michael and I stayed in his bedroom with the door closed, but other times we'd sit with his sisters and talk to them. His sisters obviously adored him. They were afraid to go visit their father without Michael with them. I had judged Michael harshly because I hadn't liked his friends. Now I understood that having two sisters who adored him was a better indicator of his character than being popular with the cool kids.

Evan Corey had never been willing to spend this kind of time with me. For Evan, a girlfriend was someone to fit in between sailing lessons and baseball practice and outings with his family. Michael, in contrast, took me into his life and into his home. He liked making puns on his last name and telling me he was my Mr. Wright.

Michael knew all about his reputation as the bad kid in the neighborhood, and seemed proud. He'd actually robbed a house once and he'd never gotten caught. Another time he and a friend had cased a small gas station. After figuring out the layout of the shop, they distracted the owner, and made off with seventy-five dollars from the cash register. He hadn't gotten caught for that, either. In fact, he hadn't gotten caught for anything since he was thirteen.

Hearing the stories of his crimes made me uneasy, but how could I judge him harshly when he accepted me so completely? The comfort I felt with him came from knowing he understood me. He knew who I was—the bad girl in my family—but he loved me anyway.

"Bretna," said Mrs. Weiss, my art teacher.

I looked up, expecting trouble. The others were putting away their paints and waiting at the sink to clean their brushes.

Mrs. Weiss said, "Your work is good. Really, really good."

"Thank you," I said.

"I'd like to enter a few of your pieces in a display at a local gallery featuring young artists," she said.

From nearby, Charlotte—a particularly sassy tenth grader—heaved a sigh. When Mrs. Weiss moved to the back of the room, Charlotte said loudly enough for me to hear, "I'll never respect anything Mrs. Weiss says again, if she likes those messes Bretna makes."

I pretended I hadn't heard. Later, Michael said, "They're jealous, that's all. One day you'll be a famous artist, I know it."

"How do you know?"

"Something about your paintings makes people want to keep looking at them."

Mrs. Weiss selected two of my paintings for the display. When the display opened, there was a reception and critics from the newspaper. A man with a fedora hat studied each of my paintings, then turned to me.

"Are you the artist?" he asked.

"Yes."

"Interesting work. Very interesting. But your youth shows in your work. You need to work through your pain so you can learn to see what is beautiful as well as what is not."

I felt stunned and hurt. I felt I should answer, but instead I turned away.

When the newspaper articles were printed, one critic said my work showed promise, but was still "just angry."

I didn't think my work was angry. I asked Mrs. Weiss what she thought. She told me not to listen to critics. Michael's response was more comforting. "Your work isn't *angry*. It's complex and emotional. Maybe those critics just don't understand genuine emotion. They just want your work to be bland and ordinary and easy to understand."

Breaking things, I discovered, was the only way to get my mother to leave me alone. It started with a jar of grape jelly. My mother was nagging me about what a hoodlum Michael was until I wanted to scream. Evidently she had learned about his police record. What really bothered her, though, was that Michael didn't believe her when she tried to tell him how bad I was.

She said, "It just figures that you'd have a delinquent boyfriend like that."

Logic didn't work when dealing with my mother, and patience didn't help. Knowing she wanted a fight, and knowing I would lose—and feeling I had to do something or I would go insane—I picked up a jar of grape jelly and said, "If you don't leave me alone, I'll break this."

We watched each other for a tense moment. She never backed down from a threat. She said, "He's a criminal. One day you'll both end up in a gutter."

I threw the jar as hard as I could. It struck the floor just in front of the cabinets. The jar shattered. Grape jelly and glass went everywhere.

Breaking the jar worked. My mother suddenly calmed. She looked at me steadily. With something like triumph in her voice, she said, "You are a violent person."

I turned and ran out the front door and up the drive way. It was twilight. Whenever I heard a car coming, I hid behind the bushes. I walked the two miles to Michael's house and knocked on his bedroom window. He let me in. I was still catching my breath when the phone rang and we heard Michael's mother saying, "No, Bretna isn't here."

A few minutes later, Michael said, "I wonder what they're talking about."

"They're still talking?"

"You can't hear them?" he asked.

"I told you I don't hear well in one ear. What's your mother saying?"

"She's just saying 'uh-huh, uh-huh,' to whatever your mother is saying."

We waited three hours because that was usually how long it took my mother to forget an incident like that one, then Michael walked me home. My mother was waiting up for me in the kitchen. I went straight to my room, but she threw open my door and said, "One day I'll be dead—"

"I know. And I'll be sorry."

She gave me a disdainful look and said, "You act so high and mighty, like you're so good. Who do you think you are, God?"

I waited for her to leave the room, afraid to look away from her. Finally she left, slamming the door behind her.

Michael said he was content to wait until we were old enough to get married before making love. He meant what he said. We spent many hours each day in his room, lying together on his bed, holding each other, talking, and kissing. When he knew I was ready for more, he gradually increased the intensity of his caresses. I trusted him completely. He taught me to relax and enjoy being touched and kissed.

This went on for months. By the time he was sixteen

and I was almost fifteen, I came to believe he must qualify for sainthood. We had been together for one full year when I decided I wanted it to go all the way. He was surprised by my decision, and waited some time to make sure I really meant it. The problem was, I kept panicking, and saying, "Please stop! I changed my mind!"

He made jokes. Once he said, "I'm looking forward to when we're thirty and have been married for years and you say, 'I'm ready, honey,' and I say, 'Not tonight, dear. I have a headache.'" Anticipating his revenge amused him. Another time he said, "I think all the problems in the world are because sixteen-year-old boys are driven crazy by their girlfriends. It's like withholding air. The world is brain damaged because so many guys were suffocated as kids."

He made jokes, but he never pushed. I understood how fortunate I was to learn about love from someone as gentle and patient as Michael.

Next time my mother goaded me about my criminal boyfriend, I kicked a hole in one of the bathroom doors. The doors, it turned out, were hollow, so when I kicked hard enough, I left a small crater.

My mother marched into the living room where my father sat reading the newspaper. "That child is violent," she said. "Did you see what she did?"

"Hmm," my father said, rattling the newspaper, but not looking up.

After she left the room, I asked, "Why did you marry her?"

"I shouldn't have," he said flatly. "But my mother said I should get married. She said it was time. I was twenty-nine and living at home."

"But why did you marry *her*?"

"Hmm. Well now. I guess it's because I found her sexually attractive."

I rolled my eyes and left the room. There was really no other appropriate response.

Next time my mother and I had a fight, I kicked a hole in the door leading to the laundry room. As before, breaking something did the trick. She quieted immediately and backed away from me. After a while she said, "If you break one more thing in this house—" but she seemed too flustered to continue her threat. Maybe she felt the helpless futility of threatening me because I was no longer afraid of her.

During one of the lulls when a few weeks went by without a fight, her good humor returned. At the store she found several stickers shaped like feet. She put the stickers over the holes I had kicked in the doors, but she never let anyone forget that I had kicked the holes. "That child is *violent*," she was fond of saying.

Next, I broke a swan-shaped glass vase. She ordered me to sweep up the pieces, which I did. I stared at the pieces of broken glass in the dust pan. The vase itself had been the sort of thing my mother liked but I despised—a piece of pure kitsch. In the dustpan, though, the pieces of glass were glittering and lovely. Instead of dumping them into the trash, I brought the pieces of glass into my room and put the glass pieces on my dresser under the lamp. The vase had been an orangish color like salmon, but the shattered pieces contained every color from teal to yellow.

My mother flung open the door and pointed to the broken glass on the dresser.

"Are you crazy?" she demanded. "Are you out of your mind? Bringing broken glass into your room, and sitting there staring at it?"

I thought maybe I was mad. It was clear one of us was. Angrily she swept the pieces of glass back into the dustpan and marched out of the room, slamming the door behind her. In her haste, she'd left a piece behind, part of the swan's neck, curved and graceful. I picked it up, and turned it toward the light to watch the colors play through the glass.

17

Shortly after Thanksgiving dinner with the Willets, I was bothered by a growing pain in my ear. I went to Student Health, where a doctor examined my ear and asked, "When was the last time you saw an ear specialist?" I told him about the time I was five and had the procedure that restored most of my hearing, and about the series of ear infections I'd had when I still lived at home.

"Something is going on in there," he said. "I'm referring you to Dr. Kessler at Massachusetts Eye and Ear. He's the best surgeon in the state—and there are a lot of good surgeons in Boston. If he'll take you as a patient, you'll be in good hands."

To reach Massachusetts Eye and Ear, I took the subway from Cambridge, then switched to city buses. Dr. Kessler, it turned out, was the chief physician of Head and Neck Surgery. "Dr. Kessler takes very few new patients," the receptionist told me, "but he took you from the waiting list because of the doctor who referred you. You're lucky."

I didn't feel lucky when Dr. Kessler looked into my ear and asked me the name of the doctor who'd done the procedure when I was five. "I'll call for your records," he said. "Come with me."

He took me into another examining room and told

me to lie down. The room smelled faintly of rubbing alcohol. He poked inside my ear with sharp instruments, then put a suction into my ear that made me dizzy. "Hey," I said. "That hurts."

"This will just take a minute."

It was the longest minute I had ever lived through. The suction in my ear made my head swirl until I was so dizzy I thought I'd throw up. At the same time he pinched deep inside my ear. The pain was so sharp my eyes stung.

When he finished, he told me to close my eyes until the room stopped spinning. Then he said, "You have a disease growing in your ear called cholesteatoma. We're going to have to take out the disease."

"What does that mean?"

"It means surgery. I'll schedule you for a second opinion, but I have no doubts."

Surgery. I felt stunned. "What about my job?"

"You'll miss less than a week."

Hanukah fell in mid-December, before the winter break began. Curtis invited me to his house for dinner and lighting the candles. His family would be in their New Hampshire home. We arrived early Saturday afternoon. The house was located in an area of Concord that reminded me of Beacon Hill, with narrow streets and brick sidewalks and antique lamps. His home was one of a row of Federal–style homes with a large bay window jutting over the street.

We walked into the house and his father hollered out, "Is that my friend Bretna?"

His parents had been sitting on the couch in the living room, but when Curtis and I stepped into the front hallway, they came in to hug us. Mrs. Willet wanted to know if I was hungry.

"I'm fine, thank you."

"No one turns down freshly baked bread," Mr. Willet thundered. Once he mentioned it, I smelled the warm bread.

"Come on," said Mrs. Willet. "Dinner won't be for hours. You have to eat. Here, I made some hot soup." She signed as she spoke. She took me by the hand and led me toward the kitchen. A pot was clattering on the stove. She lifted a lid and out wafted the smell of chicken soup.

"Sit down, both of you," she said, again signing as she spoke. "It's so nice to have you here."

I smiled, thinking I could definitely get used to Mrs. Willet's brand of exuberance.

"How is Alex?" Mr. Willet asked.

I told them about the Sign Language Club and ended with: "So he's fine. Except that he's in love with a girl named Mona."

"You never know," Mr. Willett warned me. "Maybe she's in love with him, too."

"Maybe," I said, feeling doubtful.

Curtis's Aunt Melissa and her family came for dinner. Aunt Melissa's family was every bit as boisterous as Curtis's. There was the usual noise and confusion when the two families greeted each other, with hugging and kissing and shouting.

If Melissa were a color, she'd be the color of Orange Crush: energetic, sweet, glowing. Mrs. Willet, on the other hand, would be burgundy: red with blue undertones, a deeper, richer color.

I sat quietly on the couch next to Curtis while Stacy, Curtis's cousin, lit the candles and said the blessing. Then gifts were exchanged. I brought Curtis a sweatshirt from the Museum of Fine Arts gift shop, and he gave me an art book. I was touched that Curtis's mother had a gift for me, a set of baskets for my dresser top.

Curtis sat back, watching everything but not participating much. He had that look that meant he was taking everything in. He had a way of narrowing his eyes as if to focus better.

After the gifts were exchanged and the young children were busy playing with their toys, Curtis signed, "We can leave now, if you want."

"All right," I said, thinking he wanted to leave. I stood at the door, again feeling uncomfortable. Curtis said good-bye to each person. At first I stood awkwardly, then realizing I was supposed to do the same, I imitated him. I said goodbye to each family member, giving and accepting hugs, feeling entirely self-conscious.

His parents walked us out to the car, his mother dabbing her eyes and his father singing—and signing at the same time—"We're glad you're going, you rascal you!"

We drove back to Cambridge without trying to talk. I'd noticed that after getting together with his family, Curtis was usually subdued. At first I thought he was sad, but he seemed tense and angry. I could not understand this. At all.

We were at a red light on Brattle Street when I asked, "Do you like visiting your family?"

He shrugged to show that he wasn't completely sure.

I was amazed. Here he was, with the warmest and most loving family on the face of the earth and he didn't even seem to appreciate them, or realize how lucky he was. In fact, he was positively glum.

"They're so nice," I said.

"I never completely understand what is going on. I

give wrong answers because I didn't understand the questions. I feel like a different species or something."

"I understand what that's like."

He shot me a look and signed, "I know you had it rough and all, with difficult parents, but you can't possibly know."

Difficult parents? The word seemed woefully inadequate to describe my parents. I was taken aback by the harshness of his signs, feeling hurt and a little angry. I forced myself to form my reply gently, "Maybe I do know something about it, Curtis."

He shook his head no. I didn't answer. How could he think that only the deaf suffered, that only the deaf understood isolation and bewilderment, and that my own pain didn't qualify?

The following Thursday I was sitting in Dr. Kessler's examination room. His secretary checked the arrangements for my hospital room, when she realized I was not a full time student at the College of Art, even though I still carried their special insurance coverage for graduates. Janae joked that the college knew its graduates would be working odd jobs and would need insurance for a long time. The secretary checked into my insurance and went to talk to Dr. Kessler, who came back and said, "You're not covered for hospitalization here."

"What can I do?"

"You can take care of it through the clinic." He wrote down a building and room number and said they were expecting me. "You'll have some paperwork to fill out over there," she said, "but it shouldn't be a problem."

I hated everything about the clinic. I hated how impersonal the receptionist was, and I particularly loathed the doctor who came in and looked at my ear. Unlike Dr.

Kessler, who was brisk and professional, this doctor's shirt was wrinkled and partly tucked in. I didn't like the way he smiled, which seemed more like a leer. He didn't respond when I complained that he had hurt me. Then I realized, from the way he talked about the upcoming procedure, that he thought he was going to operate on me.

"You're not doing my operation," I told him. "Dr. Kessler is." The secretary specifically said there was a problem with the hospitalization on my policy. She hadn't said anything about doctor's fees.

He frowned and looked back at my chart. "No, you've been transferred to the clinic."

I stood up and left the examining room, ignoring the doctor when he tried to stop me.

Once in the lobby, I called Dr. Kessler's office. His secretary said, "He's in with a patient right now."

"This is Bretna. Will Dr. Kessler be doing my operation?"

She told me to hold the line. When Dr. Kessler came to the phone, he said, "Come on back over here."

"What's happening?" I asked.

"Nothing. Don't worry. There was a mix up. Just come on back over."

I was waiting in Dr. Kessler's waiting room when the receptionist said I could go into his office. I went in and sat down. He said, "There's a small problem with insurance coverage, but we'll be able to take care of it. How old are you?"

"Twenty-five."

"You may be covered on your parent's insurance. Do you know what kind of policy they have?"

"I don't think I'm covered on their insurance." In fact, I was one hundred percent sure that I wasn't on their insurance.

"What did your parents say when you told them you needed another operation?"

"I didn't tell them."

He blinked, evidently surprised. "Why not?"

"I don't think they would care, to tell the truth."

I could see that he didn't believe me. He picked up a pencil. "What's your father's phone number?"

I gave him my father's work number. I had no idea where he was living. He had moved out shortly after I left home. Dr. Kessler wrote the number down and said, "I'll see you next week, at the usual time."

The next week I sat in the patient's chair. Dr. Kessler came in and examined my ear as usual. Then he asked me lots of questions about myself. He wanted to know what I was doing in Massachusetts, so far from home. I explained that I'd come for art school, then asked, "Did you call my father?"

"I did."

"What did he say?" I asked, even though I had a pretty good idea what he had said.

Dr. Kessler's voice became strained and angry when he said, "He said you left home so he has no further financial responsibility."

"What's happening with my insurance?"

"Everything is taken care of. Your hospital room will be paid for by the clinic. Officially the clinic physician will be listed as the surgeon, but I'll perform the operation."

"So my policy covers doctor's fees?"

"Don't worry about it, Bretna." He set an instrument on the table and then picked up a file.

My voice was shaky when I said, "Tell me. Does my insurance cover doctor's fees?"

"In fact, it doesn't."

"Then who is paying you?"

He turned back around and considered me. "I'm not getting paid."

"But that isn't right! You have to get paid!"

"It doesn't matter," he said. "I don't keep my money, anyway."

On the verge of tears, I insisted, "You have to get paid!"

"Bretna, it's all right."

"No, it isn't all right." I now understood that I had bulldozed Dr. Kessler into performing an operation for which he wouldn't get paid. I felt ashamed, and stupid.

"It's all right," he said again. "I don't keep my money." He wrote something on my chart and said, "We have one more prep appointment next week," and walked briskly from the room.

When I got home, I googled "Gershon Kessler" and learned that he was one of the city's most generous philanthropists. He kept enough money for his family to live modestly and for his sons to go to college, and donated all the rest to the Jewish community. I scrolled through articles and learned that his father had been in a Nazi concentration camp as a very small child. His grandparents, who had escaped to Switzerland, spent their entire fortune bribing officials until they got their son released. When Gershon Kessler learned what his father had endured, and what his grandparents did to save him, he decided to become a doctor and gave all of his money to charity.

That evening, Curtis sent me a text message: *Is the insurance problem worked out?*

Ever since the last visit with his parents, there'd been a strain between us. I was touched that he was concerned about the problem with my insurance.

"*Yes,*" I wrote back. "*Have you heard of Gershon Kessler?*"

"*No. Who is he?*"

"*My doctor. A big philanthropist.*"

"*I'll ask my parents. They want us to come to dinner this weekend.*"

"*Okay.*"

18

The summer after my second year of high school, my mother announced that she wanted to go to St. Louis for a visit. She hadn't been back since we'd moved away, six years earlier. After making her announcement, she told me, "You don't have to go, if you don't want to. You can stay home with your father."

The last thing I wanted was to take a vacation with my mother, and I told her so. At the start of winter break, she packed the car and left with Teddy and Hannah. Packing put her in one of her good moods. She and Teddy and Hannah made jokes and laughed as they packed the car. I knew she'd wanted all along to take her vacation with just Teddy and Hannah—the good children—and I knew she'd chosen her words carefully when telling me about the vacation to get the reaction she wanted, but I didn't care.

My father and I were left alone in the house. We rarely spoke to each other. I was puzzled by the fact that he came home from work each day, showered and left, and didn't come back for hours. For dinner I usually made myself a sandwich or scrambled eggs or just ate from the refrigerator.

I told Michael about his strange habits. "He probably

has a girlfriend," Michael said.

The idea of my father with a girlfriend intrigued me. I'd always imagined he had secrets he was guarding. Nobody could be as vacant and devoid of life as he seemed to be.

"Let's follow him and find out," I suggested.

Michael liked anything that required cunning and plotting. We included his friend Jason because my father would recognize Michael's mother's car.

That evening the three of us waited down the street in Jason's car. When my father drove by on his way to his mystery date, we trailed him downtown to an exclusive Italian restaurant, the Café Italiano, a white stucco building with beveled windows and stained glass lanterns. I was astonished by the place he'd chosen. Did he actually have a sense of romance?

We waited twenty minutes. Then Jason went in to see what he was doing.

Jason returned and said, "He's sitting by himself."

"Is he eating?" Michael asked.

"He has a drink."

"He must be waiting for his date," said Michael.

We sat for another twenty minutes, watching everyone who entered the restaurant but no one who entered could have been his date. Jason went inside to see what was happening.

He came back and reported, "His food came. He's sitting alone."

"Maybe she stood him up," Michael suggested.

"He doesn't look bothered."

"Very strange," said Michael.

"You must know by now," I said. "My father is strange."

When he came out, about forty minutes later, we

followed him back to the highway. He turned westward, away from home.

"Aha," said Michael. "Now we'll see what he's up to."

We followed him to the parking lot of a Hilton. Jason got out and followed him inside.

A half hour passed before Jason returned. He plopped into the driver's seat and said, "He is in one of the bars, watching television and drinking a martini."

Michael said, "Maybe he's trying to pick up a woman."

"I don't think so," said Jason. "He's not paying attention to anyone."

"Is he watching the news?" I asked.

"How did you know?" asked Jason.

"It's what he always does." This was too absurd. I said, "I want to see."

I borrowed Michael's jacket and baseball cap. "Come on," I said to Jason.

I must have looked outlandish walking through the plush Hilton lobby wearing a boy's jacket and baseball cap. We stopped at the entryway to the bar. There was my father, watching the news on television and sipping a martini, just like he did at home.

I had hoped to learn something exciting about my father—that he had desires or a secret life or a fantasy world, or anything. I'd hoped to discover some clue to his aloofness and detachment. What I found was nothing.

I was nearing the end of my junior year, which meant that Michael's graduation date was approaching. He started talking about moving to Los Angeles and joining one of the gangs there. Such talk irritated me to no end. Then he started acting as if his group of friends were a real gang, and he was the leader. He swaggered more, and smoked more. He never smoked with me, but I knew he was smoking more because I smelled it on his clothes and in his car.

Next he talked about joining the Marines or the Air Force. His excursions with his friends were becoming more frequent, which caused us to quarrel even more. I could not accept his talk of gangs and the military. My only wish was to get away from the tension in my house. I had no desire to go looking for bigger battles.

"I just don't get it," I told him one afternoon. We were in his room. He was sitting on his bed, and I was in the desk chair. "You say you hate when your dad drinks, but then you drink. You say you hate your dad's violence, then you want to go where there's more violence."

"Maybe the Marines can straighten out my head."

"Maybe you should just straighten out your own head."

He looked sad. "You don't understand. I steal things. I need to stop. I need the discipline."

"If you don't want to be a thief, just stop being a thief."

"It's not that easy, Bretna."

I turned away from him. I didn't understand why it wasn't that easy.

Michael enlisted in the Marines and got his ship-out date. He found out he'd most likely be stationed in Texas. I cried, for hours on end, day after day. He often came over and sat with me while I cried. "You can join me later," he said, "after you graduate. We'll get married. I'll make sure you have a place to paint."

I shook my head. The last thing I wanted was to go live on a Marine base as a military wife. I didn't know what life had in store for me, but I knew that wasn't it. I cried harder.

"Bretna," he said sternly. "This is something I have to do—"

"I know," I said, sobbing.

The night before he was supposed to leave, he wanted to take me out, to say good-bye. I told him no. The pain would just be too much.

It was half past eleven and I'd already gone to sleep. I woke up to a tapping at my window. I opened the window.

"Hello," he whispered through the screen.

"Hello," I said.

He said, "Maybe you'll change your mind later and join me."

"Maybe," I said, but I knew I wouldn't. I didn't want to live with someone who talked about joining gangs or who needed the discipline of the military to straighten out his head, even if he loved me and accepted me completely. I didn't want discipline or a regimented life or flag-waving. I wanted serenity and peace and loveliness. In particular, I didn't want to live on a military base in Texas. I wanted to believe that life held something more magical for me, something shimmering and luminescent. For that, I knew, I needed to go far from home.

What I needed was a fairy godmother to emerge from the pages of a book and say, "Come with me and fondly stray, over the hills and far away."

One day, shortly before my high school graduation, my mother said, "My sister Myrna is in town."

My father laughed. The dining and living areas were open, so from where I stood I had a clear view of him sitting in his favorite spot on the couch, reading the newspaper. He had a way of laughing under his breath, a chuckle that was both bitter and ironic.

"Myrna is a nut case," he said. "She's as loony as they come."

This was what I'd always heard about my mother's sister, but I figured crazy didn't have much meaning in my family, and really, who were my parents to talk?

I'd always accepted without question that my aunt Myrna must be crazy, if both my parents said so. Now the fact that they didn't like her was a strong point in her favor. I looked forward to meeting her.

Myrna came into the house that evening like a whirl of energy. Her laugh sounded like the ringing of bells. She spoke with an affected European accent, rounding and lengthening her vowels. Unlike my mother, who never wore makeup, Myrna wore vivid lipstick and eyeliner. Her face was small and round, with high cheekbones, and the bow-shaped lips you see in photos from the twenties. She wore a magenta business suit, with her nails polished to match. Myrna kissed me and Teddy and Hannah, and said how delighted she was to meet us.

If Myrna were a color, she'd be green: full of vitality and life and energy, the first green of spring, that clear vivid green touched with yellow.

After all the introductions and greetings and small talk, we sat down to dinner. My mother told Myrna about her job in a doctor's office and how much she liked it. Myrna responded by talking about her job at the university. "I'm an assistant dean now," she said. She looked at me and said, "That does not mean I am assistant to the dean. I'm like a dean in my own right." I had the feeling she wanted to impress me.

Next Myrna talked about her house. She and her third

husband had bought a thirty-one room mansion near the university. After the divorce, she kept the house. She helped raise money for the upkeep by renting out rooms to university students. At the moment she was short of students, so she had to advertise, which was tricky because renting rooms in her neighborhood was illegal and the neighbors were getting suspicious.

"The house is more than one hundred years old," she said. "It's a beautiful turn of the century Victorian. It's marvelous."

After dinner I offered to take her to Twin Peaks so she could see the view of the city. She said, "That would be great fun. Let's go."

We parked, and I showed her the look-out spot. For a really good view, you had to hike the rest of the way, but from here you could see all the landmarks: Alcatraz, the Golden Gate Bridge, the Transamerica Building. She squealed "Oooh!" She walked around, snapping pictures, saying how marvelous the view was.

"Hey, Bretna, I think I need a day at the beach tomorrow. Want to join me?"

"Sure!"

Next day, sitting on a beach blanket, I told Myrna how I just couldn't get along with my mother.

"Lenora has always been impossible to get along with," Myrna said. "She's never been able to control her tempers."

Myrna's words hit me like a revelation. The simple statement that my mother had never been able to control her tempers meant the problem predated me, so couldn't have been caused by me.

"Mom said she was the obedient daughter," I told her. My mother told me that Myrna used to steal lipsticks from the five-and-ten cents store, wear lipstick to school, and wipe it off before returning home.

Myrna said, "Yeah, right." She told me about the time they were in high school and my mother picked the lock on Myrna's safe, found a package of cigarettes, and planted them in Myrna's pocket and left it on the mantle for their mother to find. "She did it to make me look bad, not caring what it did to our sick mother. She showed no concern for our mother's illness. She disrupted the peace in our house. She put our father into an early grave and she knows it."

I looked out over the ocean. The sky overhead was blue, but the horizon was misty, soft, and gray. There is something calming about being able to see so far.

"Hey, listen," Myrna said. "Why don't you come to St. Louis? You can have one of the rooms in my house. The best room is coming vacant in July. It has a walk-in closet and a private bathroom."

That settled it. Now I had my destination. As soon as I graduated, I'd take off. St. Louis was almost two thousand miles from home, which I considered far enough.

I should, maybe, have worried about going to live with an aunt who I'd always heard was crazy. But after years of dealing with my mother, I felt no fear.

My mother gave me a going-away present wrapped with the comic pages. Using the Sunday comics was her way of economizing: She thought gift paper a waste of money. "You spend all that money for fancy paper, then tear it up and throw it away," she often said.

The card was signed: "Teddy, Hannah, Mom & Dad," in my mother's writing. Inside was an assortment of objects: a pair of kitchen scissors, a card holder for recipes, an address label maker, a toothbrush holder, an electrical extension cord.

I looked at my mother to see what she meant by these gifts. "Kitchen scissors?" I asked.

"You'll need kitchen scissors," she said.

I didn't understand.

"When you're on your own," she explained, "you'll need kitchen scissors."

"An electric cord?"

"You'll always be able to use an extra cord."

"A toothbrush holder?"

"You share one with Teddy. When you're in your own place, you'll need one of your own."

I looked at the things in the box, then back at my mother. She must have seen my bewilderment, because she left the room and went downstairs and started the washing machine.

I knew from the price stickers that she'd gone to Pic'n'Save and bought from the bargain rack. I would soon be boarding a cross-country Greyhound bus, venturing forth into the world on my own, to make my own way, and what she thought I needed was a pair of kitchen scissors and an extension cord?

I bought a one way bus ticket to St. Louis, and sorted through everything I owned, deciding what to throw away and what to bring. My mother gave me two old suitcases. The rest of my stuff I packed into a barrel I'd found on the street. I figured one day I would return, triumphant. I would be Bretna Barringer, the famous artist. People would admire and respect me. My parents would realize they'd always been wrong about me.

On a Monday morning in early July, my parents went to work as usual. They acted as if it were a day like any other, as if I weren't catching a Greyhound bus at ten a.m. and leaving indefinitely. Teddy and Hannah left to find their friends. Nobody said good-bye. Not that it mattered. It wasn't as if I expected a marching band to see me off.

19

"Of course I have heard of Gershon Kessler," said Curtis's mother, who insisted that I call her Joan. "His tennis partner, Sylvia Salfield, says he acts unassuming and modest, but if you ask him who is the best surgeon in New England, he says, 'me.' He donates tens of thousands of dollars each year to the Jewish children's hospital, to Jewish schools, and to the Hadassah soup kitchens, so he doesn't need to pretend to be modest."

"He's doing my operation," I said.

Curtis's father—who said I should call him Jared—leaned back comfortably in his chair and patted his stomach. He was a large man, and obviously enjoyed his meals. The men I had known in the past had always faded into the background, and I couldn't get used to how present Jared was. He filled the room. As soon as he talked, he seemed to grow larger. If he were an animal, he'd be a rhinoceros. At the same time, you had the feeling his skin was not as thick as he pretended. If I painted him as an animal, I'd paint him as an affectionate rhinoceros.

Jared said, "Are your parents coming to town?"

"For what?" I asked.

"What do you mean, 'for what?'" Jared said. "For your operation!"

I wasn't sure how to answer, so there was an awkward

silence with everyone looking at each other.

"What did they say when you told them?" Joan asked.

"I haven't told them."

All three of them looked astonished, even Curtis, who knew enough about my parents so he shouldn't have been surprised. To make sure he understood, Joan repeated for Curtis what I said.

"Bretna," said Curtis. "Maybe you should call them."

"*Maybe?*" Jared thundered. "Are you out of your mind? She should *definitely* tell them!" He turned to me and said, "Bretna, call them."

I wasn't accustomed to people telling me what to do, and I didn't like Jared's tone when he said, "Pick up your phone, right now, and call your parents."

My first impulse was to argue and explain, but I had a better idea. "Can I just send a text message?"

"All right," said Jared. "Go ahead."

I sent my mother a text: *"I need an ear operation. It's scheduled for Jan. 27."*

When I finished typing, I set my phone down. Joan said, "She'll call soon. Let's have dessert. We have French vanilla ice cream."

We were eating ice cream when my phone vibrated. My mother had written: *"Do you have a good doctor?"*

I wrote back, *"best in the city."*

She responded, *"That's what's important. Let us know how it goes."*

I handed my phone to Curtis, who read the messages, and handed the phone to his parents, who also read the messages.

"What about your father?" Jared asked.

"I don't have his phone number." Again Joan and Jared looked at each other, so I explained, "I know the number at his shop, but he isn't there now."

"You need to tell him, too."

I picked up my phone and sent my mother another text message: *"Can you tell Dad?"*

She wrote back, *"OK."*

We resumed eating without speaking until Joan said, "Who paid your college tuition?"

"I did," I said. "Mostly scholarships, but some loans to cover living expenses, and on-campus jobs."

We returned to our meal. There was something different now in the air, a feeling of sympathy and warmth coming my way, particularly from Joan and Jared, but from Curtis as well. He was studying me closely, as he always did, but I saw something new in his face, something like sadness. My parents had conveniently demonstrated precisely what was missing in my family without me having to say much at all.

Joan said, "It's just so hard for me to understand. If one of my kids was sick, I'd be there. I'd certainly say more than 'I hope you have a good doctor.'"

It was like she moved in her own private, protected bubble, enclosed in a world of perfect familial love that I thought only existed on old T.V. shows like *The Brady Bunch* and *Leave it to Beaver.*

The day before my surgery, Curtis rode the bus with me to the hospital and waited while I went through the admission paperwork. After I was checked into my room, he took a few paperbacks from his briefcase and put them on the dresser. "I brought plenty to read," he said.

"I won't be feeling well, Curtis. I doubt I'll be able to read those."

"They're for me," he said.

"How long are you staying?"

"I've taken today and tomorrow off, so I can be

here."

I was touched by this. At the same time, I thought it unnecessary. "You can just come after the operation. When I'm in surgery, I won't even know you're here."

"I will be here," he said firmly.

"Thank you," I said, realizing how completely unaccustomed I was to any such displays of caring and love.

"It's hard to believe your family isn't here," he said.

"That's because you don't know them. If you knew them, you'd believe it. I told you something is weird about them."

The nurse came in to give me a pill. When she left, visiting hours were over. Curtis came back at six in the morning, before the nurse came to wheel me off to the operating room. He was sitting in my room five hours later, reading a book, when I was wheeled back. Each time I opened my eyes, he was there. A nurse came in to give me a shot. I tried to make a joke: "They think I'm a pin cushion."

"Just sleep," he responded.

Curtis's parents came to visit later that evening. There wasn't space in the cramped hospital room for everyone to be comfortable: Joan had the only chair. Jared tried to perch on the arm rest, but was too large, so he leaned against the wall. Curtis sat at the end of the bed. My roommate on the other side of the canvas curtain, an elderly large-boned woman, snored loudly.

After some small talk, Joan said, "Will you need anything else from your apartment?"

"No," I said. "I'm being released in the morning."

"You're coming back to our house," Joan explained. "I'll pick you up tomorrow. If you need any other clothes for a few days, Curtis can get them from your apartment."

I looked at Curtis to find out what this meant. "I could only take off two days," he explained.

Joan said, "I understand you live with two roommates who are busy all day. I'll be home, so you'll stay at our house."

I considered arguing. I was fine, really, and wouldn't need any caretaking. Seeing my expression, Curtis said, "Don't bother arguing. When my mother makes up her mind, that's the end of it."

I turned to Joan and said, "Thank you."

After two days in the Willet's house, I came to think of Joan and Jared as Beauty and the Beast. In fact, I wondered why Joan, who was so gentle and beautiful and kind, had married Jared, who seemed rather crass and overbearing. He might be an affectionate rhinoceros, but his natural way of expressing himself was to shout. The first evening I was there, he marched into the room and said, "Is your finger broken?" Startled and alarmed, I said, "No. Why?" He said, "Then why don't you turn off the lights when you leave the room?"

I apologized, and looked over at Joan, who shrugged and made a playful expression as if to say, "That's the way he is."

Jared also had strong opinions I disagreed with: He said boys were naturally better at math than girls. It took all my self-control not to argue with him. He said that he still wasn't convinced that Curtis was right in his opinion that raising children with ASL was better than raising them in a strictly oral environment. When he said he planned to vote Republican in the Senate election, I feared that if I spent too much time with Jared, I'd argue with him constantly.

Later, when we were alone—afraid to complain outright—I said to Joan, "He *booms*."

She laughed. "I love it! Perfect description! He does boom." Then, in a more serious tone, she said, "After you're around Jared for awhile, you'll see past the booming. Sometimes it takes a while to understand what he's all about."

It didn't take long for me to see what she meant. One evening soon after, when the three of us were at the dinner table, Joan again mentioned the fact that my parents hadn't called again to see how I was. In a quiet voice that reverberated with emotion, Jared said, "A man who doesn't take care of his children isn't a man."

Next afternoon, when Jared was at work, Joan offered me hot chocolate. She invited me to sit with her on the couch, and pulled a woolen afghan over our legs. She wore a sweater and fluffy pink slippers. Talking to Lucinda had been like talking to a cool and elegant professional. Talking to Joan was like talking to Mother Earth.

Joan said, "Curtis probably told you he was mad at us for years."

"No, he didn't." Well, not really.

"After he lost his hearing, the doctor warned us that if we weren't careful, he'd forget how to talk. It made sense at the time that if he was going to get along in the world, he'd need to know how to speak and lip-read, so we sent him to the school the doctor recommended. Curtis spent a lot of time hurting and feeling alone. I'll always feel badly."

I was about to offer her reassurances, but abruptly she said, "I'll never understand your parents. If one of my children were in the hospital, I'd be there no matter what."

I felt I needed to disclose the full truth. "Maybe there's a reason they don't want much to do with me. I was no angel."

"What could you have done bad enough to justify their behavior? Commit murder? Torture animals? What could you have done?"

"I got angry—really angry—and I broke things: vases, jars, even a window once."

Joan waved her hand as if breaking things was of no consequences. "You would not have broken things in a house full of love."

20

The Greyhound bus traveled from California to Missouri along the historic Route 66, sometimes on the old roads, sometimes on newer highways running parallel to the original route—passing through Kingman, Winslow, Amarillo, and Tulsa. There was plenty of room on the bus, so I had my choice of seats. The other passengers included an elderly couple, two women with children, and a man wearing a Marine uniform.

In the cafeteria during our dinner stop in Flagstaff, the Marine set his dinner tray down next to mine.

"I'm Tom," he said. "You're sure cute." I didn't bother answering that. I thought he was cute, too, but I didn't tell him. His uniform bothered me because it reminded me of Michael.

"Can I sit here?" he asked, even though he had already sat down and picked up his fork.

"I guess."

He made small talk. After we ate, he walked with me back to the bus. He wanted to sit next to me. "Just till it gets dark," I said. "Then I want the seat to myself."

"We'll have a meal stop tomorrow in Albuquerque," he said. "It's a great town."

"Hm," I said.

"We should get off there for a while. We could have a good time."

"I can't. My aunt is meeting me at the bus in St. Louis."

"Call her. Tell her you'll be late."

"No," I said, but I felt flattered. My smile must have made him think I could be convinced, because he kept talking about how Albuquerque was such a great town and how much fun we could have there.

The sun set over the Arizona desert. I took out my sketch pad and some pastels and drew the landscape. I planned to use my sketch pad as a photo album, recording the change of landscape between California and Missouri.

"Hey," he said. "How the heck did you do that? That looks just like a cactus!"

I knew he was flattering me so I'd get off the bus with him in Albuquerque. I smiled because I knew flattery wasn't going to work.

Once the sun had been down a while, Tom wanted to sleep with his head in my lap, but I told him no, so he moved back into an empty seat. The bus stopped at a few rest stops during the night. At each stop, I got out for a walk. Tom didn't wake up. I slept intermittently between rest stops, but I was awake at the first light of dawn. I watched the sun rise over the plateaus of New Mexico. In the early morning light, the magnificent pink and peach tones of the plateaus looked like a cardboard movie set. I opened my sketch pad and took out my pastels.

We reached the stop before Albuquerque, and the driver announced a half hour rest stop. Tom wanted me to go for a walk with him. We were behind the building when he tried to kiss me. Curious, I let him. His kisses were wet, and not exciting.

"Come on," he said, "just a few hours in

Albuquerque."

"No," I said.

Seeing that I didn't respond when he tried to kiss me again, he gave up.

After he got off in Albuquerque, I had the seat to myself again. The place we stopped for lunch served chili so hot that my eyes watered. Texas, I found boring: endless grassy fields, cows and more cows. We drove mostly with windows open and I became accustomed to the smell of cows and grass. By the time we reached Oklahoma, which didn't look much different from Texas except that we passed through more towns with wooden houses and red barns, I'd filled five pages of my sketch pad. We traveled through Oklahoma on the most local of roads, passing crumbling sheds, houses in need of paint with shutters in need of repair, and rusted tractors left abandoned by the side of the road.

Missouri had its own smell and a familiar damp heaviness in the air, which brought back my early childhood summers. The trees were deep green, a uniform color utterly unlike California with its richly varied vegetation. I was, at once, going far from home and returning home. Perhaps here, I would find what I was missing. Or perhaps—even better—I might come to understand what had gone so very wrong in my family.

Myrna's neighborhood was lined with lovely turn-of-the century homes with turrets and stained glass and well-tended lawns. Her house, in contrast was in serious need of repairs. Her lawn needed mowing. Her windows were dusty. Weeds were growing out of cracks in the front porch.

In the driveway was an old convertible, robin's egg blue, with the hood up. On the ground was an assortment of tools and rags.

Myrna told me there were thirty-one rooms in her house, so when she gave me a tour, I started counting. She pointed out the exposed brick wall in the kitchen, real hard wood floors, and plaster work ceilings. There were three staircases and no apparent order to the confusing sprawl of rooms and corridors. The second floor had a large landing with a window overlooking the back courtyard. Some of the rooms were beautifully painted and decorated, others looked as if they hadn't been dusted for decades. It turned out the thirty-one rooms included the unused and unfurnished rooms in the basement with crumbling walls and concrete floors and no heating.

"I invited all my kids for dinner," she said, "so you can meet them."

When her kids arrived, I had the feeling they were looking at me curiously and rather suspiciously.

"So you're mom's latest find," said Robbie, the middle son. "Lenora's daughter. The famous Lenora."

Robbie, an anthropologist, brought a piece of a rug, the latest addition to his collection. He proudly showed off the rug, tattered and caked with dirt, with holes that looked as if bugs had eaten through. I gathered from the way he talked that it was an authentic Indian rug.

"Isn't it beautiful?" he asked, holding it up.

At first I thought he was joking. When the others agreed that it was beautiful, I understood that he was serious. Nobody noticed that I didn't respond.

Billie, the only girl, came with her boyfriend. Myrna grimaced when she heard the sound of motorcycles in the driveway. "When will Billie grow up?" she said.

"Mom" said Robbie, "when will *you* grow up?"

She laughed merrily. "What fun is growing up?" To

me she said, "What I like best about being an adult is that I can eat ice cream whenever I want. I can even eat ice cream for dinner if I feel like it."

Billie and her boyfriend Raymond wore black leather jackets, had tattoos on both arms, and smoked long, thin, brown cigarettes. I was surprised to learn that Billie worked in a bank. She wasn't my idea of a banker. "I'm good with numbers," she explained.

The oldest son, Ryan, was not what I expected either. I thought an electrical engineer and company vice president would be skinny with glasses, but Ryan had a solid build with broad shoulders. His hair was black, parted on the side, and thinning on top. I thought he looked older than twenty nine.

The youngest, Peter, didn't say much except to boast about his studies at Fayette University. He was always using big words that I had the feeling he was mispronouncing. I thought he was the strangest of all.

"How's Toimoda?" Billie asked Ryan as we sat down to eat.

I supposed Toimoda was an animal, but it turned out Toimoda was the name Ryan had given his eight-year-old Toyota, a car on which he did all the repairs himself.

"I wish I could do that," Myrna said. "What a lot of aggravation I'd save if I could fix my own car."

"You could learn," Ryan said. "It isn't hard."

"I just don't have your brain," Myrna said.

Billie and her boyfriend exchanged annoyed glances. After dinner, when Billie and her boyfriend invited me for a walk to show me around the neighborhood, Billie told me why she had made an annoyed expression. "She never paid attention to Ryan before. Now, suddenly, he's her favorite."

"Why?" I asked.

"Because he got an engineering degree and he's earning the big bucks, that's why. You should hear her go on and on about how *marvelous* he is. She didn't used to think so, you can bet on that."

When we got back, Ryan had the hood of Myrna's car up and he was explaining something to her. She was looking at him as adoringly as Scarlett O'Hara looking at her beaux. "I can't thank you enough," she said. "I'm going to have you check out everything after I get the mechanic's opinion."

Billie rolled her eyes. She whispered to me, "She'd marry him if she could."

Sometime later, Billie asked me, "Why did you come to St. Louis?"

"I wanted to get far away from my mother. She's impossible to live with."

"And you came to *my* mother?"

21

Monday morning after my operation, I was back at work in the high school, wearing a white gauze bandage wrapped around my head. I walked into Alex's science classroom and he grinned. "You look like a truck ran into you," he said.

"I feel like a truck ran into me."

He looked more closely at my bandages and his expression changed—he was still grinning, but awkwardly now, as if realizing I was not wearing some sort of Halloween mummy costume. "Does it hurt?" he asked.

"No." I lied because I didn't want to alarm him. Besides, it didn't hurt much anymore.

"They operated on your ear?" he asked. "To make you hear better?""I don't think it will help my hearing much. But everything is fine now."

The problem, it turned out, was that the bandages made my hearing worse. The bandage and whatever cotton was packed around my ear made it so difficult for me to hear what the teacher was saying, I had to turn my chair to face the teacher so that I could catch more. As a result, I wasn't watching Alex so I didn't know what he was paying attention to, which meant I didn't know what he missed, which made tutoring harder. I looked forward to getting the bandage off.

"Everything is healing fine," said Dr. Kessler. He'd removed the bandage and was looking into my ear. Hearing him speak reassured me that my hearing was back to normal. I was therefore surprised when he took out a pad and wrote something on it. He tore off the paper and handed it to me. "I'm referring you to an audiologist."

"Why? I already know I don't hear well in one ear."

"Go on across the hallway. Show the receptionist this referral. They'll give you a hearing test."

Across the hallway was a receptionist, who led me to a room in the back. A nurse dressed in scrubs came in and put a pair of padded earphones on my head. "Raise your hand when you hear the beep."

I concentrated on the beeps. Each time the tone sounded, I raised my hand. She took off her earphone and wrote something on my referral notice. I expected her to say, "Well, your doctor was worrying about nothing."

What she said was, "Have you had this problem long?"

I looked at the notations she had made on her graph. She'd charted a forty-five decibel hearing loss in my right ear, and a thirty decibel hearing in my left ear. I'd done enough reading on deaf education preparing for the job with Alex to know those numbers meant a significant hearing loss. I felt nothing had changed since the operation, which meant—if that graph was correct—that I'd always had such a hearing loss. It was impossible. If I had such poor hearing, how had I lived such a normal life? How could I use the phone? How was I getting through school?

"I really think there's a mistake," I said.

"We'll give you a more complete test," she said.

"Come this way and I'll introduce you to the audiologist, Emily."

Emily led me into a glass enclosed booth fitted with a more elaborate headset with knobs and buttons. She held a device shaped like a microphone. She told me to press the red button on the device whenever I heard a sound. The tones grew softer, coming at regular intervals. I could predict when the next pitch would come and what it would sound like. The pitches grew fainter until I wasn't sure whether I was hearing them or not. Unsure, I didn't press the button. The test went on until I was tired from straining to hear.

She stood up and opened the door.

"How did I do?" I asked.

"Have you ever worn hearing aids?"

The graph she had drawn gave the same decibel range loss as the nurse's graph. The graph had to be wrong because it showed a significant hearing loss in both of my ears. I remembered waking up one morning and listening to a bird chirping outside my window. I rolled over and put my other ear into the pillow, and the chirping stopped. I lifted my head, and heard it again. The obvious conclusion was that one of my ears was fine.

"I need to be retested," I said. "There were sounds I wasn't sure about."

She stood akimbo, giving me a look I couldn't read.

"Really," I said. "There's a mistake. I need to be retested."

She went back to her chair. I sat back down in the booth and listened for the pitches. This time, wanting to be sure the results were not falsely negative, I pressed the clicker when I wasn't quite sure, just to be safe.

After a few scales, she stood up and opened the door and said, "Now you stop that. You're not a child."

"Stop what?"

She gave an annoyed grunt and said, "Tell me. What good does it do to cheat on an audiogram? Honestly." She explained that after working down the scale, she started at the bottom and worked up, to test the results. She could therefore see I was pressing the button when I wasn't really hearing the beep.

I laughed, embarrassed, and she laughed, too.

"Come on out," she said. "Sit over here."

Another doctor came in and peered into my ears with an otoscope. Then he went to talk to the audiologist, who had been standing behind me. I tried to listen to what they were saying, but when I heard something about New England Telephone, I concluded that they weren't talking about me so I stopped trying to listen.

The doctor walked around to stand in front of me. He handed me an official form with New England Telephone written across the top. "This is for an amplifier," he said. "Just send this to the phone company, and they'll give you an amplifier for you phone."

I understood that he was treating me like a deaf person—assuming that I hadn't heard talking behind me, which indeed I had not, then coming around, standing in front of me, and talking distinctly.

Handing the form back to him, I said, "I don't have any problem with the phone. I use it all the time."

He pulled up a chair and sat down. He handed the form back to me and said, "You're straining to hear and you don't know it. You're missing more than you realize. You have a hearing loss and it isn't mild. You need hearing aids."

"If that's true," I said. "How have I gotten by all this time?"

"You can't know what you're not hearing. It isn't like

bad sight, when print becomes blurry and you know there's a problem."

"But one of my ears is good. I know it is."

"It feels that way because you *can* hear out of the left ear. Not well, but you *can* hear. Wait a minute. I want to send you home with some hearing aid information."

On my way out, I passed Emily. She handed me a packet of information, and evidently wanting to make polite conversation, said, "What kind of work do you do, Bretna?"

My sense of irony got the better of me. I smiled and said, "I work with a deaf boy who denies his handicap."

She drew back, surprised. While she was off balance, I said, "Bye!" and breezed out the door.

Next day I checked into hearing aids. They cost thousands of dollars and my insurance did not cover them. That was that. There was nothing I could do. I put the audiogram into a manila folder and put it on the top shelf over my desk.

The following Saturday morning Curtis and I were in his apartment when the red light in the hallway blinked on and off. He went to the door and opened it. In came three guys about seventeen, signing rapidly. They all appeared to be signing at once. One asked Curtis in the ASL style, "What-think-you-I-do?"

Curtis asked several rapid questions, none of which I could understand. As always there was a difference in how Curtis signed with deaf people. His face was more animated, his gestures more relaxed.

"I'll see what I can do," Curtis told them. He sat at his TTY and made calls. I wanted to ask the guys what was the matter, but I didn't want them to see how awkward my ASL was.

I concentrated on my drawing. The pastel drawing I was working on was a snowy landscape all in whites, clear translucent blues, and black. I liked drawing snowscapes because they reminded me of my first winter in New England, when I was both overcome with the beauty of the place and awed by the harshness of the weather.

One of the boys wandered over and looked at my drawing. Curtis was still busy with his TTY. The boy startled me by making the sign for "silence" and pointing to the picture.

I signed, "Yes."

Curtis got off the phone and handed one of the boys a piece of paper. After some more rapid signing, the boy signed, "Thanks!"

Curtis walked them to the door. He returned to the living room and explained what had happened: One of the boys was unable to find an interpreter for a job interview Monday. "There are not enough interpreters in this city," he signed. "If you ever really learn ASL you could earn good money."

I smiled, wondering if indeed a person with a forty-five decibel hearing loss in one ear and a thirty decibel hearing loss in the other could get registered as an interpreter.

I went back to my drawing. For the first time since knowing Curtis, I wanted to return to my apartment to get away from him. The entire situation struck me as so complicated: He was uncomfortable with my ability to hear. Even if he didn't admit it, I knew he was. My hearing loss was worse than I had known, and worse than I let on, and I didn't want to tell him about the audiogram, afraid that it would make a difference when it shouldn't.

22

My room in Myrna's house was furnished with a four-poster bed, a small dresser that also served as a night stand, and a chifferobe. The walls were papered with a faded chintz print, and the wood floors were scuffed. Attached was a bathroom with a bear-claw tub. In the open area just outside my bedroom was an impressive bookcase filled with books.

I was unpacking and hanging my clothing in the chifferobe when Myrna came in and flopped down on the bed like a kid. She said, "Rent is four hundred and fifty dollars. There are twenty-four days left this month, so that will be four hundred and thirty-nine. Rent includes utilities."

I was flat amazed. I hadn't thought to ask what she was going to charge me. A friend's sister in California had paid nine hundred dollars for her entire apartment including utilities—a bedroom, living room, kitchen, with use of a swimming pool. And that was in California.

"I can pay you with traveler's checks," I said, "or you can wait until I open a bank account."

"I'll take the traveler's checks."

As I counted out the money, more than a third of all I had, Myrna made small talk. "Don't you just love the wallpaper," she said, and explained that when she and her third husband bought the house ten years earlier, they wallpapered the entire second floor, trying to match the Victorian style of the original. I said I liked the wallpaper, even though I wasn't particularly fond of floral prints.

Next time I had a chance, I asked her oldest son, Ryan, what he thought of four hundred and fifty dollars a month for that room.

"Outrageous." He said. "Highway robbery. She tried to make my brother pay, too, but he just moved out. You don't have to stay long. After you get to know your way around, you can find another room. Lots of people rent out rooms around here, mostly for under three hundred dollars."

"I better figure out how to get a job."

"Go to the University," he said. "There are always jobs there.

Uncle Willie and Aunt Dorothy lived less than a mile from Myrna. Dorothy and my maternal grandmother had been sisters.

"My goodness," Dorothy said, when I called and told her who I was. "Lenora's daughter. How long will you be in town?"

"I'm staying. I'll start looking for a job Monday."

"Well, goodness. You must come for lunch tomorrow." She gave me the address.

Next day, I borrowed Myrna's bike, rode to their house, and locked the bike to a lamp post in front. I must have visited their house as a young child, but I didn't remember it. The house was brick, trimmed with white.

Dorothy opened the door, leaning on a walker. "Come in," she said.

She was dressed in a button-down blouse and slacks. Her hair was silver and pulled into a knot behind her head and held in place with a net. The dining room table, in a corner of the living room, was set for lunch. The living room was decorated with hooked rugs, brass clocks, and painted china bowls. From the kitchen came the warm spicy smell of cooking meat.

Uncle Willie came in from the kitchen. We greeted each other, and sat on the couch and made small talk. They asked how everyone was, although they didn't remember the names of my brother and sister. I said everyone was fine. Uncle Willie had an easy smile, and struck me as the sort of person who went through life laughing at everything. Dorothy seemed fussy and formal.

Dorothy went into the kitchen and came back with soup. We moved to the table. "It's lentil," Dorothy said. From the murky color of the soup, I didn't expect to like it, but it smelled faintly of tomatoes and had a satisfying tang.

After some more small talk, I said, as casually as I could manage: "I never really got along with my mom."

"Really?" Dorothy asked politely.

"Really," I said. Then: "What was she like when she still lived here?"

Dorothy looked thoughtful for a moment, then said, "What will you do in St. Louis."

It was a clumsy evasion, but I went along. "I'm trying to get a job at the university. I want to take art classes there."

They both nodded approvingly. "That must have been Myrna's idea," Dorothy said. "She can give you good advice about such things."

"Myrna has a good job at the university," Uncle Willie said.

"I'd better check on the meat," Dorothy said, and went into the kitchen.

She came back and served each of us a slice of

meatloaf. The meatloaf had a hard-boiled egg cooked inside and what tasted like bits of onion. Meatloaf with egg tasted surprisingly good.

I said, "My mother told me she was an angel of a child."

"Your mother," Dorothy said firmly, "was a hellion, always running around and screaming."

"I'm not surprised," I said, and I wasn't.

"When we told her that her mother needed peace and quiet she said, 'Who do you think you are, God? I'll listen to you when you are God.'"

"Dorothy," Willie said quietly.

To Dorothy, I said, "My mother told me she had wonderful parents."

"She did," she said. "Annabelle and Charlie were the sweetest, most loving people in the world. Nobody knew how two such loving people—"

"Dorothy," Willie said again. They looked at each other.

"What?" I asked.

They both looked uncomfortable. I said, "Nobody knew how two such loving people what?"

"I think it's time for the pie," Willie said

Dorothy sighed, stood up, and went into the kitchen. I wanted to get up to help her, but there was too much awkwardness.

When Dorothy came back, I said, "Please tell me. Nobody knew how two such loving people, what?"

Dorothy said, "Nobody knew how two such loving people had three such self-centered and mean children."

I wouldn't have described my Uncle Oliver as particularly mean. Detached and unknowable, maybe. Certainly he'd never shown any interest in me. I said, "Myrna doesn't seem mean."

Dorothy said, "Myrna got her first divorce when the children were little. She went back to school. Neighbors used to find Billie running around the neighborhood in her diapers. They'd bring her home and Myrna just laughed."

After that, we ate in silence. Later, when Dorothy went into the kitchen, Willie said, "Dorothy is a little hard on Annabelle's children. It isn't fair what she says. Your grandmother had a disease, and your grandfather had a heart attack. The family was under a lot of strain."

Dorothy came back into the room and said, "When your grandfather had that heart attack, he was only forty-two living under the constant stress of a sick wife, two uncontrollable daughters, and a son who didn't give a damn about anyone. Willie can think what he wants, but I saw what they went through with those kids."

"We really shouldn't be talking about this," Willie said to me. "I'm sorry."

"But I want to know," I said. In fact, that was why I had come.

"We've said more than we should," said Willie.

After that, I couldn't get another word out of them about my mother. Dessert was an apple pie with strips of crust woven across the top. The pie was warm and cinnamony.

"This must have been a lot of work to make," I said.

Dorothy said, "I bought it at Schnucks."

"Schnucks?" I asked.

"A grocery store."

Willie said, "Do grocery stores in California have strange names?"

"Not so strange. Safeway. Albertson's."

I said, "I remember Grandma Annabelle's house. I remember a drawer in the kitchen where she kept cookies. But for the life of me, I can't remember the name of the street they lived on."

"McNab," Willie said. "McNab Road."

I was pedaling down McNab Road for the second time when I noticed an elderly woman sitting on her front porch. I stopped on the sidewalk in front of her house and said, "Hi! My grandparents used to live on this street."

"I've lived in this house forty years, since these houses were first built," she said. "I knew everyone here. What were their names?"

"Annabelle and Charlie Zetner."

"Of course I knew Annabelle and Charlie! I probably knew you, too. What's your name?"

"Bretna. My mother is their youngest daughter, Lenora."

"Of course I knew Lenora. Everyone on this street knew Lenora. Come on up. Make yourself comfortable. I'm Betty Rosen."

Betty Rosen's voice was chilly. She had thin lips, an aquiline nose, an animated expression, and ice blue eyes. If not exactly beautiful, she must have once had an interesting, expressive, and arresting face, the kind of face you wanted to keep looking at.

I laid the bike on the lawn, climbed the stairs to the porch and sat on a lawn chair.

She pointed to a house across the street and about halfway down the block. "That house with the white trim was their house."

I looked at the house, trying to recall having seen it before, but I couldn't. Then I remembered something: "The kitchen was white with frilly blue curtains." I suppose I remembered the kitchen so well because of the cookie drawer. I also remembered that the cookies were kept in a drawer low enough for me to reach.

"The kitchen is still white," she said. "The folks who bought it left it just the same: white tile, white refrigerator, white floors. The new folks moved in just after Annabelle died. That would have been—" she paused and said, "almost twenty years ago! Time certainly flies."

Then I asked what I really wanted to know: "What was my mother like when she was a child?"

"Your mother was a wild thing. She didn't walk, that child, she ran. She didn't talk, she shouted. As soon as she was old enough, she went tearing up and down this street on her tricycle. She had more energy than five children."

That I could easily imagine.

Betty said, "She liked to pin the bathroom towels to her shoulders like a cape and run in and out of the house shouting that she was Vampire Girl so everyone had better watch out. She took her mother's lipsticks and put war paint on her cheeks and nose and rode around the front yard on her broomstick-horse, giving war whoops."

I laughed.

"Yup, she was something else. Full of energy. When she was a teenager, she was full of rage. Here's one thing I remember: She wanted to get married in the worst way, and she wanted to marry a doctor—" She looked at me and asked, "Is you dad a doctor?"

"He's a television repairman."

"So. Lenora didn't get what she wanted. Well, no surprise."

"What were my grandparents like?" I asked.

"Your grandmother was sick. Had some disease, I forgot the name.

"She needed peace and quiet," I said.

"That's what she said she needed. Don't we all?"

"The doctors said she needed peace and quiet or she'd die sooner."

"I don't think the doctors knew much about that disease. Nobody expected her to live to see her grandchildren, that's for sure. When the word went out that there was a death in the family, we all sent cards and flowers, thinking it was Annabelle. Imagine the shock to find out it was Charlie, died of a heart attack on the golf course one morning. A surprise. A shock."

"I heard that Charlie and Annabelle were wonderful people."

"Who told you that?"

Come to think of it, the source was not exactly unbiased. "Annabelle's sister. She also told me that nobody could understand how two such sweet and loving people had three such difficult and selfish children."

"Don't believe that. Something like that can't be true. If two people have three selfish and difficult children—particularly children as selfish and difficult as Oliver, Myrna, and Lenora—all I can tell you is that something went wrong in that house. I can't tell you what, but something went wrong."

23

"I have the most perfect idea," Rosie said one evening. "You can arrange a day hike, a retreat, for the sign language club. We offer hikes perfect for a high school club retreat—less than three hours of walking with a beautiful place to rest. It's a great way to break the ice and bring a group together."

"That's not a bad idea," I said.

"Let me get you a brochure." She bounded into her room and came back with an Outdoor Adventures brochure. There would be a fee to pay, including a fee for the guide, but it wasn't much money, and the librarian had mentioned that they had funds for enrichment activities.

"I'll talk to the librarian," I said.

"I've lived in Massachusetts all my life," Rosie said. "So I know the hiking and camping in this state like the back of my hand. The hike I recommend is near the Connecticut River. You can see actual dinosaur footprints."

"No kidding?"

"No kidding. The tracks are set in slabs of sandstone."

She pulled down her can of espresso roast from the cabinet and went on, "My parents weren't big hikers or campers. My mother liked to say that her idea of roughing it was staying in a Hyatt Regency. I didn't really discover hiking and rock climbing until high school."

She tamped the grinds and I could smell the bitterness of the coffee. "So, Bretna. Where are you from?"

"I was born in a suburb of St. Louis called Creve Coeur. The name is so perfect, you'd think I made it up."

"Why?"

I looked at her. "Creve Coeur is French for 'broken heart.'"

Rosie said, "Oh! How sad. So what was Creve Coeur like?"

Sometimes I found Rosie's chattering tiring, but I was here in the kitchen, so there was nothing to do but answer. "We lived in a subdivision called Arrowhead Meadows. I remember looking for Indian arrowheads with a friend in a vacant field."

"Did you find any?"

"Never. But my friend was convinced we would, so we kept looking."

"There may not have been any arrowheads in that field," Rosie said. "But I promise there are real dinosaur footprints by the Connecticut River."

The meeting of Alex's education team was held in a special conference room accessible only through the principal's office. The room was paneled with dark wood, making it look more like a bank conference room than a room in a high school. A framed portrait hung on the wall. It wasn't the kind of room that inspired spontaneity. It wasn't the kind of place I could raise my hand and say, "Excuse me, but I think you are all making a mistake."

I greeted a few of the teachers who were already there and selected a chair near the door. Alex came in next, his face glowing. I knew it was because of his final grades. He'd been on the verge of changing his mind about going into all intermediate classes—until he finished the semester with more A's than he expected. Never mind that one of his A's was in remedial reading, one in speech, one for showing up every day at the Learning Center for tutoring, and one in PE

Next entered Karen, one of the counselors. Elaine had arranged for Alex to meet weekly with Karen, stressing that his meetings with Karen were confidential. Elaine also had Alex meet with her weekly as well.

Lucinda and a man who I assumed was Esteban, Alex's father, entered next. Lucinda smiled at me, and chatted pleasantly with Elaine. Watching them, I thought that nobody would ever guess that they talked about each other with pure scorn.

Alex shuffled in and took a seat to the right side of the table. I signed, "Maybe you should sit on that side so you can see me when I interpret."

He spelled, "OK," on his fingers. I was surprised at his compliance. Ordinarily he refused an interpreter on occasions like this because he wanted to show he could follow the discussion on his own, even though in fact, he couldn't.

When everyone was seated at the table, Elaine shuffled through some papers and said, "Our first item of business is to congratulate Alex on an excellent semester."

I interpreted for Alex, who was sitting up straight and alert, watching me more intently than he ever did in class. After each of Alex's classroom teachers talked about how well he had done that semester, Elaine distributed his new schedule and his revised ed plan. She explained that he'd be moving up to intermediate English and algebra, and adding intermediate history.

In anticipation of this, I had spoken to each of Alex's teachers frankly, explaining how much each of us did for Alex, how much time he and I had for tutoring this semester and how little time we would have next semester. Now I looked around to see if anyone was going to say it was flat absurd to so dramatically increase Alex's workload. Nobody moved at all.

Elaine said, "Are there any comments?" Again, I looked around. It felt like a moment at a wedding ceremony: "Speak now, or forever hold your peace." If anyone said anything, I would jump in, but I couldn't speak first. I'd been invited as the interpreter, not a participant. Besides, Elaine and everyone else knew my opinion.

Alex said, "I want to say something."

"Yes, Alex," said Elaine.

"I want to thank Ms. Barringer for everything she did to help me. My success this semester is because of her."

He pronounced each word so perfectly that I knew he must have rehearsed. I smiled, but I wasn't happy.

"We would also like to thank Bretna," said Lucinda. I didn't know if she planned to speak just then, or if she saw and understood why I had looked pleadingly at the teachers. "Because of Bretna," she said, "we feel ready to face the challenges of the coming semester. We owe her so much."

I happened, just then, to look at Elaine, who was watching me with something like pity, as if she knew I was trapped on a train heading for a brick wall.

"What are you doing later?" I asked Curtis the following Saturday morning.

"Tonight there's a sign language performance at the

Deaf Association called Art Sign. I'll bet you didn't know we have our own poetry."

"No, I didn't." I didn't like how I felt when he made the sign for "we." The sign itself, first touching one shoulder, then swinging the hand around to touch the other, formed a circle, and seemed to shut me out.

After I gave a few hints, he invited me to the performance.

Walking into the Deaf Association that evening, I wondered if I had made a mistake. Curtis stood near the stage with a group of people who were signing too rapidly for me to understand what they were talking about. I recognized an occasional sign, but that was all. Curtis saw me and waved. A moment later, someone tapped his shoulder and absorbed him in a sign conversation.

Two guys about my age leaned against the reception desk. As I approached, one made the salute for "Hi," then signed rapidly.

"Please—slow," I signed, using the ASL idiom. Then, "My ASL is rusty."

"Are you hearing?" the other one asked. My non-expressive face and my signing—which was straight Signed English with a few ASL idioms thrown in—must have been the giveaways. I'd gotten used to Curtis understanding me, but Curtis and I had probably invented our own hybrid way of communicating, the way Alex and I did.

"What's your name?" one of them asked me.

I finger-spelled my name, then he spelled his own name. A woman joined us. The guy signed, "This is Bretna. She's hearing."

The woman looked at me, her expression, polite and distant. "Why do you know sign?" she asked.

"I tutor a deaf boy in a public high school."

She made the sign for "interesting," snapping her thumb and middle finger out from her chest.

I looked back at Curtis, who still stood near the stage, deep in a sign conversation with a group of people. Would he ignore me all evening?

"Where are you from?" one of the guys asked me. He had dark straggly hair, pale skin, and acne.

Surprised by the question, I signed, "I was born near St. Louis."

"My brother is from Illinois. Chicago. Pretty far from St. Louis."

"Same general neighborhood," I signed. I was trying to be funny, but nobody laughed.

"Who do you know here?" the woman asked me. She signed slowly and deliberately, the way one would speak to a foreigner.

Instead of spelling out Curtis's name, I made his name sign. She looked genuinely surprised. "How do you know Curtis?"

"I was in his sign language class over the summer." Well, I *had* walked into their club. I supposed it was her right to cross-examine me.

She looked at me more closely, and signed, "Nice hat." Then: "Great jacket."

I was wearing one of my thrift store finds, a multicolored tailored jacket in shades of salmon with a matching hat from the 1960s, the kind of suit Jacqueline Onassis might have worn.

"Thanks," I signed.

I hoped Curtis would rescue me, but he was still signing with the group of people near the stage, acting as if I weren't there.

More people entered and soon I was surrounded by

so much signing that I couldn't follow any of it.

Another man wearing a blue work shirt and trousers with a nametag that said "Xavier" stitched over his breast pocket introduced himself to me and asked where I was from. When I said I was born near St. Louis, he said he didn't know anyone from St. Louis. I thought it a strange introductory ritual. Then he started signing about the performance. I nodded, occasionally making the sign for "really," or "interesting."

He grinned and asked, "What's the greatest problem facing deaf people today."

I supposed that by some miracle he hadn't guessed that I was hearing, probably because I'd kept my own signing to a minimum.

"I don't know." I imitated the way Curtis formed the signs.

"It's a joke," he said.

"I still don't know."

"The greatest problem facing deaf people today," he said, grinning, "is hearing people."

I tried to match his grin even though I didn't think it was funny. The group moved to admit a newcomer, a man in a tweed jacket. The man looked familiar. When he started signing rapidly, I recognized him from the jerky motion of his hands: He was Reuben, the man who'd begged five dollars from Curtis the evening we'd gone to that Chinese Restaurant. I hadn't noticed him because he'd cleaned up—his hair was combed, his beard trim, his clothing without tatters.

"Aw," Xavier groaned, and signed, "We've all heard that one before." He pointed to me and said, "Tell her. Maybe she hasn't heard it."

"I have a great joke," Reuben signed to me. "Pay attention."

"Sign slowly," I told him.

He signed very slowly, exaggerating his signs and mouthing the words so I easily followed the joke: "A deaf husband and wife stopped at a motel for the night. It was late and they got the last room. After they got their keys, the innkeeper closed the office and went to bed. Across the street was a twenty-four hour market. The man said, 'I'm hungry. I want to go to the store for food.' The wife said, 'I'm going to bed.' When the man came back with his groceries, he could not remember which room was his. He looked up at the dark building, and tried to remember but he couldn't. Then he got an idea. He got into the car and started honking. Honk! Honk! As he honked, the lights in the motel came on, one by one. Soon all the lights were on except for one room. He knew which room was his: the room that was still dark."

I didn't want to laugh, but I did. "Very funny," I told him.

"Even hearing people laugh at that one," he said.

Curtis appeared and sat next to me. Anyone watching would have thought it was coincidental. I looked at him, then faced forward. In my peripheral vision, I saw him ask, "What's the matter?"

"Nothing. I shouldn't be here."

I waited for him to ask why, but he just sat with his hands resting on his knees, not looking at me. He knew why. Then he signed, "I invited you."

"No, you didn't. I pushed you into it."

He hesitated a moment too long. "That's not true."

"Say you're glad I'm here. Say you're not ashamed to be seen with a hearing person."

"I'm not ashamed."

I looked at him in the unwavering manner of the deaf, understanding now why they did it. After a few moments, he fidgeted, betraying himself. A person could reveal so much under the intensity of a quiet stare.

"I'm just not used to it," he signed.

"Your friends seemed surprised to see me here."

He grinned. "I guess so, after all those times I swore I'd never date a hearing woman."

When I noticed the people around watching us, I felt too self-conscious to answer. You cannot have a whispered conversation in sign language. From across the room, people can eavesdrop, which meant plenty of people in the room knew what we'd just said to each other.

A man wearing a sports jacket and red tie walked onto the stage. I caught enough of what he was signing to know that he was introducing the performer, Annette Anders. Then a woman walked out on the stage, dressed in black leggings and a flowing black skirt of transparent crepe. She stood for a moment looking at the audience, then, as if completely absorbed in her own thoughts, she looked up at the ceiling.

She began a kind of dance with her upper body, her hands flowing, her arms circling forward and forming an arc over her head. I caught a few signs: 'a long time ago," and "a young girl," enough to know she was telling a story. Her expression changed dramatically as she told her story. First she was frightened, biting her lip, staring into space. Then she was dazed.

She signed, "I know silence." The sign for "silence" was usually made by moving both hands down and to the side, but she spread out her hands to include the entire space around her. "I know sound," she signed, but she didn't form the sign in the usual way, originating from the ears. Instead she made a gesture as if sounds were all around her.

I mentally translated: "Silence is the moment nothing moves, a moment caught in a photograph. I know a whisper. A whisper is the leaves moving. I know laughter—" as her tempo increased, I lost her meaning. I thought Alex should see this. If he knew how beautiful signing could be, maybe he'd stop mumbling his signs, embarrassed for the hearing kids to see.

After the performance there was a light murmur and the scraping of chairs as people stood up and went to the reception area where a burgundy cloth-covered table was set with silver warming trays. I smelled the faint, spicy scent of curry. Curtis and I stood awkwardly together.

A man tapped Curtis on the shoulder and he turned aside to answer. Jake, the hearing guy who usually sat at the reception desk, approached me and said, "Hi. What are you doing here?" He signed as he spoke.

"I came—" I looked at Curtis.

"That's what we thought." As before, he signed as he spoke. I wondered about his use of the word 'we.' What entitled him to lump himself with the deaf people?

"Are we the only hearing people here?" I asked, not signing as I spoke, even though by not signing I was breaking an important rule of etiquette.

He didn't answer, so I repeated, "Are we the only hearing people here?"

"No. Barbara's husband is hearing."

"Who is Barbara?" Rebellious, I kept my arms at my side. Curtis approached us, but when he saw me speaking, my hands by my side, he stopped. I looked away from him.

Jake pointed to Barbara and her husband. Barbara's husband's hands were moving rapidly.

I said, "People are looking at me like my face is green. Why don't they look at you like that? Or Barbara's husband?"

"We're not here with Curtis. You are."

Someone tapped Jake's arm and began signing rapidly.

I drifted toward Barbara and her husband, watching their conversation but unable to figure out what they were talking about. They kept repeating one sign that I had never seen before, and that I guessed was idiomatic ASL: the sign for "think" the index finger pointed toward the temple, followed immediately by the sign for "hearing," the index finger rolling in a horizontal motion in front of the mouth in imitation of words spilling out. The snapping of the hand between "think" and "hearing" made the sign seem bitter and angry.

"Think-hearing," I translated.

I looked at my watch. If I hurried, I could make the hourly bus back to Kendall Square. I grabbed my coat, and walked toward the door. All I wanted was to be home, in my own room, surrounded by the comforting smell of paints and charcoal pencils.

I was almost to the sidewalk when I heard footsteps on the walkway behind me. I looked back and saw Curtis hurrying to catch up with me. I didn't slow down.

He caught up and, using his voice, said, "I'll give you a ride."

I shook my head and walked on, listening to the angry clicking of my heels and the lighter tapping of his rubber-soled shoes.

In the light of the bus stop, he signed, "I didn't think the evening would go this way. I thought it would be interesting, that you'd learn a lot."

"I did. What's 'think-hearing?'"

"A deaf person who tries to be like a hearing person. Why?"

"Like Alex?"

A beat of time passed. Then another. "Yes, like Alex."

"Barbara's husband is hearing."

"He's hearing," Curtis signed, "but he's really deaf."

"What are you talking about?"

"His parents are deaf. His brother is deaf. He understands deafness. He's been signing all his life" Curtis signed in the ASL manner that looked like: "His-mother-father-deaf, his brother deaf, he understand deaf."

"He's think-deaf."

I meant it as a joke, but I could see from the way his face closed off that Curtis didn't like it. "Look, Bretna I know you've had it rough—"

I knew what was coming. "I don't need you to feel sorry for me," I said.

"I don't feel sorry for you. Look at you. You left home at eighteen on a bus. You financed your own education at the Massachusetts College of Art. Your parents could care less that you were in the hospital for major surgery. You're a survivor. You're not the kind of person someone feels sorry for."

I didn't say anything. My hands were limp in my lap.

"I'm the only deaf person in my entire family," he said. "I just don't like being the only deaf person around."

"Fine," I signed, not looking at him.

"I know I'm being unfair."

I was surprised by the depth of my anger. "Good. I'm glad you know."

"I just want you to know how I feel. Sometimes it really bothers me to see how well you got along with my family, how easy it all is for you—"

"You think it is easy for me?" I felt tears coming.

"The talking part, laughing at the right times, all of that."

I didn't answer. How do you convince someone he's completely wrong?

We both looked up as the bus wheezed up. The driver opened the door. I boarded the bus and sat near the window, my cheek pressed against the cold glass.

He waved good-bye. Something about the way he waved seemed angry, and final.

The glass fogged under my breath until I could no longer see him.

24

My father's family came from Columbia, a two-hour bus ride from St. Louis. My paternal grandmother, Lillian, died when I was about eight. I remembered that my paternal grandparents visited us a few times when I was younger, but my memory of my grandfather came from photos in an album I'd found once in a cabinet in the laundry room. I knew that my great-grandfather and his brother fled Poland in the 1930s and went to England, where they worked for a year to earn boat fare to New York. In Poland, their name had been something like Barishansky. In England, they called themselves Barringer. I never knew how my grandfather ended up in Columbia, Missouri.

I found his phone number online.

"Hello," he said. His voice had a slight tremor, and sounded surprisingly familiar.

"Is this Will Barringer?"

"Yes it is," he said sharply. "Who's this?"

"Bretna Barringer."

"Bretna? Hold on while I turn off the television set." He came back and said, "Well. What do you know? Your dad told me you'd come to Missouri!"

"He did?" I was surprised he'd even registered the fact that I'd left.

"Sure he did. Just yesterday."

Surprised by the joviality in his voice, I said, "You sound good."

"Why *wouldn't* I sound good? There's nothing wrong with my *voice*."

I didn't remember him being so, well, feisty. I said, "I'm staying with Myrna—"

"Who in hell is Myrna?"

"My mother's sister."

"Myrna? Oh. I remember her. She's as crazy as your mother."

Not sure how to answer that, I said, "We never saw much of you."

"How could you see me, being way the hell out there in California? But I talked to your father every single week, Thursday morning, ten o'clock."

"You did?" I'd never really known my grandfather, but my feelings were hurt that he only talked to my father during work hours. "How come you never called our house?"

"I don't care much to talk to your mother. She never liked me, ever since the time she picked up the phone and heard me asking your father when he was going to leave her." He laughed. "What I said, in fact, was 'When are you going to unload that bitch?' She never forgave me."

I had a distant memory of being with my paternal grandparents—I think they were babysitting me and Teddy, before Hannah was born—and they talked in hushed voices about *her*. I knew they were talking disapprovingly about my mother.

"If Jack had the sense of a goat, or as much sense as Ken Schacter, he would have gotten out of there by now."

"Who is Ken Schacter?"

Silence. Then: "You don't know about Ken Schacter?

Well, yeah. How would you know?"

"Who is Ken Schacter? Now you have to tell me."

"Ken Schacter is the man who was married to your mother before she married Jack."

My mother had never said a word about a previous marriage.

He laughed and said, "I know some folks who know the Schacters, and everyone says what a nice guy Ken is. After Ken moved out, your mother told people he was violent." He laughed. "Ken? Violent? He was the nicest, calmest guy you'd ever want to meet. I guess they were married about six months. Your father was just too nice to divorce her."

"Oh, come on. There's nothing nice about Dad."

"What are you talking about. He is a quiet, gentle person."

I decided not to argue. Instead I said, "Maybe I should come for a visit."

"Why don't you do that? I don't drive anymore, but if you take the bus on out here to Columbia, I'll get one of your aunts to get you from the bus station."

"One of my aunts?" I said, trying to figure out who he meant.

"I guess your great-aunts, your grandma's sisters."

Then I remembered. "There were six girls altogether, right?" I said.

"Yes. Four have passed on, but Gertie and Bernice live in town. You've got cousins out here too, but I don't know that you ever met them."

"I didn't," I said. For that matter, I couldn't recall having met any of my grandmother's sisters, either.

The bus from St. Louis arrived in Columbia at one thirty. I called my grandfather before leaving St. Louis and told him when I'd be there. He said, "Gertie will pick you up."

I found my aunt Gertie easily enough—she was the only elderly woman at the station. She saw me and said, "You must be Bretna," and squeezed my shoulders in a gesture something like a hug. "My car is this way."

Her car was a red Pontiac convertible that appeared to be about twenty years old. She said, "What do you think of an old lady driving a red sports car?"

"Well," I said. "It's an *old* red sports car."

She laughed. "There you go! That makes it just fine, doesn't it?"

She pulled out of the parking lot and said, "So what are you doing in Missouri?"

"Well, one thing I did was spend about ten minutes listening to my grandfather tell me what a nice guy my father is."

She gave me a look I couldn't read and said, "He probably believes it."

I came right to the point: "What was my dad like when he was a child?"

She made a contemplative expression and said, "How about this? Why don't we stop by my house for a cup of tea. I'll call your grandpa and say we're running a little late. Then we can have a chat and I'll tell you whatever you want to know about your father."

"Thanks."

She drove through a quiet residential neighborhood of older houses, and pulled into the driveway of a wooden house painted white. Just inside the door, she set her purse down on a table and said, "I'll make tea." We sat at the yellow Formica table in the kitchen. There was one word for her kitchen: cute. The tile was yellow and white, accented with yellow rose tiles, the counter tops were white, the curtains yellow and blue.

When we were at the table with our tea, she said, "Tell me what you want to know about your dad."

"Was he always so, well, passive?"

"Always. Your grandmother thought the problem started with his fever."

"I don't know much about scarlet fever," I said.

"We didn't, either. Jack was ten months old when he got that fever. Lillian called me and I rushed right over. His skin glowed pink. We called the doctor, but he just said babies are always running high fevers. We sat up all night, putting cold cloths on the baby's forehead. Then his temperature spiked higher, and that sandpaper rash came up over his chest and there was a white coating on his tongue. We called again and the doctor said bring him to the hospital. When we got there, the baby's tongue had three spots the size of wild berries."

"Who was 'we'?" I asked. When she looked puzzled, I said, "You keep saying 'we.' Who was up all night?"

"All the sisters—Bernice, Annabelle, Dotty, Emma, me, and your grandmother. She called us all over. We took turns taking naps. Your grandfather slept all night. He had to be at work early and a sick baby was no excuse for missing work. After that fever, whenever Jack did something that seemed a little off—when he laughed at the wrong times or said something insulting without realizing it—your grandmother said it was from the fever. The doctors said no, scarlet fever can ruin a person's eyesight, but doesn't do anything to the thinking or feeling parts of the brain."

"Did he have any friends?"

"Not that I remember. He was on the boy's high school gymnastics team. He spent his afternoons practicing gymnastics in the backyard, walking on his hands in circles around the yard."

"I didn't know he was a gymnast," I said.

I remembered a story I knew about my father: He was an enlisted man on his way to Vietnam when an officer asked for volunteers with radio experience. As my father told the story, he couldn't raise his hand fast enough. He'd tinkered with radios in high school, so he spent the war on a mountaintop in Japan. A stupid man wouldn't have had the radio expertise to manage that job. A stupid man would have drifted off to the front and gotten killed.

I said, "I don't think the scarlet fever hurt the thinking part of his brain." Then I remembered how he used to cheat his customers, and said he'd own slaves if they were legal.

"I guess not. He's run a business all those years, after all. Anyway, the doctors said scarlet fever doesn't cause personality damage. Bernice always said if a fever can damage a baby's eyesight, it can do other things as well, but she wasn't a doctor so she didn't know."

She paused and said, "Maybe it didn't have anything to do with the fever. Who knows?" She stood up and said, "I have some pictures. Maybe you'd like to see."

"Sure," I said. She went out of the room and came back with a shoe box filled with photographs. She sat down and took out the photographs—many of them faded with age—and showed them to me, one by one. This one was my grandparents with their two sons, my father and Ricky. That one pictured all six sisters together at the marriage of the youngest, Bernice. This one was from a trip to the zoo and showed my grandmother standing in front of the monkey cage.

I'd never before seen pictures of my father as a child. There was something almost comic to the blankness of his expression, and the distortion of his eyes through his thick glasses. I was most intrigued by the photos of the six sisters, laughing, with their arms around each other. Each of them had wavy dark hair. One of the sisters wore tortoise shell glasses, and another favored pearl earrings. I couldn't even imagine what it would be like to grow up close to five sisters.

I looked closely at a photograph of my grandmother and her twin. "Did they always dress alike?" I asked.

"Always. Your father used to joke that he had two mothers."

One of the photographs pictured all six sisters together in what looked like a grassy park, with my grandmother holding my father. He must have been about two years old. There was nothing unusual about my father in the photograph. You could read nothing of his personality in his face. But the six sisters, who looked to be in their twenties, were alive with joy and love.

You wouldn't think a grandmother and granddaughter could have such different lives.

All three of us—me, Janae, and Rosie—were in the kitchen at once, a rare occurrence since we usually went our separate ways and kept different schedules. I opened one of the cabinets and said, in what I thought was an off-hand comment, "We have to figure out how to organize these cabinets. They're getting out of control."

Rosie swung around, alarmed. "Oh, no. It's starting."

"What's starting?" I asked, alarmed as well.

She wouldn't answer. She washed her cup and put it on the drainboard. She marched into her room and closed the door. Janae and I looked at each other. Janae shrugged.

Next morning, I was alone in the kitchen when Rosie came out of her room and said, "Your hostility really disturbed me." She was so angry that her face was red and her eyes blazed.

My hostility? I realized my hands were shaking. It had been years now since I'd left home, years since anyone had accused me of being violent and hostile and who knows what else, but instantly Rosie's accusation put me back to that dark place of doubting myself. I thought about asking Janae whether I'd been hostile, but I was afraid to: Janae was often so critical of me.

"You need to apologize," Rosie said.

My stomach was clenched. My instinct was to fight

her, the way I'd fought my mother, refusing to give in, refusing to say something that wasn't true, but Rosie wasn't worth it, so I said, "Fine. I'm sorry if I seemed hostile."

"Not *seemed*, was."

"Fine, Rosie. I am sorry I was hostile." Instantly, upon uttering the words, I had the uncomfortable feeling that I'd been bullied into telling a lie.

There were more than twenty kids in Alex's new English class, lined up in rows. I signed, easily keeping up—by now I could sign rapidly, as long as I followed English syntax—but I knew Alex wasn't paying attention at all. One of the better students had been appointed note-taker for Alex because a deaf kid cannot watch an interpreter and write at the same time.

Alex sat with his back straight and his expression serious. He was sitting like the other kids, imitating them, pretending to do what they were doing. I knew he had no idea what was going on.

The teacher wrote "inference" on the chalk board. Alex turned and watched as I explained what an inference was.

"That's stupid!" he signed. "How can I know what's in a sentence if it's not there?"

I ignored him and continued interpreting. If I stopped to converse with him in the middle of a lecture, I'd miss whatever was said next. He repeated, "That's stupid." The sign for "stupid" was to hit his forehead with his knuckle. The teacher caught the gesture and, startled, looked at me. I shrugged lightly.

On the board, the teacher wrote, "How old is Pip?"

The instructions were to go back through the chapter and come up with an answer. I watched as Alex read back through the chapter. He was becoming visibly frustrated. I knew he was searching for a number.

When he looked at me, I signed, "You're supposed to guess his age from the way Pip talks and acts."

He put the book down and glowered at the floor. He sat that way until the end of the class period.

In English class, Alex sat in the front row and I sat in a chair facing him. There was an assignment on the board, and all the other kids were working, but Alex was slumped miserably into his chair.

I tapped his foot. He was so surprised by the tap that his entire body jolted. I tried not to laugh at his shocked expression. Seeing my smile, his own smile almost surfaced.

"You're supposed to write a description of your favorite room," I told him.

The teacher stepped in front of Alex to find out why he wasn't working. "What's your favorite room, Alex?" she asked.

He looked at me and I signed the question.

"The bokey," he said.

The teacher looked helplessly at me. I said, "Say it again."

"The bokey," he repeated louder. The kids sitting nearby looked up.

"A room in your house," I said again, thinking he hadn't understood.

He clenched his fist and said, "The bokey."

"All right," I signed. "Fine. Write a description."

He looked at the paper, then at the top, and wrote, "The Bokey." Then he put his forehead in his hand and put down his pencil.

To prompt him, I signed, "Is it a small room or a

large room?"

He looked to the ceiling as if I'd just asked the world's stupidest question. "Small," he signed. "How can a bokey be big?"

"Upstairs or downstairs?" I asked.

"Upstairs!" He was genuinely angry. "A bokey can't be downstairs!"

Anyone else, looking at him, would have seen stubborn defiance. I saw his bewilderment and pain. "Just tell me one thing about this room," I said.

"You are not there," he signed. "But you see everything."

This was a puzzle. I thought, from this description, that the room must somehow be behind glass. I visualized his house, trying to guess what a bokey was.

Then I understood. I wrote, "The balcony," on his paper, and sketched a balcony.

Emphatically, he made the sign for "yes." But when I told him to write his essay, he sank glumly into his chair and refused.

I figured that with Alex slipping behind so quickly and growing increasingly frustrated, Lucinda and Elaine would see their mistake soon enough to move him back into classes he could handle before he fell apart.

To add to my distress, Rosie was being just plain rude—walking out of the room if I walked in, talking pointedly at Janae and ignoring me, and I couldn't understand why.

During the days that followed, I expected Curtis to call me or text me—but he didn't. I felt too much pride, and too much fear, to ask him why. Maybe because I knew why.

Everything was falling apart, but instead of creating a sculpture to reflect my state of mind, I wanted to do a study of Dr. Kessler. The only way I could approach the project was with some degree of literalness: I began with a concave glass bowl into which I layered chips of glass in varying shades of gray, creating my vision of a concentration camp—low, squat, dull buildings. Chips of dark glass became barbed wire and rows of bedraggled people, their postures suggesting anguish and prayer. But then one of them grew and became the clear blue of redemption and hope and beauty set in a larger dome in imitation of the sky and the life-giving clouds. I called the work "The Philanthropist."

Next I began work on a sculpture called "Silence" from the pastel drawing I did that day in Curtis's apartment when the boys came over, the snowy landscape all in whites, blues, and black. It wasn't right, though, so I heightened the clarity of the blues and whites. The medium—shattered glass layered with glazes—made the colors sharper, clearer, and colder.

I set the sculpture on a concave surface, as if at the top of a globe. The composition didn't feel complete, though, until I added a solitary figure inside, standing beside a tree. The figure of a man stood hunched against the cold, drawn into himself. Initially I'd imagined that the hunched figure was Curtis, but as I worked, sharpening and deepening the colors, I realized the figure was me. I kept wishing the figure would stand up straighter.

The sculpture was nearing completion when Janae wandered into my studio to look. "Nice," she said. "It has a sadness to it, but nobody can call it angry."

The problem was that "Silence" is a cliché that doesn't capture the experience of deafness. I imagined Curtis seeing the sculpture one day and saying to himself,

"I knew she didn't really understand." So I started another sculpture, beginning with a figure whose posture and expression captured bewilderment. A short distance away was a cluster of people entwined in an intricate dance. Between the figure and the dancing people was a glass curtain that distorted the images viewed through it.

I had started out trying to depict deafness, but what I captured, I realized, was how I had felt growing up. I gave the sculpture a title from Alice in Wonderland: "Uncommon Nonsense."

When I finished, I brought the sculptures to the owner of the Livingston Gallery who said, "They are *beautiful.*"

No one, I realized, had ever called my work beautiful. Creepy, disturbing, fascinating, and angry. But never beautiful. It occurred to me that what is ugly in the world is obvious. It's much harder to find the beauty.

"I can sell these, Bretna," he said.

I felt enormous relief. He was still looking at the sculptures when he said, "People ask me why you work with broken glass."

"I like the way the light plays through glass," I told him, but I realized the answer wasn't nearly poetic enough. I'd have to come up with something better.

Alex entered his math class smelling of peppermint and cigarettes, wearing the expression that I knew meant trouble. He sat down and didn't look at anyone. The teacher handed out the quizzes. He worked on his quiz, then looked at me and signed, "Please help."

"With what?"

"I don't know number two."

I looked at his paper and saw that he'd left about half

the quiz blank. I repeated the second question in signs hoping that seeing the signs would jog his memory. He shook his head. "Tell me," he signed.

"I can't. Any more help would be cheating. Raise your hand and ask the teacher."

Harshly Alex repeated the sign for "help," slapping his hand against his palm. I shook my head. He didn't ask the teacher for help. Instead he turned in his quiz with several questions blank.

Next day, when the teacher gave back the quizzes, Alex had a C minus. It was better than I'd expected, so I signed brightly, "There's nothing wrong with a C."

He slumped deeper into his seat and scowled. "People don't get into college with C's."

"Sure they do!"

"Maybe for a deaf college. Not for Harvard." Then he picked up his pencil and said, "I will smoke." He pretended to smoke his pencil, holding it between his fingers and puffing on the eraser end.

I wrinkled my nose. "Smoke stinks."

He took another puff on his pencil.

"Athletes don't smoke," I told him.

"I'm not an athlete."

"You didn't even try out for basketball," I said.

"Why bother? I just sit and watch. I can do that with a T.V."

It was too bad sports weren't going to work out for him. Being good at sports may have helped earn him respect.

That afternoon, just because I felt like getting out, I walked through Harvard Square and paused in front of a café window. The café looked like a brightly-lit glass cube with couples holding hands, groups of college kids clustered in booths, families at the square tables in the center. When I saw hands moving, I had the startled feeling that people were signing—but they were just hearing people in animated conversation.

One of my college assignments was to draw an unusual interior. I had drawn a goldfish bowl from the viewpoint of the goldfish. I became aware of how the glass would distort the goldfish's view. And of course, you couldn't hear from inside the bowl, particularly under water. I discovered that a goldfish bowl, ordinarily a cliché for being on display, was in fact the perfect image for isolation.

I walked on, and paused at the window of a book shop. Reflected in the glass was a pair of hands moving gracefully and confidently. This was no hearing conversation.

I turned and saw Curtis sitting near the subway entrance on a low brick wall, wrapped in his fleece-trimmed coat, absorbed in a sign conversation with a woman with a round face. Neither of them noticed me. I turned back around to watch them in the glass.

As Curtis signed, the woman thrust her hands into her pockets, waiting her turn to respond. Neither of them wore gloves. I felt the chill in my own fingers. I recognized the woman from the pictures tacked up in Curtis's office. I turned and walked the four blocks back to the subway stop.

At home, Janae was waiting for me, excited. "They called from the Livingston Gallery," she said. "It sounds like one of your sculptures sold!"

My hands were shaking when I returned the call. Yes, indeed, "Uncommon Nonsense" had sold for $800, and the buyers wanted to commission another work for a space in the entry hall of their Louisburg Square townhouse. They were willing to pay $1,200 for the commissioned work with the understanding that I would visit their home and create the work to suit the scale and color-scheme of their home.

I arranged to visit the buyer's Louisburg Square home the very next day, a Saturday. I brought a sketch pad and measuring tape. Their entry hall and living room was done in deep golden hues, a tone-on-tone color scheme, and the wife told me she wanted rounded shapes. I promised to bring sketches and colored glass chips for their approval by the end of the month.

A few days later, "Benji" also sold for $800.

To put the icing on my triumph, a writer from *Boston Art*—having seen how my work had changed during the past year, from "just angry" to sublimely beautiful—wanted to interview me. Giving the interview was surprisingly easy. When she asked me why I worked with broken glass, an answer came to me: "Creating sculptures from broken glass," I told her, "is a way to create beauty from what has been shattered."

Alex was not in school on Monday or Tuesday. Lucinda called Tuesday to say he was sick. I didn't believe a word of it. Elaine said I could tutor kids in the Learning Center, or I could just reduce my hours for the week and go home. I tutored kids in the Learning Center.

When Alex didn't show up on Wednesday either, I called Lucinda at home. "I hope he's okay," I said.

"Can you come over to tutor him? We'll pay you, of course. It would be nice if he doesn't fall too far behind."

"All right," I said. "But I don't need payment. I haven't been doing much at the school."

"I'll pick you up in front of the school in ten

minutes."

Lucinda picked me up in a gray Lexus with an interior as soft and lush as a pussy willow. We rode back to her house in silence. She opened the door and we were greeted by the blaring of a sports game. Alex was in the family room watching television. Lucinda walked over and turned off the television. He groaned. When he saw me, his scowl changed to an embarrassed grin.

"You have to study now. Ms. Barringer is here to help you."

"I can't. It's too hard for me."

I looked at Lucinda, expecting her to see her folly. She said, "It's not too hard for you. That's what you said last summer about basic skills algebra. And look how well you did."

Alex pounded the end table with his fist. Lucinda turned to me and said, "Maybe you should wait in the dining room."

I was in the dining room standing by the window when Esteban walked in. He held out his hand for me to shake, and said, "Hi, Bretna." Then, gently, "What is going on?"

"She's trying to get him to work."

From the next room, Alex let out a loud, "Noooo!"

"So tell me," he said quietly. "How is Alex coping in his classes?"

I took a chance and told him the truth. "It's horrible," I said. "He shouldn't be in those classes."

"But he did so well last semester."

"I helped him a lot, maybe more than I should have. The teachers helped him, too, sometimes even giving him answers on tests. Everyone meant well. In basic skills, there's no harm—kids get points just for trying. But he expects the same in intermediate. I'm sure he's been mad at me—"

"He thinks you stopped helping him."

"He wants me to give him answers! That would be cheating!"

Esteban looked at me for a long time. "That depends on how it's done. Of course, if you give him answers that would be cheating. But sometimes a child with learning disabilities needs extra help."

In a flash I understood all of Elaine's warnings.

Lucinda led Alex into the room and said, "He's ready to work now."

Alex spread his books and papers out on the dining room table. The change in him was dramatic. For two hours, he sat, patiently finishing one homework assignment after another. Lucinda certainly knew how to get him focused.

By the time he finished the last math assignment, we were both exhausted. Now I was sorry I'd said anything to Esteban. Alex seemed to understand the material. Maybe I was wrong and Lucinda was right.

26

One week after I arrived in St. Louis, I landed a job at Fayette University as an assistant in a microbiology laboratory. Because I was an employee, I could take art classes tuition-free. I signed up for Watercolor and Introduction to Sculpture. The sculpture class was taught by a retired professor from the prestigious Massachusetts College of Art. I'd heard of him. He was the author of an important book on the history of sculpture.

I was in my room reading the book the professor had authored when Myrna tapped at my door. "Come, look what I bought!"

She took me by the hand and pulled me to her bedroom. Laid out around the room was an assortment of clothing: a chocolate-brown velvet skirt with a matching blazer and vest, two blouses, and a pair of lace up brown velvet shoes. It was clear, from the way the rich velvet shimmered in the light, that these were clothes of the highest quality.

"Look at how many different outfits I can make," she said, showing me all the combinations she could put together.

I touched the skirt, admiring the silky softness. Myrna said, "Make sure your hands are clean." She tried on the jacket and showed me the flattering cut. I told her she looked like a princess. She laughed happily.

The doorbell rang. Myrna frowned. "I wonder who that is."

"I'll go see." I ran down the steps. At the door was her son, Ryan.

"Hey," I said. "Come see the clothes your mom bought. They're gorgeous."

He made an expression that I couldn't read, something between dismay and concern. "She's upstairs," I said.

Myrna had closed her door. I knocked, then peeked inside. She was hanging the blazer in the closet, her shoulders hunched, her manner furtive.

"I'd better go," said Ryan.

I followed him down the stairs and out the front door. "You just got here. What's the matter?"

"Bretna. Please."

"Nobody shows up for one minute and then leaves. Tell me."

He looked at me, then looked up toward the house. "Let's go for a walk," he said.

We were around the block when he said, "She asked me for money. She told me she needs help with her electricity bill. She also said she has to get the plumbing repaired. I wrote her a check for one thousand dollars."

"Oh," I said. "Do you think those clothes cost one thousand dollars?"

"Where did she get them?"

"The shopping bags said 'Famous Barr.'"

"If she got them at Famous, they cost at least a thousand dollars. You've obviously never shopped in the designer department of Famous-Barr."

"I shop at thrift stores. But why would she lie? Why didn't she just ask you for money for clothes?"

"Maybe she thinks I wouldn't give it to her. I've been

helping her with her bills and repairs for three years. I suspected she lied about what she wanted the money for."

"Then why did you give it to her?"

"What else could I do?" he asked.

"You can say *no*."

"How can I do that? She's my mother. Because of her job at the university, I got my college education free."

"But this is just weird," I said. "It's a lot of money."

"She knows I get quarterly bonuses."

We were around the corner, out of sight of the house, so we stopped walking. "So what if she knows you get quarterly bonuses?"

"She tells me I owe it to her. After our father left, she slaved night and day to support us."

I shook my head sadly. "You're like my brother."

"What do you mean?"

Indeed, what did I mean? My brother knew how to live at peace with my mother. My brother wasn't tormented the way I was, traveling two thousand miles in a need to get far away, setting out on a quest to understand our family, doubting himself to the point where he felt he was going mad. Maybe I shouldn't criticize Ryan for accommodating his mother, since I often wished I could be the same way. On the other hand, asking for money for plumbing repairs and using the money to buy fancy clothes was just plain wrong.

Myrna was on the telephone in the kitchen. When I came in to make myself something for dinner, she went into the dining room. From the kitchen, I couldn't hear what she was saying. Curious, I stood near the doorway and listened. She was telling someone all the details of a date she'd had the night before. I'd noticed she hadn't been home the evening before, but I had no idea she'd been on a date. She described the way the man kissed her, and how she had to think long and hard about whether to go home with him. From her tone, I figured she was talking to a girlfriend.

She hung up and came into the kitchen and put on a kettle for tea. My plan was to try to get her talking about her childhood so I could learn more about my own mother. First, though—because I was curious—I said, "Who was that?"

She said, "Ryan."

"Ryan, your son?"

"Of course Ryan my son."

The idea that she'd been talking to her own son about her date gave me such a creepy feeling that I ate my canned soup in silence, then went upstairs to my room.

Next time Ryan came by the house, I took him aside and said, "I heard your mother's side of a conversation. She was telling you about her sex life."

"I know. I ignore her."

"How do you ignore her while you're on the phone?"

"I hold the phone away from my ear while she talks."

"Why don't you tell her you don't want to hear about it?"

"I can't, Bretna, okay? I just can't."

I didn't understand why not, and I could see from his closed expression that he wasn't going to say anymore.

Later one of Myrna's boarders, a graduate student in biology, told me that the year before, Ryan told her he wanted to transfer to his company's Paris office but he had to withdraw his transfer request because Myrna threatened suicide if he left.

The leaves changed and I felt as if I inhabited an entirely new world. I walked the few blocks from Myrna's house to the University, my feet crunching through the fallen leaves. I hadn't seen a real change of seasons since my tenth year. I wasn't prepared for the beauty of the trees turning or the musky smell of damp leaves.

I was in the kitchen with Rebecca, one of Myrna's graduate student boarders, when she pointed to my sweater and said, "I hope you have something warmer than that to wear this winter."

I tried to remember what snow and ice was like. Some mornings in California were so cold there was a layer of frost on the ground and windows. "I guess it will get really cold," I said, "like putting your hand in the refrigerator."

"No, Bretna," she said. "It will be like being all wet and sitting in the freezer."

I assumed she was exaggerating, so I was unprepared for the shock of the first snow fall. I was so cold I didn't think I'd survive the walk to work. By the time I arrived at the office, my feet were so numb, it hurt to walk. After work I went to three different thrift stores until I found suitable gloves, hat, coat, and boots. I understood the instinct to hibernate. I wanted to crawl into a warm, quiet place and rest for a long time, bringing a sketchpad, an easel, and paints.

I was in the kitchen washing and putting away my dinner dishes and pots—I'd made spaghetti for the third time that week—when Myrna walked in. I said hello. She turned away and sorted through boxes in the pantry, pointedly ignoring me.

I put a pot into the cabinet and was walking toward the door when she said, "You haven't been doing your ten hours of work."

"My ten hours of what?"

"I thought I told you that each of my boarders are required to put in ten hours of work each month. How else can I keep this place in shape? Besides, you're always leaving your stuff around the house."

I thought it was enough that I kept my room and bathroom clean and paid an outrageously high rent. I tried to remember to pick up after myself in the common areas, but I often forgot. Still, ten hours each month seemed like way too much.

I called Ryan for advice. "Just don't do it," he said. "She won't kick you out over that. She wants the rent money."

"How do I find another place to live?" I asked.

"Go to the campus housing office. They have off-campus listings."

Next day, I went to the campus housing office and looked through the listings. I didn't make any calls, though. Just then I lacked the energy or will to move in with strangers.

One morning I was walking across the campus when someone behind me called out, "Bretna!"

Ryan caught up to me. Surprised, I said, "What are you doing here?"

"I figured I'd take a class, too. I've always wanted to learn French."

"That's great!"

"If you see my mother, please don't tell her. I don't want her to know I'm considering transferring to Paris."

"I won't tell her. Transferring is a good idea. I hope you do it." Anyone with a crazy mother could count on me as an ally.

"I figured I should follow your advice, and your example. Look at you. You just got on a cross-country bus and went two thousand miles from home."

In his voice was something like admiration. I said, "It was easier for me. I didn't have a mother hanging on to me."

"Yeah, but I'm almost thirty. You're *eighteen*."

Myrna knocked angrily on my bedroom door, then threw the door open. "What have you been doing? What kind of trouble have you been stirring up between me and my son?"

"Me?"

"I know you've been talking to Ryan, turning him against me. You're a little snit. You're a troublemaker, that's all you are."

I was shaking. I'd tried to get as far away as I could from my mother, and here I was, dealing with my mother all over again.

I said, "Your relationship with your son is sick, sick, sick."

Unlike my mother, Myrna didn't lose her temper. Calmly she said, "I want you out of this house by the end of the week."

I wanted to throw something at her. Instead, I closed the door and flung myself across my bed and cried. Part of me understood that something was wrong with Myrna, just as something had been wrong with my mother. Hadn't others said just that? Another part of me, though was afraid that Myrna, my father, and my mother were right, and that the problem was that something was deeply wrong with me.

27

After moving out of my Aunt Myrna's house, I had a rough time of it for a while. I rented a room from Mrs. Simon, an elderly woman with a four bedroom house near the campus. Mrs. Simon was like a cat—watchful and condescending. She liked sitting in the warmest place in the house, a chair in the living room near the heater. She insisted that I be a "good girl," which meant she bolted the front door at nine p.m. every night. Not that I was dating—I wasn't—but it bothered me just the same.

One evening I forgot about the bolted door and went to a late movie and came back to find the door not only bolted, but Mrs. Simon standing in an upstairs window shaking her head disapprovingly. When I rang the bell, she turned out the lights and ignored me. I spent the night in a Motel 6 and next day went back to the housing office to find another place to live. Meanwhile, I was bored in my job, so I transferred to another office, and was soon bored there, too.

What turned the year around was Professor Wilkins, the teacher of my sculpture class. By the middle of the first semester, he asked me to remain after class and said, "You shouldn't be here. You should be at the Massachusetts College of Art." He told me to get an application and start getting my portfolio together. He said he knew a few people he could call.

With his help, I won a full scholarship. My first glimpse of the campus was on their website, a photo featuring a cluster of maples turning bright shades of yellow, orange, and red with a white steeple in the background. As lovely as the photo was, I was unprepared for the startling charm of New England. Traveling northward on a bus, I felt I was entering a quaint paradise of lakes, hillsides with white-washed church steeples surrounded by ancient maples, and wooden rail fences that looked as if they dated all the way back to the time of the Pilgrims.

The college was located west of Boston along Highway Two, past Walden Pond, where Thoreau had isolated himself to live deliberately.

I applied for special permission to take sculpture in my first year. That was when I began working with shattered glass, starting with mosaics, then advancing to three-dimensional forms. I sculpted my paternal grandmother holding her baby, knowing something was wrong with him. I sculpted a boy walking on his hands through a crowded park, and in so doing, I came to feel a connection, or perhaps point of sympathy.

I often walked along, absorbed in the beauty of the New England landscape, thinking nothing could be lovelier than the row of maples covered with a layer of ice so thin it seemed like fragile glass, when I felt the pang of what I lacked. I stopped, rested my cheek on my shoulder the way a bird tucks its beak into his back feathers, and cried.

I loved the colors of winter—white, the sharp blue sky, black branches spreading like lace. The cold was unlike anything I'd ever known, the entire world frozen and lifeless and still. It amazed me that people took the harshness of these seasons as a matter of course.

Compared to this relentless cold, a St. Louis winter was mild. I wondered, with a touch of awe, what would have happened if I'd gone straight from California to Massachusetts. The shock would probably have sent me running back to California, even if doing so would have meant sacrificing my sanity forever.

Sometimes I liked looking at a map just to see how far Massachusetts was from California. I felt like a fallen leaf carried by the wind to the ends of the earth, or like a creature tucked into a cocoon, growing and healing.

Seeing the first nubs on the branches that would become blossoms, I understood why a poet might consider April the cruelest month: Emerging from the comfort of hibernation to find the world struggling back to life can shock the body. When spring came, I felt I was coming out of a siege. I was startled one day in April to take off my glove and realize I could have my hand in the air without it hurting—and what a glorious feeling it was not to hurt.

I didn't fully emerge from my self-imposed isolation until a few years after graduation, when I lost my fellowship and had to look for a real job, and found myself intrigued by the ad for an interpreter and tutor for a deaf student. Perhaps the job appealed to me because I was finally ready to emerge from hiding.

28

A week after I saw Curtis in Harvard Square, I learned from the owner of the Livingston Gallery that the Museum of Fine Arts wanted to add three of my sculptures to their display featuring artwork using glass. Shortly afterward, *International Artists* interviewed me for an article. I said the same things I had said before, about how working with broken glass allowed me to create beauty from what had been shattered.

The same day I gave the interview, my mother emailed me to say "How are you? We are all fine." That sort of thing. "Fine," I wrote back.

A few days later, she sent another email, this one longer. After the usual "How are you? We are all fine" stuff, she wrote, "Teddy just started at San Diego State and he is getting married to a girl we all like. Things have changed, Bretna, they've changed a lot. I've mellowed. Maybe you should come home for a visit."

I didn't know how I felt about the email until I tried to do a glass mosaic entitled "Letters from Home." The work I created was a mixture of carnation pinks and sky blues—a sparkling medley of hope. I reread the email, and thought she was apologizing. She seemed to be acknowledging that she'd been wrong about me, and wrong for the way she treated me. I couldn't remember a single time when my mother had apologized for anything.

Maybe she *had* changed.

The algebra teacher, Mr. Perkins, handed out the midterm exams, two pages stapled together. Alex slouched into his chair, his feet extending into the aisle. He stared at a spot on the floor near his sneaker.

The other students bent over their desks, working on their exams, but Alex didn't move. Mr. Perkins walked over and tried to talk to Alex. Alex grinned but refused to look up. Mr. Perkins waved his hand in front of Alex's face.

To me, Mr. Perkins said, "He's being distracting. Please tell him to get started on his exam."

I waved my hand, but he wouldn't look up. I tapped his foot, but he looked away. Finally, knowing he could see in his peripheral vision, I signed, "I suggest you pull yourself together."

"Shut up," he said aloud. His speech was garbled. I understood it, but I doubted anyone else would.

"You are not to speak to me this way," I signed.

"Shut up," he said again, louder and more distinctly. He stood up and bounded out of the classroom. I gathered up my things and, to no one in particular, said, "Please excuse me."

I found Alex sitting at his usual table in the Learning Center. I sat down across from him and waited. He turned and stared at the clock. Then he said, "Look at that."

I made the sign for, "What?"

"The minute hand just sits there then jumps to the next dot."

When it was clear that all he was going to do was watch the clock, I picked up a book and started reading. Then he kicked my foot and said, "It's too hard."

"It's too hard if you don't try. Not even Einstein can pass a test without trying."

"Who is that?"

"Einstein, the smartest scientist in the world."

"Where is he?"

"Now? He's dead."

"I'm Ein-Ein. Call me Ein-Ein."

I felt something like a chill. I said, "Okay, Einstein, let's get working."

Then he said, "I'll be dead like Ein-Ein."

"Don't joke like that. Remember how well you did last semester?"

"In basic skills. In bonehead classes." He grinned.

"Tell me what you want," I said. "Do you want to do well in school?"

He made a gesture as if to stab himself and said, "I want to die."

My hands were shaking. Was it that humiliating to move back to basic skills? Was it that terrible not to go to an Ivy League school? I was angry at Lucinda for pushing him, and angry at Elaine for not doing something to stop this.

"That's not funny," I signed.

"That's not funny," he repeated, exaggerating his signs.

I felt a deep tiredness. "Maybe you should rest for a few minutes," I told him, and went to find the teacher in charge of the Learning Center. Seeing my face, she said, "What's the matter?"

"Alex is making suicide jokes. He said he wants to die."

"You have to tell Elaine."

"Isn't there anyone else I can tell?"

"Walter will just turn the problem over to Elaine.

223

You'd better tell her. I don't think you have a choice. You have to tell someone."

"What if I tell Lucinda?"

"His mother? Nope. You work for the school. He made the suicide joke here. You have to tell one of the administrators."

Well then. If I had no choice, I had no choice. I went to the special education office and knocked on Elaine's door. Through the window I saw that Elaine was standing at the filing cabinet in her office. She opened the door and I said, "I need to talk to you."

"I'm very busy. If this is not an emergency, we can schedule an appointment for tomorrow afternoon—"

"There's something I need to tell you now."

She sighed heavily. "Fine. Come in." She sat down, and I sat across from her. She must have sensed my hesitancy because she said, "What?"

"Alex is making suicide jokes."

She held still, then picked up a pencil. "What did he say, exactly?" Her tone was clipped. "There are legal issues involved."

I recounted the conversation about Einstein and described his gestures. Elaine, softening, said, "Don't worry. You did the right thing. I'll take over." She looked at her watch and said, "I'll be talking with Alex, so you can leave early if you like."

"What's going to happen?" I asked.

"What do you mean?"

"With Alex? With his classes? He's not going to make it in these classes."

"Eventually Lucinda will see that and she'll move him back to basic skills. Between now and then things will be rough."

The phone rang at ten forty-five. I'd already gone to bed. In my haze of sleep, before remembering that Curtis relied on text messages, I thought he was calling.

I turned on my phone and said, "Hello."

"How could you do this to our family?" It was Lucinda, and she was furious. "This humiliation. After everything we did for you. I've never had to endure anything like this in my life."

"How could I—?"

"Elaine has wanted to get her hands on something like this for a long time."

"I was worried about Alex."

"You were worried about Alex. *You* were worried about Alex?"

"I tried talking to everyone, but nobody listens. He is in classes that are too hard for him!"

"You're the one with the attitude, Bretna. You're the one making him think he can't do it."

I held the phone away from my ear, but I could still hear the angry chirping of her voice. I put the phone back to my ear, and she was saying, "—this played right into Elaine's hands—"

"I just don't get it. What did Elaine *say*?"

"She was careful with what she said to *me*. You know Elaine. But she had a smug attitude as if she was right all along. All because of you—"

My voice was shaking when I said, "Lucinda, I was just trying to—"

"I don't want to hear what you were trying to do. You've caused enough damage already." Click. The line went dead.

29

Alex was at school the next day. He looked beaten up, but he was there. I interpreted, and he ignored me. The teachers pretended not to notice anything.

After school was a meeting of the Sign Language Club. Alex came to the meeting. He sat toward the back, his arms folded over his chest. On the blackboard, I made a list of the equipment each student would need to bring including a daypack with water, a bagged lunch, sturdy shoes, and rain gear just in case. "If any of you have trouble getting what you need," I told them, "let me know."

The next item to discuss was transportation. "Please see if any of your parents can drive," I said.

Mona's hand went up. "Both my parents can drive. That's two cars. And my boyfriend can drive. That's three."

I interpreted without looking at Alex. Others said they'd ask their parents. When I dared steal a peek at Alex, I could see he had recovered himself—he sat stony, but with an alert expression pasted into place. I figured that was the first he knew that Mona had a boyfriend. For the entire rest of the meeting, he sat very still.

Instead of discussing the suggested list of do's and don'ts for the hike, I distributed a handout at the end of the meeting. I had no desire to discuss with this group—

which included Rodney and Costa as regular members—
how to handle the fact that there were no toilets along the
trail.

Later that afternoon, I was in my studio working
when my phone vibrated. It was a text message from
Curtis. *"Hi, I saw you in Harvard Square last week. I want to
talk to you."*

I felt shaky and surprisingly happy. I wrote. *"Ok,"*
which didn't come anywhere near expressing how I was
feeling.

Next, across the screen of my cell phone, came the
words: *"meet me at the Café Milano at 3?"*

"OK," I wrote again.

When my phone vibrated again, I thought Curtis was
sending another message. Instead, it was the gallery
owner calling to tell me that he sold "The Philanthropist."
Oddly I felt a pang of regret. I'd been thinking I should
give the sculpture to Dr. Kessler as a gift for doing my
operation, but I'd been so eager to start selling sculptures
again, I'd left it for sale. I also considered keeping it for
myself, and never before had I wished I could keep one
of my own sculptures.

I sat in the café by a window, watching the street and
waiting for Curtis. When he entered, I felt the slightest
jolt—I'd forgotten how appealing he was, with his curls
and large rounded shoulders and eyes that seemed to take
in everything. He wore a nylon jacket, with a blue plaid
scarf hiding the lower part of his face. He hung his coat
on the rack near the table and asked if I wanted tea. I said
I did, so he went to the counter and stood in line.

He returned with the tea, and we sat for a few

minutes in silence. Then he said, "I saw you walking away that day in Harvard Square. I should have said something. I just didn't know how to explain myself."

He paused and looked at me.

I sipped my tea. The fact was, he'd disappeared for two months. I wasn't going to make this easier for him.

He made the sign for "sorry." Then: "Did I ever tell you the story of the deaf woman on the Cape who got her hearing back?"

I shook my head no.

"She was married for twenty years to a deaf man. Her deafness, it turned out, was just a middle ear problem. She got an operation and could hear. After that, everyone kept asking her to tell them all the secrets of hearing people. She kept saying, 'There aren't any hearing secrets. I swear there aren't.' But nobody believed her. Finally she and her husband got divorced. He couldn't accept the fact that she could hear but wouldn't tell him the hearing secrets."

"There aren't any hearing secrets," I said. Did he really think there were? Could anyone really believe there were?

"I know that here," he pointed to his head. "But not here," he pointed to his heart.

I wasn't sure what to say, so I watched him and waited.

He sat back in his chair. "Where's Benji?"

The question so startled me that I thought he meant the actual dog.

"Your sculpture," he said. "It isn't in the gallery any more."

"It sold," I said. Then: "You went to the gallery?"

"Three times. Well, actually, four. Lately I've been looking at the one called 'Uncommon Nonsense,' the one about trying to understand what other people are doing."

I needed a moment to absorb the fact that he'd been going to the gallery looking at my sculptures. All right, so he was apologizing and going to look at my sculptures. What the heck did that mean? Was he back to stay? Were we together again?

I took another sip of tea.

"How's Alex?" he asked.

"Up and down. Mostly he blames me for his failures. He thinks I should help him more."

"Will he pass his classes?"

I thought about the way Lucinda had gotten him working and said, "I don't know. Probably not." All I had to do was think about Lucinda and a weight came into my stomach. I knew from the science teacher who was also head of the union that Lucinda was trying to pull her support for me so my salary would go back to eight seventy-five. Now that my sculptures were selling, I was tempted to quit—but I wasn't ready yet.

"Is the Sign Language Club hike still on?" he asked.

"It's next weekend."

"Can I come?"

"Why?"

"I want to meet Alex."

His face was unreadable, inscrutable. We stared into each other's eyes for a long time. It was like a game of chicken: Who was going to look away first?

"It won't work," I said.

"What won't?"

"Alex is not going to join your deaf pride groups. Trust me."

"Does he even know there are organizations where he will fit in?"

"He was in a program for the deaf last year. He most

229

certainly did not fit in there. When I told him about the Art Sign performance and said he should see it one day, he rolled his eyes and used the phrase 'deaf ghetto.'"

"That's because of his family. I think I can talk to him." Then, "I really want to go."

"That wasn't a good enough reason," I said. "Think of another."

"I want to be with you."

"But what about how deaf people and hearing people shouldn't be together because they can't really understand each other?"

"I used to think that. It was a phase I went through."

"A *phase?*"

"All right, so it was a fifteen-year phase."

At that, we both laughed.

When we entered my apartment, all was quiet. Janae was in her studio, painting, and Rosie was out somewhere. Seeing us come in the front door, Janae waved and we waved back. Curtis walked around the common area, and looked into my room, as if to make sure nothing had changed. "Can I see that email from your mother?"

I was searching for the email on my phone when the front door opened. Rosie breezed into the apartment, singing loudly, "Hello, people! I have amazing, awesome news!"

She certainly did live on an emotional roller coaster. I told Curtis what she had said, using only signs. Curtis and I stood in the door to my bedroom, watching her. Janae, too, emerged from her studio, her hair pinned on top of her head, wearing a paint-smeared apron and holding a paintbrush. We were all waiting for her amazing, awesome news.

"Rocco told me he's in love with me," she said, positively glowing. "He's been in love with me for two years! He's making plans to move his practice to New Hampshire. Nobody there knows him, so that's where we're going!"

If her life was a roller coaster, it was clear she wanted it that way. I explained to Curtis privately that Rocco was her psychiatrist. He raised his eyebrows in surprise, but then quickly neutralized his expression. Well, I was surprised, too. Just when I thought nothing Rosie could say or do would really surprise me, she came up with this. I could see from Janae's expression that she, too, was startled.

That was when it occurred to me that if Rosie were a color, she'd be the color of saffron, a bit of orange, a bit of red, and a lot of spice, an emotional color that changes with the light. The same color as my mother.

"I just know I'm going to love living in New Hampshire," she said. "It's one of my favorite states! Fabulous hiking! Beautiful scenery!"

"Wait a minute," I said. "What about our hike? You're supposed to lead the sign language club hike."

Rosie dug through some papers on her desk and handed me a map and a brochure. "Here's the trail. There's nothing to it. Just make sure nobody gets lost and the kids drink plenty of water. They'll be all excited about the dinosaur footprints, but remind them to look for warblers. The warblers will be very exciting for them, too. The warblers will be migrating. This brochure explains all about it."

I wondered how she could be so out of touch to imagine ninth graders excited about seeing warblers. Still, she couldn't leave us in a bind like this. "Rosie," I said, my voice sharp.

"All right. I'll tell them at Outdoor Adventures to assign another leader, but really, there's nothing to it."

Curtis wandered over to my desk and idly picked up the manila folder from the top shelf and opened it. Inside was my audiogram. He read it, and looked at me, amazed. "This is yours?" A silly question, since my name was written at the top.

"Yes," I signed

"Why didn't you tell me?"

I shrugged.

He looked back at the audiogram and said, "You need hearing aids."

"They're expensive. Maybe one day I'll get them."

"With hearing aids, you might hear perfectly."

"Oh, terrific. Then you'll really hate me."

He set down the paper. "I know you're joking, but it makes me sound, well, it makes me sound like—" he broke off, unsure.

"Like an angry deaf person?" I asked.

"Yeah, I guess," he said.

He reached for my hand. I wondered if he expected to stay the night. Well, he wasn't going to. He couldn't just disappear like that, not call for months, and then just waltz right back as if hardly anything had happened.

"I'll let you know if you can go on the hike," I said, and walked him to the door.

That night, I dreamt I was in a dimly lit room surrounded by dozens of people who wouldn't talk. They weren't deaf—they heard me perfectly, but they chose not to answer. Their hands made swift motions, and when I didn't understand them, they laughed at me. My first hazy sensation was that I was back at the Art Sign performance. As I came fully awake, I imagined people asking if I was hearing, and probably also, "What's *she* doing here?"

Next day, Curtis invited me to dinner at his place. His roommates, as usual, were away. I was setting the table in Curtis's apartment and he stood in front of the stove, stirring a pot. The smell of his chili was mouth-watering.

"I think you should go home for a visit," Curtis said.

"Maybe. I should see if my memories match the reality."

"I want to see, too," he said. "So I'm going with you."

Then the lights went out.

"What happened?" I spoke into the darkness before remembering that speaking aloud would do no good.

I heard him moving the pot. Then he bumped against me, and took my hands. Bending my forefingers, he tapped my knuckles together, making the sign for "electricity." He swept my hands outward, making the sign for "finished." The electricity was out.

He probably had candles somewhere. In the top kitchen drawer, I'd seen matches.

When I made the sign for, "What now?" he followed my motion with his hands.

He touched my chin and kissed me, then took my hands and formed the words, "What else?"

He led me to the next room and drew me down to the rug, his body covering mine, and kissed me again.

There, on the floor in the darkness, he undressed me and turned me around, bending me into positions that might have embarrassed me with the lights on. As we made love on the rug, the feel of his hands made me forget—just for a moment—that any time the lights could come on. I thought I heard a bird whistling outside and as I wondered what kind of bird would sing at night, Curtis took my hands and crossed my arms over my chest, making the sign for "love."

30

Mona bounded up to me, handed me a sheet of paper, and said, "What do you think of this design for a poster?" Her plan was to write "Beautiful Hike" in large letters, followed by when and where, with the edges of the poster decorated with cutouts of trees.

"Nice," I said. "Maybe you should add that we'll see actual dinosaur tracks."

"Good idea! That might even attract some new members. Can you draw some dinosaur tracks for me?"

"If I know what they look like. Your mom can probably find us a book with some pictures of dinosaur tracks."

We went to the library to find pictures of dinosaur tracks. Using the photographs as a guide, I made her some dinosaur footprint stencils, exaggerating the lines and curves for emphasis. "These are great!" she said. "Thanks!"

Next morning, entering the school, I was greeted by a series of posters decorated with dinosaur footprints announcing that the Sign Language Club was going on a hiking retreat where we would see actual dinosaur footprints—and new members were welcome.

Alex entered math class positively glowing. "Good news," he signed, keeping his motions small. "Mona's mom is looking into getting us a bus to the hike because she doesn't have enough drivers."

"Great." Then, wondering why he cared whether he went in a bus or car, I asked, "Why is that such good news?"

"Mona's boyfriend was going to drive, but now he's not because he's not Mona's boyfriend any more. They broke up." He made the sign for "broke up" with a triumphant flourish.

What a long way he'd come: Earlier in the year, he would never have been able to find out something like that without me hearing it and telling him.

He didn't say anything more about Mona until we were in the Learning Center for tutoring when he told me, "I am going to ask Mona to go out with me."

"Really?" Keeping my face carefully blank, I tried to imagine Mona agreeing to date Alex, but couldn't do it. It was like imagining a twenty-year-old dating a twelve-year-old.

That afternoon, I went to the library to talk to Mona's mother, to see if it was okay for Curtis to come along for the hike. Seeing me, she waved and said, "We have quite a group so far. Seven boys signed up. That includes Costa and Rodney and a few other regulars, and two new boys, juniors. We have twelve girls, bringing the total number of students to nineteen."

"I want to bring a friend, too. He's deaf so it should be appropriate for the hike."

"That will be just fine," she said. "Do you and your friend want to ride the bus? Or will you drive separately?" I sent Curtis a text message asking which he preferred. "Let's drive," he responded.

Janae and I entered the apartment at the same time. The moment we walked into the apartment, I knew something was different. The kitchen counters were empty, Rosie's afghan was gone from the living room chair, and her plants were gone. Her bedroom was empty—she'd taken her futon, plastic drawers, rugs, wall hangings, and had emptied out her closet.

"We'd better run another ad," Janae said.

We sat silently in the kitchen, drinking tea. After a while I said, "There is something I want to show you." I went into my room and came back with the manila folder. I handed it to her. "It's my audiogram."

I let her read it, unsure how much explanation she would need. She looked at me, her face all wonder and astonishment. "You have a significant hearing loss," she said.

"I never knew it was that bad."

"Well. That explains a lot."

"What?"

"For one thing, maybe that's why you never reacted to Rosie's passive-aggressive behavior."

"What passive aggressive behavior?"

"She would get so frustrated with you. Like, a few weeks ago, she opened the refrigerator and said, 'Everyone keeps putting their stuff on my shelf.' So right away, I moved my peanut butter off her shelf. You didn't react at all. In fact, next day, when you were unloading your groceries, you put a bunch of stuff right there on her shelf, right in front of us."

"I never heard her make that comment! I just saw all the extra room she had—"

"Right. But I thought the same thing she thought, that you were either ignoring her or totally oblivious."

My mother had often accused me of living in my

own world and being oblivious. "I may need therapy of my own," I said. "To find out how much trouble my hearing loss has caused all my life."

"That was the way she operated. She muttered under her breath and expected us to respond. I found her incredibly manipulative. Sometimes I watched you, wishing I could just ignore her, too."

Janae looked into her teacup and idly stirred her tea with a teaspoon. Then she said, "You always told me you didn't hear well out of one ear, but most of the time it seemed like you heard perfectly so I never thought much about it. But I remember something you said about a year ago."

Janae and I were so much alike. We both held on to things people said for years, until we finally understood. "What did I say?"

"Actually, it was sort of funny, but at the time I didn't know what to make of it. Early one morning, in the kitchen, I said something to you. The sun wasn't up yet. You pointed to the switch and said, 'Turn on the light so I can hear.'"

31

Curtis insisted on buying us both plane tickets. I pointed out my sculptures were selling, and the way things were going, I anticipated winning the fellowship again, so I had enough money.

"Save your money for hearing aids," he said.

Our plane arrived at the San Francisco airport early on a Thursday morning. We'd both taken Thursday and Friday off work, and planned to stay through the weekend. I was surprised by my first sight of my mother. She seemed smaller than I remembered. My mental image of her was how she had looked looming frighteningly over me when I was a child. Now she seemed insignificant, not the kind of person to have inspired in me such terror.

She wore a floral print blouse so old that the pattern was completely faded, giving the blouse a grayish-blue hue. I remembered that blouse when the blues had been more pronounced. Her hair was cut short in a boyish style, dyed a shade too dark, and she wore no makeup. There was something pixyish, or even childish, about her.

The way she reached for me and said, "Bretna!" embarrassed me and took me aback. She wiped her eyes with the back of her hand, then gripped my shoulders and said, "In spite of everything you've done, Bretna, I still love you."

From his angle, Curtis would not have been able to read her lips, so I signed for him.

Ben, my mother's new husband, who had been standing awkwardly by, shook my hand, then Curtis's hand, and said, "It's nice to meet both of you."

I looked at Ben, curious about what kind of man would marry my mother. Ben seemed sweet, if rather simple, with a kind smile and unexpressive eyes. I didn't have much chance to form an opinion of Ben because my mother pulled me close again and said, "No matter what you've done, you're still my daughter."

On the drive home, she talked about how much she loved her job at the office and how well she was doing in general. I tried to tell her about life in Massachusetts, but whenever I started to talk, she held still for a minute, then, as if I hadn't spoken, she continued talking about her job in the doctor's office. "I've been promoted to office manager," she said. I interpreted for Curtis as she talked. "The doctor I work for is wonderful. He's a great boss, the best I've ever worked for. I don't think I've ever been happier in a job."

She turned around to look at me and Curtis in the back seat. She talked about each of the people she worked with. Mechanically I interpreted, feeling bewildered. I expected my mother to be curious about my life, but she only wanted to talk about herself.

"When is Teddy getting married?" I asked.

"Oh, we're not sure yet," she said, and gave Ben a look that seemed to have meaning. Then she went back to talking about the office.

Teddy and Hannah were at home when we arrived. They said hi and went about their business as if I hadn't just returned after an almost eight-year absence. I wanted to ask Teddy about his fiancé and when he was getting married, but he just waved absentmindedly and left the room.

In my view, Hannah had always been the prettier sister, but now she seemed awkward, or maybe it was simply that she wore such dark eyeliner, and her hair needed washing.

I thought I should call my father and tell him I was in town. It was before five, so I called him at his shop. "Bretna?" he said. "Can you hold on a minute?"

When he came back to the phone, he said, "A customer just walked in. I'll call you back."

I said fine, told him where I was, and hung up.

Curtis was on the couch, watching everything. I asked if he wanted me to interpret.

"No need. I can follow it. It's like watching a movie without subtitles."

I must have given him an uncomprehending look because he said, "You'd be surprised how much you can get by just watching."

So I wandered into the kitchen to help my mother set the table. "I can't believe how different Teddy and Hannah look," I said.

"Teddy and Hannah are very close," she said in the tone of an important confidence. I had no idea, from the way she said it, whether they really were close, or whether she wanted me to think they were.

After dinner, Teddy said, "I have to go. Ariana is waiting."

At least someone decided to share with me the name of Teddy's fiancé, even if it happened inadvertently.

My mother said, "We all like Ariana so much," and went back to talking about her work at the office. I didn't bother interpreting for Curtis, who seemed content to just watch. She didn't say anything directly to me or

Curtis for the rest of the meal. I felt as if I were viewing a strange farce. I also felt as if I was seeing my mother for the first time.

Discretely, using only signs, I asked Curtis what he thought of the movie without subtitles. He said, "Your mother creates an emotional hurricane and pulls everyone in."

If the others noticed us having a private conversation, they acted as if they didn't.

After dinner, my father called back and invited me and Curtis over to his apartment for a visit. Hannah, who wanted to use the car to visit her boyfriend, offered us a ride.

My father lived in a new complex with a well-tended yard. His condominium was neat and tidy—actually, obsessively neat. The furnishings were sensible, as if he'd gone to a furniture store and said, "Just send me some sturdy, sensible furniture." He had a few pictures on the wall, prints that looked like they had come with their frames.

"So, Bretna, look at you. Here you are, doing so well. And you used to be in so much trouble all the time."

The familiar tension came into my stomach. "Why do you suppose that was?" I signed my questions as I spoke, but didn't try to interpret my father's responses. Curtis was watching my father speak, so I knew he was getting some of it, and I could fill him in later.

"Why do I suppose what?" my father asked.

"Why do you suppose I was always in trouble?"

Instead of answering, he said, "I think it's funny how things turn out. My brother did everything for Joshua. He begged Joshua to go to college, offered to pay for everything, but Joshua didn't want to go. We didn't do anything for you, but look where Joshua is, and look where you are. You're doing much better. It just goes to show that it doesn't matter what you do for kids."

"Do you think you're a good father?" I asked.

"Absolutely not. I told you. But I never did anything wrong to you. All that stuff, when your mother was hitting you, was happening when I was at work. I didn't know about it. Besides, you were a difficult child. Do you remember all the things you did? How you yelled and broke things?"

He was repeating my mother's words, retelling her stories. I felt myself being carried back to the place of deepest confusion.

I asked, "What about that time you kicked apart the speaker?"

He laughed quietly. "You know what your mother is like. She needles you and needles you until you can't stand it and you explode."

There was no point trying to point out the contradictions in his reasoning—why his behavior was excusable but mine wasn't.

"How about the beatings?" I said.

"Beatings?" he appeared genuinely puzzled. "What beatings?"

"Before we went to California, she said you beat her."

He laughed again, a quiet, amused chuckle. "You know how she lies!"

"Maybe she lies about me, too," I said.

"Oh, no. I saw your anger. I heard the way you talked to her. You were always challenging her, always standing up to her."

I waited until I knew my voice would not quiver, and said, "Dad, can I ask you a question?"

"Go ahead," he said jovially. "Ask me anything."

"Have you ever thought something is wrong with you? Have you ever thought you're different from other people?"

"Yes," he said. "Absolutely. I've always felt inferior to other people."

I had expected him to deny this, or say something like, "I stay calm when other people get upset," as if he possessed greater virtues. His quick and certain answer took me aback.

"Why do you feel inferior?"

"Because I just don't connect with other people."

"Do you think you're as caring as other people?"

"No, absolutely not. I lost the ability to be caring."

"How?"

"Hmm." He paused to think this over, then said, "We never had much money when I was a kid, and that was hard on us all."

"Did you have a bad childhood?"

"No, absolutely not! I had wonderful, loving parents!" He chuckled. "I'm not going to ask you that same question. I'm not going to ask you if you had a bad childhood, because I know what you'll say. And then I'll say, 'Well, Bretna, I just don't think your childhood was all that bad.'"

There was no point explaining this contradiction either—that his childhood with loving parents had been bad enough for him to lose the ability to care, yet my childhood—with a father who didn't care—hadn't been 'all that bad.'

I was ready to go, but there was one more thing I wanted to know: "What's going on with Teddy? When is he getting married?"

"In three months." My father laughed and said,

"Whenever I want to upset Ariana I say, 'I'm inviting Bretna to the wedding.' She gets all scared and upset. She's heard all the stories, and she doesn't want her wedding ruined with flying dishes and tantrums and windows being broken."

My stomach felt like it turned over and my arms were suddenly trembly, but I concentrated on interpreting this for Curtis.

I stood up, signing as I said, "We should go now."

Curtis and I said good-bye to my father—he didn't offer to hug us or even shake our hands. Outside on the street, I called the phone number Hannah had given me and asked if she could give us a ride home. She said she'd be there shortly.

"It's humiliating," I told Curtis. Ariana, who I had never met, knew only the stories of me, filtered through my mother's perceptions. "This was what it was like growing up. I was embarrassed and ashamed to face neighbors or anyone else she told stories to."

"You know," Curtis said. "You can see right away that your mother is disturbed. The way she talks, the way she moves. But your father is really the one who is sicker. He is also more honest. He straight-up told you that he isn't normal."

"I went on a three-thousand-mile quest to find out what was wrong with my family, but all I ever had to do was ask my father and he would have told me. It's sort of funny when you think about it."

Hannah's car rolled into the parking lot. Curtis got into the back seat, and I sat in the passenger seat. I looked out the window for a few minutes. I had the idea if I treated Hannah the way Curtis's mother treated her sister—they frequently met for lunch—and if Hannah and I could get away from the others, maybe we could reach each other, so I said, "Hey, Hannah, maybe we should have lunch together tomorrow, just us."

"Okay," said Hannah.

Good. I had an opening. It seemed to me that I'd been like a big sister to Alex, and not a bad one, either. Maybe I could do it with Hannah, too. "So tell me about your boyfriend."

"His name is Matt. When we get married, we'll be a family."

Just from the way she said it, I knew the marriage would never come about. I looked at her sharply to see if she knew this was fantasy. She didn't. So I changed the subject. In what I thought was a big-sisterly tone, I said, "You're so pretty. You know, I think you'd look much better with lighter eye makeup."

"Oh, shut up."

"Well, excuse me."

"You know, Bretna, the truth is that I don't like you. I tried, but I don't. You act so prissy, asking me to lunch like you're a movie star. Mom's right. You think you're so much better than us."

My fury at all of them rose to the surface. "You know," I said, "you might want to think about why I always got the worst of it. You might want to think about how sick this whole family is. Sick, sick, sick."

Hannah swerved to the side of the road and slammed the brakes. "Get out! Get out of the car!" She reached across my lap, opened the door, then gripped my arm and shoved me out. Curtis scrambled out as well.

Once we were both out of the car, Hannah reached over and slammed the door, then zoomed away.

Curtis said, "What in hell happened?"

I felt weak and trembly as I recounted the conversation to him as best I could.

"It's just like you remembered," he said.

"I always thought I was crazy."

"I see why."

I called home. Teddy answered. "Can you come get us?" I said. "Hannah put us out of the car."

"Where are you?" He sounded cheerful, as if he already knew what had happened.

When Teddy picked us up, he had a smile in his eyes that could have been amusement or even gloating.

My mother said Curtis could sleep on the couch in the upstairs living room, and I'd sleep in the family room downstairs. Hannah had taken my old bedroom. Two of Ben's daughters, who were then visiting their mother, had taken over Hannah's old room.

Ben said, "I think Bretna can sleep in Rene and Liz's room. I don't think they'll mind."

"This is your house," my mother said, "and your daughters' house. I can't put anyone out of their bedrooms."

She had a genius for creating rivalries. I hadn't said a word about sleeping in Hannah's old room. Had she always so shamelessly set members of the family against each other?

Curtis came into the family room with me. The house was strangely quiet. I crept to the door and listened. My mother and Hannah's voices came from my mother's bedroom. They were talking loudly enough for me to know they were talking, but not loudly enough to hear a single word. I stepped into the hallway to listen. Their tones were conspiratorial, as if designed to show me the tight bond of their friendship.

Curtis made the sign for "What?" so I told him that I could hear my mother and sister's voices and their tone, but not their words.

"You know," I said. "I don't think my mother was exaggerating when she said she still loves me in spite of everything I did. I think she truly believes I've done something horrible to her and that something is wrong with me."

"Maybe you should try talking to your brother," Curtis said.

"I have no idea what I could possibly say to him."

What I needed was to get away again, to sort things out. Maybe one day I would know what to say to my brother, or maybe even my sister, but now there was an emotional hurricane, and I saw no way to reason with wild winds.

"I think we should leave in the morning," I said.

"I agree."

After Curtis went upstairs, I put sheets on the couch, got into pajamas, and took out a sketchpad. My mother rarely allowed herself to be photographed, and kept no pictures from her own childhood, so I did a series of sketches, imagining how she might have appeared as a young girl. As I sketched, I mentally sifted through the clues I'd gathered about my mother, particularly what I'd learned during my quest for knowledge in St. Louis. In searching my memory and imagining what had been, I felt as if I were sifting through a box of old photographs—not the clean and bright photographs of today, but the photographs of forty years ago, the kind that fade and soften with time.

After I finished my sketches, I took out a box of pastels. I almost hadn't brought them. Now I was thankful that I had. The drawings needed to be in color.

I stayed in bed the next morning, pretending to be asleep while everyone got ready for work. When I was sure nobody was in the house except Curtis, I got up, showered, and dressed. I was remarkably calm.

Curtis was on the balcony off the kitchen, waiting for me. "The flight isn't until late tonight. What should we do until then?"

"Have you ever been to San Francisco?"

"Never."

"We'll do the whole shebang. Ride cable cars. Walk on the cliffs overlooking the ocean. Eat chocolate at Ghirardelli Square."

"How about Chinese food?"

"The very best."

The balcony was surrounded by lush tropical plants: birds of Paradise, broad-leafed palms, flowering cactus. The first time I left home, I wondered if I would miss all that was familiar. Now I understood that I'd never really gotten away. I might go far, all the way to the ends of the earth, carrying with me all the sins of my family like the goat in the story of Leviticus, but I'd always have my special place here, too.

I handed Curtis the best of the pastel drawings I had done during the night. In it, a young girl wore a fiery orange dress. She had red undertones in her face and hair. Her eyes were deep brown and her smile was merry. If you looked closely at the darkness in her eyes—but only if you looked closely—you saw that she was anguished. In the background was a white kitchen with frilly turquoise curtains—a charming old-fashioned kitchen. The tension came from the gaiety of her smile contrasted with the anguish in her eyes, and the fiery orange surrounded by turquoise and white.

Curtis looked at the drawing for a long time. "It's—"

he faltered, then said, "It's startling. It's beautiful."

Yes, it was. Art was supposed to be beautiful, even if it came from someplace twisted.

"It's called 'The Girl who Killed her Parents.'"

He looked alarmed.

"She didn't really," I said. "But she was told she did, and the guilt destroyed her." I'd always thought of my mother as a dangerous powerhouse. Even Curtis said she was an emotional hurricane. But really, she was as brittle as an old piece of iridescent hand-blown glass.

The cab driver honked from the street. Curtis waved to the driver, and we went through the kitchen to the front door.

I stopped and put the drawing on the counter.

"You're leaving it here?" He seemed surprised.

"As a gift," I said.

Why not? All anyone would see was the delicate drawing of a wide-eyed little girl in a fiery orange-red dress. Nobody would know the title of the picture, or that creating pictures such as this one redressed the balance in my life.

32

The trailhead was just off Route Five not far from the town of Holyoke. A kiosk with a shingled roof explained how more than one hundred separate dinosaur footprints had been preserved in layers of sandstone, and that the entire Connecticut River Valley used to be a sub-tropical swamp.

Curtis looked up at the sky, which was mostly blue with thin, high-floating clouds. In the distance, on the northeast horizon, dark low hanging rain clouds were forming. Curtis went to his car and came back with an umbrella, which he put into his back pack. "Almost forgot this," he said.

I had mine in my knapsack, but it occurred to me that most of the kids probably hadn't brought one. "Let's hope it doesn't rain," I said.

"It probably won't."

A guy came up behind us, startling both of us. He extended his hand and said, "I'm Jason, from Outdoor Adventures. I'm leading the hike."

I interpreted for Curtis, who extended his hand, and using his voice, said, "Nice to meet you. I'm Curtis."

I looked up just as the bus pulled into the parking area and rolled to a stop. The doors swung open and nineteen kids tumbled out. I could see from the brightness of Alex's expression that nothing had happened on the bus ride to dampen his hopes that Mona would soon be his girlfriend.

I motioned Alex to come over so I could introduce him to Curtis.

Alex and Curtis greeted each other. Alex used his voice supplemented by slurred and difficult to read signs, while Curtis signed sharply and clearly.

Jason clapped his hands for attention. "All right everyone. Listen up."

I interpreted for Alex and Curtis as Jason spoke: "I did the hike this morning, and it isn't difficult. Here are the instructions. I'm in the lead, Bretna walks in the middle, and Curtis is the sweep—he brings up the rear and makes sure no one gets left behind. Rule number one: Nobody leaves the trail without letting me, Curtis, or Bretna know about it. Rule number two: Anything you bring in with you, goes out with you. Do not leave anything, even the smallest piece of trash, behind. There's a fork in the trail about halfway to the footprints. We'll all stop at that fork and wait until everyone catches up to make sure nobody goes the wrong way. The trail goes alongside the river, but you can't get to the river because it's illegal to cross the train tracks, so we're not going to the river. Everyone got it?"

There were nods of agreement. To me, Alex signed, "What did he say about forks?"

Curtis tapped Alex and explained. The result was that we started off on the hike with Alex lagging toward the back with Curtis, a situation that appeared accidental, but I knew was Curtis's design.

The trail was about three feet wide, easily enough room for two people to walk side by side, but I walked alone. A group of two girls walked in front of me and a group of three came behind. Occasionally I turned around and saw Alex and Curtis deep in conversation, but I could never watch long enough to catch what they were talking about.

The landscape was stunning, reminding me of why I loved New England. The trail was calming and tranquil with its canopy of white cedar and red maples, and sprinkling of willows. The white cedars were just coming into bloom.

After about forty minutes of walking, we gathered at the fork in the trail for a break. I sat on a large rock and Curtis joined me. From the damp, mossy smell, I knew we weren't far from the river.

"What did you talk about?" I asked Curtis, using only signs.

"Mona. I worked on him to get him to open up, and eventually he revealed to me that he planned to ask her to go out with him. Don't worry. I didn't let on that you told me."

"You talked all that time about Mona?"

"No. It took all that time to get to Mona. I gave him some advice."

"What advice?"

"Not to take her by surprise. I said if you're going to ask a girl a thing like that, you need to give hints first so she knows where you're going. That gives her a chance to get out of the whole thing gracefully if she isn't interested."

"Clever."

"Not really. Any guy who's been rejected figures that out."

He opened his water bottle and offered me some. "Thanks," I said. Then: "What did Alex say?"

He turned to face me and signed, "He kept saying, 'Maybe I should see what Ms. Barringer thinks.' I asked why he wanted to know what you think. I figured it was because you're hearing, and Mona is hearing, so you would know better than me. He said, 'Because Ms. Barringer is smart. She helps me a lot.'"

I laughed out loud. "Curtis," I said by making his name sign. "When will you stop thinking everything is about hearing-deaf?"

"Never. Because everything *is.*"

I shot him a look. He signed, "I'm joking! Really!" To prove it, he grinned and made a gesture of helplessness. Then he signed, "I guess I'm like one of those feminists who think everything is about male-female."

"But everything *is.*"

Now he gave me the stern look. "I'm joking," I told him.

Jason clapped his hands for attention. He gestured toward the trail and said, "We can have a longer rest when we get to the footprints." I interpreted for Alex and Curtis, and we set off again. This time Alex trotted ahead to walk with Rodney toward the front of the group.

I hadn't expected to be walking alone this way. I expected to be walking with Curtis. I became so absorbed in the stillness of the trees and calm solitude of the canopy overhead that I was startled when I heard the girls giggling and talking excitedly.

Rounding one corner, I heard one of the girls behind me mention someone named Dylan. Taking a guess, I slowed down until I was walking near enough to enter the conversation.

"Is Dylan one of the new guys who just showed up today?" I asked.

"He's the tall dude with the sunglasses," Emily said. "He thinks he's hot."

Another said, "That's because he *is* hot."

"I wondered why those two showed up," I said. "They're older, right?"

"They're juniors. It's sort of obvious why they're here. At least it's obvious why Dylan is here."

"He likes dinosaur footprints?" I asked.

"He likes *Mona*," Emily said. "Can't you tell? He looks at her and practically *drools*."

The next time Jason called for a rest, I told Curtis what I'd learned from the girls. Curtis said, "I noticed that guy—Dylan? Is that his name?—watching Mona. She was looking at him, too. Maybe we should warn Alex."

"No," I signed.

Curtis drew back and gave me a look as if maybe I'd said something like, "Let's push Alex into the river."

"Why not warn him?" Curtis asked.

"Alex needs to take his own falls. I learned my lesson about that."

"But Alex is so childish compared to some of those other kids."

"No interfering," I said. "This is up to the goddess of love, or whoever is in charge. For all we know, Mona will pick Alex."

Curtis looked at me to see if I was joking. I said, "It could happen."

"My bets are on Dylan," he said, "but I'm rooting for Alex."

At one o'clock, an hour and a half after leaving the parking lot, we came to what appeared to be a glade but was actually a clearing with large slats of sandstone. Jason led the group across the sandstone and stopped. "Here are the footprints. Before we wander around and eat lunch, these are the rules. See that tall sycamore?" He pointed to a tree towering over the others. "You can wander around, but make sure you stay within sight of that treetop. Understand? We came with twenty-two people, and we're leaving with twenty-two people. We're heading back at two o'clock, so in exactly one hour, I want everyone here, on this slab of sandstone. Got it?"

There were nods and murmurs of agreement. The footprints—some of which, it turned out, we were actually standing on—were about fifteen inches long with three large toes, like a bird. The stencils I'd made were nothing like these tracks. Some of the tracks were more distinct than others and some were etched deeper into the sandstone. Most were facing westward, toward the river.

Curtis came up beside me and made the sign for "amazing," and I agreed.

"See those?" Curtis pointed to a smaller set of footprints. "Those are the footprints of small meat-eating dinosaurs, ancestors of modern day birds."

I looked at him, impressed. "How did you know that?"

"I read the brochure."

I looked around and saw a few groups of kids here and there, but most—including Alex, Mona, and Dylan—were not in sight. It was clear most of the kids were drifting in the direction of the river. Either Jason pretended not to notice, or he really didn't notice. He wandered over toward me and Curtis, evidently expecting to be invited to eat with us. I spread out a plastic tarp and said to Jason, signing as I spoke, "Will you join us?"

"Certainly," he said.

Having Jason there made conversation difficult. We talked about the dinosaur footprints and how beautiful the hike was. Occasionally I looked around, wondering what was happening with Alex, Mona, and Dylan. Each time I looked, Curtis looked, too.

Once when Jason didn't seem to be paying attention so that a private conversation didn't seem rude, I signed, "Any luck converting Alex to your side?"

"None," he said. I looked at his face to see how he felt about that, but I couldn't read anything at all. "As you said, he's stubborn. But he did tell me something that I think will interest you."

"What?"

"His mother tried to get you fired, but couldn't."

We'd been sitting together facing the same direction, and I'd been watching his hands. Now, stunned, I turned to face him. "Who stopped her? Walter? Elaine?" I couldn't think of a single person who would come to my defense.

'He did."

"*Alex?*"

"He told his mother if she got you fired, he'd stop coming to school. He told his mother you're a good interpreter."

At first I was too stunned to answer. But once I thought about it, I could easily imagine Alex facing down his mother. What I said was, "He's a kindred spirit."

Just then, Jason stood up and glanced at the sky. The wind had picked up and the sky was darkening.

"We should head back," Jason said. He walked to the edge of the sandstone, cupped his hands around his mouth for volume, and shouted, "Time to head back!"

Mona and Dylan came from the direction of the river, holding hands. To Curtis and Jason, I said, "Excuse me. I want to look around."

I jumped down from the sandstone slab and ducked behind a cluster of shrubs so Jason wouldn't see me jump over the railroad tracks and walk toward the river. I chose the path that most of the kids seemed to be taking back from the river, not the path Mona and Dylan had come from. Rounding a corner, I came face to face with Alex. His expression was set in something like defiance, his shoulders erect. I supposed that during the past hour, he'd gotten his heart broken.

"Did you get a chance to ask her?"

He gave a brisk nod of his head. "She was polite. She said no *thank you.*"

"At least you asked."

"Yeah. I asked."

Just when we joined the others, the rain started—a light pitter patter at first. The kids ducked under the trees, which helped at first. Curtis took out his umbrella and invited me under. Alex shrugged off his jacket and used it for an umbrella. So many kids did the same, I figured there were not many umbrellas among them.

I took out mine and offered it up. About a half dozen kids came forward for it. I offered it to Alex, who hung back. I figured I could show favorites. I was his interpreter, after all. He opened the umbrella and was suddenly very popular as three girls crowded under with him.

Dylan, it turned out, had an umbrella. He and Mona sat on a boulder under one of the trees, huddled under their umbrella.

Alex then did the chivalrous thing. When another girl nearby looked around for a way out of the rain, he offered his place and went to stand off by himself, with his jacket pulled over his head.

For what seemed like a long time but was probably no more than ten minutes or so, we stood there like that, huddled under umbrellas and jackets, with Mona and Dylan snuggled together under an umbrella. Alex was across the slab, directly in front of me and Curtis. I looked at him now with a new respect. You could see how brave he was, lifting his chin, acting as if he wasn't even aware of Mona and Dylan together.

The rain slowed to a drizzle, then stopped. Jason climbed up on the sandstone slab and called out, "The shower is over. We can head back now." He clapped and indicated that everyone was to draw near, to listen.

I interpreted as he gave his instructions for the hike back—again, we would gather at the fork, nobody was to leave the trail without telling him, and Curtis would bring up the rear.

We stopped twice for rest, and reached the trailhead at four o'clock.

We gathered in the parking lot. I thanked Jason, on behalf of the Sign Language Club. The kids—who appeared entirely worn out even though the entire hike had been less than four miles—clapped politely. I pretended not to see Mona and Dylan in my peripheral vision, again holding hands. Alex was one of the first to board the bus, Mona and Dylan were among the last.

The bus pulled onto the highway. I asked Jason, "Do we need to do anything else? What about the fee?"

"It's all taken care of," he said. Then, "Great group."

"Thanks," I said.

Curtis and I watched him walk toward his car. Curtis said, "How about a cup of something hot in Holyoke before we head back?"

"Good idea," I said.

A half hour later, we were sitting at a corner table in a coffee shop called "Common Grounds," a name that struck me as perfect under the circumstances. I cupped my hands around the paper cup to feel the warmth.

Curtis signed, "He's a tough kid. He has gumption."

"Yes," I signed.

"When I was his age, I wouldn't have had the nerve to ask a girl with looks like Mona."

"Alex doesn't lack for nerve."

"He can hold his own with a bunch of hearing kids. He can hold his own with anyone."

"Yes, he can." I couldn't tell how Curtis was feeling just then.

"I wanted to talk to you about something," he signed.

He reached into his coat pocket, and took a flyer from his pocket and handed it to me. The flyer announced an art exhibit and art sale at the Deaf Association to be held on Memorial Day weekend. "I want to put some of your sculptures on display. If there are any you want to sell, you can mark them for sale."

I looked back at the flyer, which simply said, "Art Exhibit."

"I'm not deaf," I pointed out.

"So?"

So? I wanted to say, *What do you mean, so? Wasn't that the entire problem—that I'm not deaf?* Instead, I just smiled. "Isn't this exhibit for deaf artists?"

"That was the original idea. In the past we featured only deaf artists. But I told the board that it shouldn't matter whether the artist is deaf or not. What matters is the work."

I looked directly into his eyes. He was watching me steadily, triumphantly, almost as if to say: *Surprised you!*

"Which brings me to the point," he signed. "I want to display your sculpture, 'The Philanthropist.'"

"You can't display that one," I said. "Someone bought it."

"Yes, I can." He paused for effect, and signed, "I

bought it."

I wasn't sure what surprised me more, that he bought The 'Philanthropist,' or that he said it doesn't matter whether an artist is hearing or deaf.

"Where is it?" I asked.

"On the little table in my apartment under the window."

That was where he'd had the lovely model of the stopping place in the woods.

We drank the rest of our tea in silence. Then I said, "If I did a sculpture of today's hike, I'd do it in shades of peach and aquamarine—relaxing, opposites coming together, but harmonious. Those aren't the colors you'd expect since Alex has a broken heart right now. But today was definitely a day of aquamarine and peach."

"I would have thought it's a day of light green."

"That's because you're being literal. If I did a sculpture, I'd have to include the dinosaur footprints, even though I can't figure out what they're supposed to symbolize. I'm not sure what dinosaur tracks have to do with an unrequited childhood crush."

Curtis waved to make sure I was paying attention, and signed, "Hello. Not everything is a deep symbol. Sometimes a dinosaur footprint is just a dinosaur footprint."

I smiled, but I believed he was wrong: One day, maybe years from now, I'd understand the symbolic significance of the dinosaur footprints—and when that happened, I'd create a sculpture of the hike.

ALSO BY TERI KANEFIELD

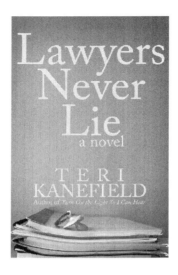

A boy on the roof. A house in shambles. A new baby. A lawsuit.

Just when Susan — an idealistic new lawyer and mother of three — thinks she's getting it all under control, the police arrest her husband for a crime he didn't commit.

Susan and her family struggle to put the pieces together, prepare for a courtroom showdown – and discover the reason for all those lawyer jokes.

ABOUT THE AUTHOR

Teri writes short stories, essays, novels, books for young readers — and lots of appellate briefs.

Her books include the critically acclaimed *The Girl from the Tar Paper School,* and *Guilty? Crime Punishment, and the Changing Face of Justice.* Her essays have appeared in Scholastic's *Scope Magazine, The Recorder* (San Francisco's Legal Newspaper), *Education Week, Jewish Currents,* and other periodicals. Her essay "The Best Interests of the Child," was included in *Reaching for the Bar: Stories of Women at all Stages of their Law Careers,* published by Kaplan Books. Her short stories have appeared *in The Iowa Review, American Literary Review, Cricket* and other periodicals.

Her law practice is currently limited to appeals. She accepts clients only through the Appellate Defenders Inc. and The First District Appellate Project, non-profit law firms dedicated to improving the quality of indigent representation in criminal, juvenile, dependency, and mental health appeals.

She lives in San Francisco with her family.

Made in the USA
Charleston, SC
19 November 2014